Real Vamps Don't Drink O-...

D1302147

$12.95

mm

SOS622

Also by Tawny Taylor

SEX AND THE SINGLE GHOST

Published by Kensington Publishing Corporation

Tawny Taylor

Real Vamps Don't Drink O-Neg

KENSINGTON BOOKS
KENSINGTON PUBLISHING CORP.
www.kensingtonbooks.com

KENSINGTON BOOKS are published by

Kensington Publishing Corp.
850 Third Avenue
New York, NY 10022

All Kensington titles, imprints, and distributed lines are available at special quantity discounts for bulk purchases for sales promotion, premiums, fund-raising, educational, or institutional use.

Special book excerpts or customized printings can also be created to fit specific needs. For details, write or phone the office of the Kensington Special Sales Manager: Attn. Special Sales Department. Kensington Publishing Corp., 850 Third Avenue, New York, NY 10022. Phone: 1-800-221-2647.

Kensington and the K logo Reg. U.S. Pat. & TM Off.

ISBN-13: 978-0-7582-1509-3
ISBN-10: 0-7582-1509-6

First Printing: September 2007
10 9 8 7 6 5 4 3 2 1

Printed in the United States of America

To my husband,
who handles my crazy schedule,
a perpetually messy house,
and shortage of home-cooked meals
like a champ.
And my children, who have heard
"Mommy's trying to work"
more times than any kid wants to hear.
Thanks for being so patient with me.

And my editor, Audrey,
and agent, Natasha.
You've helped make my dreams come true.
Thank you.

Chapter 1

"I know, I know, I'm a rotten friend—" Sophie Hahn stumbled through her best friend's front doorway in the hurried, less than graceful gait of a deer that has suffered a near fatal confrontation with a semi truck. "Dao? Where are you?" She rushed through the living room, shouting, "Really, there should be a law against leaving a message that begins with 'I need you to get over here yesterday,' and ends with, 'It's life or death' at five A.M. on a Saturday morning. I'll have you know I ran at least three red lights on the way here, and I think I'll need a rotate and balance. I'm pretty sure my right tires are shot. Dao? Lisse? Hellooooo!"

She rounded the corner, heading toward the kitchen at a fast jog; however, the sight of her friend—pale, bedraggled, and slouching against the wall as if he lacked the strength to stand upright—brought her to a screeching halt. "Holy smokes! You weren't exaggerating. What the heck is wrong with you?" She lunged forward and pressed the back of her hand to his forehead. No fever. "You'd better lie down. Is it serious? Darn it! I knew I should've come over last week—"

"No, no. Nothing's wrong." Dao Wen Dong knocked her hand away like it was a pesky fly, gave her an unconvincing shake of his head, and practically dragged his limp-looking body across the living room to shut the front door. "I've never been better." He held her in a stiff, cold hug for an instant, then dropped his arms, motioning her toward the kitchen with a tip of his head.

I've had a warmer welcome at the secretary of state's office. "No offense, but you look like hell," she said as she leaned back against the kitchen counter and crossed her arms over her chest.

Her friend's responding smile was hollow, his eyes flat as day-old Pepsi, as he poured a cup of coffee. He offered it to her, but, not a coffee drinker, she refused it with a shake of her head. Despite her best effort, she couldn't help staring at the deep purple shadows hanging under his eyes like bruises. The dark circles contrasted sharply with the wan tone of the rest of his face.

Had her teetotaling friend gone on a bender?

"Seriously, you don't look well at all," she repeated.

"Thanks," Dao grumbled. "It's good to see you too, not that you look much better."

Having forgotten her mad rush to Dao's house, and the lack of time and attention she'd paid to her hair, clothing, and make-up, Sophie raised a hand to tame her bedhead. "Well, you said it was life or death. Honestly, if you'd wanted me to take the time to get all pretty, you should've avoided the words 'Get over here yesterday.' So, what's the big secret? Are you hungover? Did you go on a binge, down a beer or two, lose your head, and do something crazy— like take a midnight road trip to KFC?"

"You know I don't drink. And even drunk I wouldn't touch deep-fried food."

"Then are you sure you're not sick? Maybe you should go see a doctor. Seriously."

"Oh. No. I'm quite certain I'm fine. I'm just tired. Been working a lot, between—" He chuckled. "Well, let's just say I'm not getting much sleep these days. But I'm taking vitamins. Lots of B for fatigue and C to fight off infection.

Anyway, I wanted to show you my latest work in progress. It's sheer genius." He motioned for her to follow him down the hallway.

"I bet. I've loved every book you've written. Brilliant. Absolute genius. I wish I could write like you do. Then I could quit my crappy job, stay at home, and work in my jammies. What a life!" Sophie hurried behind him to his office. Despite the fact that the man had to have lost a good twenty pounds or more the past couple of months and looked like a walking skeleton, he could move pretty quickly when he wanted to. Must've been those B vitamins kicking in. "Speaking of geniuses, where's your lovely wife?"

"Er . . . Lisse had a . . . late night." Dao gave Sophie an odd grin and guilty chuckle as he pulled out his desk chair and slouched into it. He added, "She's sleeping but last night—"

Sophie waved her hands. "Ah. Too much information there."

"You asked." He motioned toward an empty chair.

"So, let me get this straight—Lisse doesn't know I'm here? Even with all my bellowing?" She glanced at the empty chair, then at Dao. "I don't know. Maybe I should leave. It's early, Saturday morning, she's asleep. You've only been married a couple of months. I wouldn't want her to think—"

"No way. First, Lisse could sleep through a natural disaster. Second, she would never think anything about you and me. I've told her over and over again that after being friends for so long, sleeping with you would be plain creepy. Like sleeping with my own sister—if I had one, that is. Besides I doubt she'll wake up for at least a couple of hours." Dao scooted his chair up to the desk, swept his cluttered desktop clear with one arm, then fired up the Dell. "If I'd known what an effect marriage would have on my writing, I would've married Lisse months ago. I can't believe how inspired I've been lately—"

"Please," Sophie interrupted before he went into any

details about the subject of his inspiration. She pulled up a chair and sat. "If I agree to stick around for a few minutes, you must promise me, no more talking about your sex life. I can't remember the last time I had any conjugal—or even nonconjugal—action. I don't need to be reminded about what I'm missing."

Dao laughed, his eyes squinting into the little upside-down smileys she'd adored since the first time she'd met him, on the middle-school playground. "Fair enough." Those little smiley eyes had always been able to make her feel better, even on her worst days.

"Good, because if you said another word, I'd never be able to look Lisse in the face again without blushing."

Dao chuckled as he punched keys and clicked the mouse, finally opening a word-processing document. "I want you to give me your honest opinion." Looking extremely proud, he nudged the monitor so that Sophie could read the screen. "Go ahead."

She read the first page, or the part of the first page she could see. It was . . . awful! Some kind of strange story about a freaky woman who was traveling the globe with the sole purpose of having sex with anything she could— male, female . . . and not always human. Could a woman really do *that* with a donkey? She shuddered. Granted, Sophie could accept the fact that she was a little uptight about sex. Unlike Lilly, the character in Dao's book, she took the wheres, whos, and whats of sex seriously, hence the lengthy dry spell. But she couldn't imagine this creepy story selling anywhere, at least not outside of a porn shop.

She glanced at Dao. This had to be a joke, some kind of trick to get her over there, since she hadn't visited her best pal in several weeks.

The thing was, she couldn't find a hint of amusement on his face. Lots of hope, a little nervousness even, but not a bit of laughter. She glanced deeper into his eyes.

Oh boy, he was serious.

"I . . . wow. I don't know what to say. It's very . . . um, different. Why the change in, er, genres? I mean, you've done very well with your mysteries. I love your mysteries. They're so gritty and real."

"I felt it was time for a change."

"And what a change it is," Sophie said, making every effort to keep her reaction tamed down for the sake of her friend's feelings. She knew Dao had a very delicate ego, at least when it came to his work.

"So, what do you think?" he asked as he scanned the page with his cute little brown eyes. "I'm on fire for this one. Can't stop thinking about it, even when I'm sleeping."

It's garbage, if you want to know the truth. "On fire? Really?" *Yes, burning it sounds like a good plan.* Sophie sighed. "Well, who am I to say what'll sell and what won't?" Not the least bit interested in reading any more, she leaned back in her chair. "I'm just a lowly secretary, not an editor. Have you shown this to your agent yet?"

"No, not yet. I'm waiting. Want to get it perfect first. It's almost there."

"Yeah? Almost perfect, eh?" *Better do another read through.*

Dao leaned forward, obviously becoming engrossed in whatever he was reading. He clicked the mouse, pecked at the keyboard, then scrolled down some more and repeated the process. "I can't stop tweaking it here and there . . . I . . . oh . . ." his words trailed off as he started typing furiously. His face twisted into a tight expression of intense effort, like one you might see on someone hanging by their fingertips from a thousand-foot cliff. "This is wonderful! Utterly amazing." His keyboard went clackety-clack as he continued typing. Sweat beaded on his forehead.

Taking that as her cue to leave, Sophie gave his shoulder a pat. "I'll come back in a few days and see how that story is coming."

"Ummm." Dao answered, not missing a beat as he continued typing.

Sophie closed his office door behind her after she tiptoed out of the room. Confused—no, more like freaked out!—by her friend's bizarre behavior and frightening appearance, she flopped back against the closed door to catch her breath.

Dao had gone from a fun-living, social guy with a sparkling smile and fairly sturdy physique to an obsessed, frail, sickly man in what? A couple of months? A few late nights couldn't have done that to him.

Something was wrong. Very wrong. And as his friend, she owed it to him to find out what. She'd never let another person she loved down again, never ignore the signs that something was wrong and assume everything would work itself out.

Making that mistake once was more than enough for a lifetime.

And this was Dao, the person who'd practically carried her through the grief of that first loss.

As she straightened up, she caught a dull thump coming from the bedroom he shared with Lisse. She tensed. Nothing like catching a new bride by surprise.

"Dao, honey. Where'd you go?" Lisse crooned from the other side of the closed door.

Not wanting to get in the way of her newly wedded friend's love life, Sophie hurried down the corridor toward the living room. Before she reached the hallway's end, she heard the telltale squeak of a door's hinges, then a female's surprised gasp. She stopped walking, figuring the sight of a woman running down one's hallway would be far more suspicious than the sight of one's husband's best friend standing all casual-like in the hallway. Still, she couldn't quite convince herself to turn around and give Lisse the reassuring smile she probably needed.

The door slammed shut behind Sophie's rigid back before she hazarded a glance over her shoulder. Figuring it was safe to look now, she turned around and said, "Sorry, Lisse. Dao called me over to check out his latest story. I'm headed out now."

"It's okay," Lisse's muffled voice came through the door. "I didn't know you were here. I'm . . . not dressed yet. I hope you don't mind showing yourself out."

"Nope, not at all. I was just heading home as we speak," she said as she hurried toward the door.

"Okay. Goodbye, Sophie. I'm sorry I can't be more social. You must think I'm very rude but my robe is down in the laundry."

"Don't worry about it. Next time I'll make sure Dao tells you before he invites me over at five A.M. on a Saturday morning." One hand on the doorknob, Sophie stooped over to slip on her clogs. As she kicked at her overturned left shoe, something opalescent and sparkly clung to the top of it. Curious, she plucked up the roundish shiny object, very thin and delicate, about the size of a quarter, and slipped it in her jacket pocket. On went the shoes and out she went, into the cool, damp early summer morning.

What a way to start the weekend, with a real-life—correction—life-or-death mystery! Regardless of her friend's insistence to the contrary, she had more than a sneaking suspicion that his health was in serious jeopardy. But how would she get him—a man who'd insisted on weathering pneumonia without seeing a doctor—to go in for a checkup?

Sophie studied the strange shimmery round thing she'd picked up at Dao's house Saturday as she set the phone back on the cradle. She wasn't sure if she'd just gotten the brush-off from Lisse or if she was just imagining things. Oftentimes, it was hard for her to distinguish reality from her fairly active imagination.

Looking for an ally in her quest to get Dao to the doctor, she'd called the one person she figured could actually convince him to go—his wife, naturally. Lisse seemed to be on her side as they discussed concerns about Dao's health, but when it came time to ask her to call and make an appointment for him, she grew very quiet. Granted, she didn't say she wouldn't, but for some reason . . .

Why wouldn't his wife, the woman who loved him, want him to go to the doctor?

The phone rang, and still lost in her thoughts, Sophie swept it up, tucking it between her chin and shoulder as she answered, "Tri County Paranormal Research Associates. How may I help you?"

Like most folks who called her work, the woman on the other end sounded breathless and panic-stricken as she detailed the nature of her problem. Sophie took down the woman's information, then put the call through to her boss, Tim, who happened to be in the office today. Most of the time he was out playing ghost buster with a truckload of electronic gizmos that as far as Sophie could tell did nothing but blink and make ugly noises.

Tim was extremely intelligent, like a card-carrying member of MENSA smart. And because she believed genius and insanity were like kissing cousins—too close for most people's comfort—she attributed his obsession with paranormal gobbledygook to this relationship. At least his stories were amusing, and the interest from his trust fund would keep her paychecks coming for a long time.

After she passed on the call, she set the shiny thing aside, figuring she'd ask Tim what he thought of it later. It had no markings like a coin, and it had a slightly irregular shape. On closer examination, it reminded her of two things—either a dime that had been flattened on a train track or a piece of fish skin or scale. Knowing Dao's propensity to eat fish, she suspected the latter.

Still, it was an odd thing. Semitranslucent, the color changed, depending on the light it was examined under. In natural light, it was mostly white and blue, but in artificial light it glowed in a wide range of colors from soft pink to deep midnight, depending on the angle she held it. Even more curious, every now and then it seemed to emit a small electrical charge. A little zap that made her fingers tingle.

Unable to resist the urge, she plucked it up one last time and ran her fingertip over the surface. The colors shimmered as she stroked it. The effect was almost mesmerizing. She stared at it a moment until Tim's voice broke the spell.

"What's that?" he asked.

"I was hoping you might have an idea. You know a little about everything. What do you think? Is it a fish scale?" She set it in her palm and lifted her flattened hand so he could get a better look.

His eyebrows shot to the top of his forehead as he picked it up and examined it. "Wow, this is amazing. Truly amazing. Where'd you get it?"

"A friend's house. It was on the floor."

"Does your friend have a pet snake?" he asked as he flipped it over to look at the other side.

"Pet snake? Heck no! He hates snakes. Why?"

"Looks like a piece of shed snake skin to me. I'd have to get a look at it under the microscope to be sure. Be right back." He walked back to his office-slash-lab, where he kept all his electronic gadgets and gizmos, and disappeared behind the closed door.

Sophie stayed put, despite her growing curiosity about the strange scale—skin—whatever, and tried to imagine how a piece of snake skin would end up on Dao's floor. She came up with absolutely nothing. That was, indeed, a mystery all in itself.

Tim returned several minutes later with the most bizarre look on his face. It was something between awe and terror. "I need to meet her. I must meet her—"

"Meet whom? Slow down, would you? What would a snake scale—"

"Skin. Definitely shed skin."

"Fine. Snake skin. What would a snake skin have to do with . . . her? It's a female snake? How can you tell? Did you get a little piece of nipple there? And how does one 'meet' a snake? Do you need a formal introduction?"

Tim rolled his eyes and looked at Sophie as if she were an absolute twit—which she was not, thank you very much.

"Don't look at me that way," she said. "I wasn't privy to whatever you saw under the microscope. I'm not a moron. Fill me in."

"Is your friend a male?" Tim asked as he continued to study the skin.

"Yes. A male *human*, that is. Just to clarify."

"Yes. Of course he's a human. Is this friend of yours dating someone . . . or married?"

"Yes. He's married but not to a snake."

Tim shook his head. "Poor guy," he murmured.

"What poor guy?" Sophie yanked on Tim's sleeve. "Poor guy because he isn't married to a snake?"

"No, poor guy because he's married to her already."

"What's Dao's marital status have to do with anything? Besides, what's wrong with marriage? I never imagined you to be one of those 'marriage sucks' kind of guys."

"I'm not, unless the wife happens to be a lamia."

"What the heck is a lamia?"

"A muse. A female vampire. Is your friend by any chance a writer?"

"Yes, but what's—"

"And since he's been married has he been more obsessed with his writing? Has he become ill yet?"

"Yes, on the writing. And yet?"

Tim looked into her eyes and again shook his head. "Poor guy. He's doomed."

"Doomed? Why?"

"She's destroying him."

"Who? Lisse? She's a quiet little thing. Maybe a tad demanding in bed from what I surmise, but hardly the kind one would expect to be a vampire. She doesn't even have a widow's peak. Don't real vampires have widow's peaks? And her teeth all look normal." Despite all the things Tim seemed to know about Dao, for which there was no reasonable explanation—he couldn't have been listening in to her conversation with Lisse—she wasn't buying the whole lamia thing. There was no such thing as vampires. Or ghosts. Or monsters. Nuh-uh.

Tim's work as a paranormal researcher was a joke. She'd seen nothing to convince her of the existence of anything paranormal. His so-called proof consisted of hazy photographs and less than credible eyewitnesses.

"Yes. She's a lamia. Half woman, half snake."

"I've seen her. She's no snake. In fact, she's very beautiful. And she definitely has two legs. Couldn't speak for her tongue, though. Could be forked. I'm not about to go ask her to open wide and say 'ahhhh.'"

"She wouldn't show her true self to anyone but her lover."

"If there's one thing I can be certain of it's that Dao wouldn't find a woman covered in scales sexy, even if the scales were rather pretty."

"He would if he was under her spell. The lamiae are extremely powerful vampires. They find their mates and slowly, over many weeks, seduce them until they are completely under their spell. Once a man marries a lamia, he's doomed to die a swift, miserable death. He'll grow weaker and weaker, his life drained from him by his wife."

"Swift? How swift?"

Tim shrugged. "I'm not sure of the time line. A couple of months, maybe."

"A couple? Like two? Because he's been married that long already." She fought the urge to panic. This was a bunch of baloney. There was no such thing as a lamia.

And Dao wasn't about to die. Dao couldn't die. He just couldn't.

Unfortunately, Tim didn't seem to know that. "Sounds like he's near the end. Sorry."

She didn't like what she was hearing. Not one bit. Which was why she preferred to look for another reason for Dao's illness. And his strange behavior. And the snake skin in his living room. Okay, there were a number of coincidences here. "There must be another explanation. That skin is from a . . . a python or something. Who knows, maybe he went to a zoo—"

"It's not the skin of most common varieties of snakes. I snapped a quick photograph and e-mailed it to my buddy who works in the zoo's reptile house. He's assured me it's not from any snake they have there. That rules out several varieties of pythons and boa constrictors. Just to make sure, he's forwarding the image to a friend of his who identifies shed snake skins for a living."

"Ick. There are people who do that for a living?"

"Sure. Out west especially. Think about it. If you found a shed skin under your porch, wouldn't you want to know if you had a venomous snake living under your house?"

"Yes, I suppose so."

Tim set the piece of skin on the desk and stared into Sophie's eyes. "Look, when I hired you, I told you I didn't require you to actually believe in what I study here. So I accept that you're doubtful. But this is your friend, and if you truly care about him, I suggest you reconsider your position on a few things. Vampires do exist. And they do kill."

A lump the size of Tim's SUV formed in Sophie's throat as she let his words pass through the baloney filter in her brain and really sink in. Even if she still didn't believe in vampires, didn't she owe it to Dao to check out all the possibilities? "So, what's the next step? Do you need to go scan Lisse with one of your gadgets? Shoot her with an ionizing ray? How do I know she's in fact one of those lamia things and if she is, how do I get her to leave my friend alone?" *Oh God. I know this is going to kill Dao. He adores Lisse. But if what Tim says is true, he's dying already.*

"Nothing I have is going to help you." He patted her shoulder and nodded. "I'm very sorry for your loss."

"Why are you saying that like he's already dead? What'ya mean you're sorry for my loss?"

"I'm saying that because I can't help you. There's virtually no way to one hundred percent identify your friend's wife as a lamia or to make her leave him."

"Virtually no way? What about Buffy? Where's a vampire slayer when you need one? Or maybe an old-fashioned stake through the heart would do the trick—on second thought, scratch that. I don't have the stomach to give someone a paper cut let alone shove a wooden stake through their breastbone. Just imagine all the blood. Have I told you that blood gives me the willies—"

"There's only one way to both identify a lamia and destroy her," he interjected, cutting off her mindless rant about television characters and paper cuts. "But each step requires the possession of an extremely rare relic, which I'm not sure even exists. They're the . . . Shoot, I can't remember the names. They're Hebrew. Never been good with Hebrew. Let me go back and get my book." He took a single step away, then glanced over his shoulder at the piece of snake skin still sitting on Sophie's desk. "I don't suppose you'd let me keep that? For research purposes, of course."

She picked it up and handed it to him. "Sure. If you'll help me. I think I'm in trouble over my non-vampire-believing head."

His eyes sparkled as he glanced down at the skin. "Like

I said, I can't help you much. But I'll do what I can. Come on." He led her back to his office. "Let's hope, for your friend's sake, the book I've read on the subject is right and the relics you need haven't been destroyed eons ago."

Chapter 2

"Excuse me," Sophie asked the librarian a couple of hours later. She glanced down at the piece of paper she'd ripped from Tim's notebook, then continued, "You got rid of the good-old card catalogue and I'll admit I'm far behind the common kindergartner when it comes to computers—a real crime considering what I do for a living, but that's beside the point. Where might I find a book on rare biblical relics?"

The middle-aged woman, slim and scholarly looking with her brown hair pulled into a neat bun at the base of her skull, gave Sophie a pleasant, if not a little condescending, smile. "Let me see what I can find." She tapped a few keys, moved the mouse around a bit, then looked up. "I'm sorry. I'm not finding anything under 'biblical relics.' However, you may find what you need under religious relics. Those are in the two-thirties. The nonfiction shelves are in this direction and they are numbered. In particular, this book *Religious Relics, Icons, Visions and Cures* by James Murrow may be of some help. The call number is two-thirty-one point seven M."

"Thank you." Sophie repeated the title and number in her head as she walked in the general direction of the nonfiction shelves. She scanned the numbers on the ends of the shelves until she found the two- to three-hundred section, then focused on the books on the shelves as she walked toward the back of the section. "Two-twenty, two-thirty, two-forty . . ." When she reached the two-seventies, she stopped and skimmed the numbers on the book spines. "Two-seventy point three, point eight. Two-seventy-one . . . two-seventy-one point three, point seven, A, B, C . . . G, P. Hey, no M?" She turned her body, and while still reading the book spines, she started walking toward the very back of the section. But a brick wall stopped her before she reached the end.

As she twisted her neck to inspect the wall, she realized immediately it wasn't your garden variety brick wall. This one was wide, tall, hard, and yummy, with a head full of blond curls and eyes the shade of a Hershey bar.

Those eyes traveled over her features for an instant, making her feel all goosebumpy inside, then returned to the book that was partly blocking her view of his face.

She wondered if the rest of his face looked as good as the part she saw. Then she shook her head and reminded herself she was on the hunt for a book, not a delish man who knew how to fill out a T-shirt and pair of snug jeans properly. "Sorry," she muttered to the wall.

"Not a problem." He stepped aside to let her pass. Naturally, his bulk took up a fair amount of the narrow aisleway between shelves, which meant to pass, she had to get mighty close to him. She turned sideways, her front facing him, of course—wouldn't want to show him her less than desirable backside—and took a single shuffling step.

As she paused, her body mere inches from his, the girly part of her—the part she'd begun to think had abandoned her ages ago—woke up from its slumber and started getting all vocal, protesting and demanding equal time as the logical part reminded her she was there to find a book, not ogle a good-looking library patron. Being she was short, his chest was at eye level—and it was the broadest one she'd ever seen. Hugged in black cotton, it was pure, unadulterated temptation. The way the thin fabric skimmed over the lines of his sculpted muscles made her toes curl.

Okay, maybe a little ogling wouldn't be out of order.

"Excuse me?" the wall said. His book slid lower, blocking a significant part of those yummy pecs.

With that lovely view obscured, Sophie went for the face, hoping it would be as pleasant as the rest of him.

She felt her breath literally catch in her throat, like in the romance novels she loved to read. Oh my. Was it ever!

Not quite as pretty as John Schneider back in his *Dukes of Hazzard* days, he had that all-American cutie pie thing going for him. But this wholesome boy next door was all grown up and one hundred percent bad boy. The angular line of his jaw and cheekbones, the coating of dark blond stubble, and the wicked glint in his liquid chocolate eyes was enough to make her inner girl swoon with delight. Immediately, without thinking, she checked his left hand for a ring.

When her gaze returned to his face, she noted that one eyebrow had lifted in question. And one corner of his mouth had lifted in amusement, which reminded her that she'd been standing there, sandwiched between his scrumptious body and the bookshelf, for probably too long for safety—his safety, that is.

"Sorry . . ." Sophie mumbled, not sure what else to say. She'd never behaved like this around a man before. Granted, she'd never seen a man this gorgeous before—at least not in real life. In the movies, yes. On TV, yes. In her dreams, oh yes. "I'll just shuffle off to Buffalo now."

His chuckle hit her right in the belly, where it bubbled and tickled her insides. Her face heated.

"I'm guessing you're either a displaced New Yorker or

a dancer then?" he asked in a low, rumbly voice that made that inner girly part perk up and take notice, along with a few other parts of her anatomy.

"Actually, neither. I'm just a secretary from Hazel Park." *Who thinks you're yummy. Want to go check out the park down the street? I know where there's a cozy, dark little corner where we could have some privacy, let our tongues get acquainted.*

Both his other eyebrow and the right side of his mouth joined the left in their raised positions, producing the kind of smile that could drop a girl of weaker constitution at fifty paces.

She took another step and cleared her throat because she was sure something very large had become wedged in there somehow when she wasn't looking. "Doing some research on religious relics. I was looking for a book called . . ." She tried to remember the title but realized it had slipped her mind eons ago, like the second she'd seen him. "Oh, shoot. I forgot. Something about relics and cures."

He held up the book he'd been reading, turned it over, and said. "You mean, *Religious Relics, Icons, Visions and Cures* by James Murrow?"

"Yes! That's the one. Oh. You're reading it then? Were you going to check it out?"

"I was thinking about it."

"Oh drat! I . . . er . . ." She dropped her gaze to his toes because that seemed to be the only body part she could look at and still be able to operate her brain and took a third sidestep, which landed her a fairly safe distance from him. "I don't suppose I could convince you to let me have it instead?"

"Hmmm. As much as I'd love to see how you intended to do that, I have to be honest and say no. I really need this book."

"What about bribery? I'm not rich but I'd be willing to clean out my bank account to get my hands on it."

To his credit, he looked genuinely remorseful as he shook his head. "Sorry again. But I promise I'll return it as soon as I'm through."

"Three weeks could be too late. I need to find the Romanick Yee-how-shoo-ah and Mawmee Dah-veed before my best friend becomes dinner for his wife."

"You mean Romakh Yehowshu'a and Mawgane Dah-veed?"

"Yes. That's what I said, er, wasn't it?"

He nodded. "Close enough."

"Anyway, I don't expect you to believe me, but I need to find out about those relics because I think I might need them to help a friend of mine."

"Your friend's married to a lamia?"

Sophie threw her hands in the air. "Why is it that everyone seems to know about those lamiae people but me? Well, at least I know now that Tim isn't completely crackers or making it up."

"Tim?"

"My boss. He's a paranormal researcher and half the time you can't believe a word he says. Good guy but if you ask me, he's a few cards shy of a full deck, if you know what I mean. The things he believes in."

"Like?"

"Oh, I don't know. Ghosts, vampires, and the like. I don't believe a bit of it but my pal's pretty sick and although I figure a trip to a medical doctor—and maybe a vacation—would probably take care of whatever his problem is, I owe it to him to check out all the possibilities. I try to have an open mind, you see. I've even been to a massage therapist once. Now, that was an experience, let me tell you. But I draw the line at believing in creatures of the night."

He looked far too amused for her comfort. "Ah, yes. Those are pretty silly superstitions, aren't they?"

"Yes! Thank you. A voice of reason. Silly superstitions,

unless you're one of those weirdos who go to the dentist and pay for bonding so you can look like a vampire. To each their own, I guess."

"Yes. That's a wise stand to take." He nodded. His eyes sparkled as his grin turned wry.

"Are you humoring me?"

In a flash the expression changed again, this time turning all innocent. She didn't buy it. Not at all. But that didn't stop it from making various and sundry parts of her warm and toasty. "Who, me? Oh, no. I never humor a woman. It's not a smart thing to do."

"You got that right, buster." She gave him a playful jab in the stomach. Her knuckles struck cotton-sheathed concrete and popped. "Youch!" She shook her hand. "Spend some serious time in the gym, do ya?"

"I used to. Yes. Been taking it easy these days." He tucked the book under his arm, caught her wrist in a grip that felt like steel bands, and stared into her eyes. Once again, she felt her breath catch in her throat. His gaze was intense. It seemed to delve deep into her brain. She giggled at the funny feeling inside her head, a soft tickling she'd never felt before, like there was a soft bunny rustling around in there. A flash of heat shot through her body, blazing a zigzaggy path down her torso, through her groin, and down to the ground. Then a wave of ice cold followed, making her shiver and coating her entire body in goose bumps.

Who was this man? More, why did he make her feel like she was going to alternately melt and freeze after the most innocent touch? Normally, she didn't get this turned on during the main event.

He lifted her hand to his lips and brushed them over her knuckles. The inner girly part dragged out the sex toys and screamed, *Let the games begin!* as she fought to resist throwing him to the ground and jumping his bones.

Ric Vogel gazed at the adorable chatterbox of a woman in stunned silence. He'd never given much credit to that whole love-at-first-sight thing, had always dismissed it as a foolish notion, something that only existed in movies and songs. But there he was, staring smack dab at it, sucker punched and reeling.

There wasn't a thing about the woman standing before him, gaping like a landed fish, that he didn't adore. Her face was that of an angel. Heart shaped with high cheekbones; a little upturned nose; and big, round eyes that were a soft golden brown. A crown of matching hair fell in glorious waves around her shoulders, beckoning his touch. Her petite body was soft and shapely under her well-fitting clothes. And her scent, sweet and clean, like a meadow in springtime, drew him to her.

He inhaled, wishing he could capture the essence and keep it forever as he brushed his mouth over her knuckles a second time.

"I . . . I . . . I . . . ohhh, Sophie," she murmured in a squeaky little voice.

The voice in his head—a much deeper and louder voice—shouted a flurry of objections to him as he briefly considered taking the cutie pie up on her offer of bribery. He could think of at least a handful of things that could convince him to part with the book still snug under his right arm.

His imagination took that thought as its cue and ran wild, sending image after image through his mind of the woman with the sweet scent and soft body lying naked before him, her legs parted, her eyes closed, her lips pursed, her chest rising and falling swiftly, sighing his name as he brought her to bliss and beyond. Naturally, those images stirred something else—an uncomfortable erection.

He needed to make a few adjustments.

He must have grimaced because the woman's expression changed from utter awe to puzzlement.

Still looking him in the eye, she gently pulled her hand free of his and tipped her head. "All better. Thanks," she whispered. Her lips pursed just a tiny bit, their ripe full-ness making his erection all the more urgent.

"That's a matter of opinion," he grumbled.

"Hmm?" Her eyebrows rose in question.

"I . . . said that's good. Glad to hear it."

"Yeah, that's what I thought you said."

Damn, he liked the way her eyes glittered when she was teasing him. He could just imagine how they would shine when she was in the throes of passion.

"So, I can't convince you to reconsider?" she asked.

Reconsider? What? Taking you home with me? It wouldn't take much to convince me to do that.

"I mean, I really, really need that book. It's a time-sensitive issue we're talking about. A man's life is at stake. Honestly, would you say you need it for anything that dire?"

Almost. My life's at stake, and the lives of my people.

"Unless you're married to a lamia," she said. "I didn't see a ring but figured a girl should never make assumptions."

"No, thankfully, I'm not. Married to a lamia, that is. They wouldn't be interested in me anyway."

"I can't see any female not being interested in you."

"That's a generous compliment, but I'm not a writer. They tend to stick with author types. Poets too."

"Oh. Silly me. Tim did say that . . . I think. I guess I'd better do some reading on the subject."

"You're more likely to find information on the lamiae on the Internet. It's not a widely researched topic," he said as he tried to convince himself it was time to leave. Although his next class didn't start for hours, he had some tests to grade. Since he wasn't fond of fill-in-the-dot Scantron forms, he had about fifty essays left to read. It would take him hours.

Still, he couldn't seem to accept the thought of turning from the woman and walking away. It made him ache inside like nothing ever had before. While he was holding her hand, she'd let him inside your mind, for a mere few seconds, but in that time, he'd seen such beauty and intelligence. Wit, caring. She was the woman of his dreams, and more.

Too bad she'd come to him now, when he was in the midst of such important work. He had no time for a serious relationship now.

He slid the book out from under his arm and forced his gaze from her lovely face, knowing that would be a good start. From there, he'd take one step away, then two. He could do it.

He watched as she combed her fingers through her hair. A long, curling strand fell over her face, wrapping around her chin. Without thinking, he captured the silky lock in his fingertips. His index finger traced her lower lip. His gaze fixed to that full lip as he lowered his head.

"Jeesh!" cut in a high-pitched voice from behind him. "Would ya get a room already?"

He jerked his hand away and spun around, finding the owner of the voice, a girl who couldn't be more than twelve or thirteen standing at the end of the row, wearing a typical preteen's scowl of disapproval.

"There's nothing grosser than watching old people kiss. Nasty," she said to a second girl who stepped around the corner to take her position beside her friend.

"They were making out back here?" the second girl asked. "Darn, I miss everything."

"Come on. They're done now. Besides it wasn't exactly pretty." The first one spun on her heels and dragged her gaping friend away.

The woman, now behind him, laughed softly. "So, what do you do?" she asked.

Figuring the show was over, he turned to face her, the sting of embarrassment still burning his cheeks.

Her eyes widened. "Oh my God! Look at how red you are. You're not a priest, are you? Did we just commit some heinous sin?"

His gaze leapt right back up to her face. "Priest? No. Whatever gave you that idea?"

"The red face for one. And the religious books, I guess. Maybe something else too, something I can't quite name." She chewed her lower lip as she studied his face. Oh boy, did he want to taste that lip of hers. He bet she'd taste sweet, like a ripe summer peach or apple. "You have a priesty air about you."

"Hmmm. Don't know if I should take that as a compliment or not."

"Considering the respect my mother has for her priest, I would."

"Fair enough. Thank you."

"I know what it is!" She lifted her index finger. "It's your soft voice and manner. You move very deliberately and don't say much, just like Father John."

"Ah. Well, thank goodness it wasn't the wrinkles and stooped shoulders."

She squinted, her lips pursed into a cute little pout as she studied his face for a moment. He was mighty tempted to kiss that pout, show her how wrong she was about him being anything like a priest. "Nope. Don't see a single wrinkle. And your shoulders are a lot of things but stooped isn't one of them."

"That I'll take as a compliment." He offered his hand, eager to know her name, just in case . . . in case he might like to contact her about the relics they seemed to be both hunting. Perhaps she'd even like to work together? It would be a strictly professional arrangement. "Name's Ric Vogel. I'm a professor of natural science at Midwestern Michigan University."

"Aha! A professor! Now that makes sense. You seem like the professor type." She tipped her head down just slightly and batted eyelashes long enough to be illegal in at least a few dozen states as she wrapped her dainty hand around his.

He really liked the way that felt. A wave of warmth washed over him. Heat settled low, below his belt. "I thought I was the priest type," he teased, adoring the way her face lit up whenever she had a lightbulb moment. He could practically see the bulb blinking over her head.

"I'm not too proud to admit I made a mistake. You definitely fit the professor image more than the priest. It's your eyes. And my name's Sophie. Sophie Hahn. It's nice to meet you." She gave his hand a single pump up and down and then wiggled her fingers until he released her hand.

"Sophie," he repeated. "I tell you what, why don't we share this book? We can go sit at a desk over there"—he motioned toward a row of tables in a quiet corner—"and read over the material together."

"Wow. That sounds great but . . ." She checked her wristwatch and frowned. "I've got to get back to the office. My lunch hour's just about over. Maybe we can meet somewhere later tonight?"

"I have an introduction to biology class tonight from six to eight-thirty."

"Poop. I don't get off until six. What if I meet you at your classroom at eight-thirty? Would that be okay? I'll need directions. I've never been on Midwestern's campus."

"Sure. That'll be perfect." He checked his pockets for something to write with but he knew he didn't have anything. Empty-handed, he motioned toward her purse, hanging from her shoulder. "Do you have something to write with?"

"Oh. Yes. I suppose that would help." She dug through the contents of her purse until she produced an envelope from an electric bill and a pen with a chewed-up cap. "Please ignore the mangled cap. My boss eats all my pens." She handed them to him.

"Not a problem." He set the book on his bent knee and used it as a makeshift desk as he wrote the directions on the envelope. "I'll see you later, then. Maybe we can get some coffee?" He handed the envelope and pen back to her. His fingers brushed hers and another wave of warmth spread through his body, leaving ripples of wanting in its wake.

"I'm not much of a coffee drinker, especially at night. I'd be up all night long if I drank even half a cup." She smiled.

He swallowed a goofy sigh. That was one killer smile. He wondered if she knew how deadly it was to a guy. His lower parts ached, and his teeth ached from gritting against the other ache. He was just an overall aching mess. "Fair enough." He stood there, book in hand, feeling awkward and self-conscious and very, very horny. The horny part didn't surprise him but the awkward and self-conscious part did. He'd had more than his share of women in his bed. Why did this one make him feel so flustered and unsure? It wasn't like she'd done anything to make him feel that way. Chatty, friendly, and cute, she hardly gave a superior air. Yet when she looked at him with those golden-brown eyes, he squirmed like a kindergartner in church.

He hoped by tonight he'd be back to his cool, composed self. More than that, he hoped he could keep his true nature from her for just a little longer. She needed more time yet. More time to accept the impossible.

Chapter 3

After work, Sophie made a quick stop at Dao's house. Lisse answered the door, shooing her away by telling her Dao was sleeping but had a doctor's appointment in the morning. Sophie wasn't sure if she believed her, but at the moment she was willing to trust Lisse was telling the truth.

She hurried home, picked at a Lean Cuisine, and freshened up, changing into a comfy pair of jeans and white top that showed off the hint of an early summer tan. She slid on a pair of high-heeled mules to make her stumpy legs look a little longer and headed out to the campus.

It had been a while since she'd been on a college campus, eight years to be exact. But she still remembered the feeling of being a student, racing across campus to make her next class, cramming for exams, going to parties in cramped dorm rooms. The memories made her smile. The parking situation, however, didn't.

She found Adams Hall without a problem. A three-story structure of glass and steel, it sat in the middle of a circle of similar buildings. The shared parking lot was at least a couple of football field lengths away. And crammed to capacity. Sure, if she'd waited until after eight-thirty to arrive, it probably would've been empty, but Sophie had to admit she was so anxious to see the good-looking professor—for a number of reasons—she hadn't wanted to wait. As a result, she was twenty minutes early and forced to search the back fifty for an empty spot.

After she found one, a tight spot between two mammoth SUVs, she parked her subcompact, did a final hair and make-up check, and then hurried toward the building. About halfway across the parking lot, the sky opened and half an ocean—or so it seemed—dumped from the clouds in the kind of torrent Michigan is apt to see in early summer. Within seconds, she was drenched to the skin and the victim of a nasty case of goose bumps. If only she'd thought to bring an umbrella!

She briefly considered turning around and heading home, but as she stood, dripping, just inside the doorway, Ric's smooth, deep voice coming from a classroom close by inspired her to cast that notion aside.

So what if she was a tiny bit wet and her shoes made obscene noises when she walked? A little water never hurt anyone. For all she knew, Dao was near death, being Lisse's primary food source. She owed it to him to buck up and do what she must to find him some help, whether it was from a more traditional source or nontraditional.

If a professor of science at a university believed in a lamia, who was she to question it? A guy with the initials PhD after his name had to know more than she did, with her BA.

Sophie stood outside of room 103 and listened as he answered a couple of last-minute questions about the next day's assignment. Then she heard the telltale sounds of zillions of shuffling feet as the attendees headed for the door. Feeling out of place, she stood like a sentry outside the door, waiting for the last few stragglers to leave before she ventured inside. The curious stares she was gathering by students as they wandered past made her nervous and uncomfortable on top of cold. All in all, within seconds she was so miserable, she was ready to make a hasty exit. Maybe she could borrow a copy of that book from another library.

She did an about-face and took a step down the hall.

"There you are . . . oh. Is that you, Sophie?" she heard Ric say behind her.

Too late. Oh well. Gathering what remained of her dignity, she pasted on a smile and turned around. "Yes. It's me. I was just waiting for your students to clear out before I came in." A huge droplet of water dripped from her bangs and landed on the bridge of her nose. Following the law of gravity, it slid down to the tip and hung there.

Ric's gaze followed its path until she swiped the stupid thing away.

Within a heartbeat, she was wishing she had a second water droplet to distract him.

His warm gaze wandered lower, following the line of her neck to her shoulders. It dropped about four inches lower, then didn't budge. All it took was a quick glance down to see why. The torrent in the parking lot had made her formerly cute white shirt absolutely obscene. It was almost completely translucent now. The lines of her bra showed crystal clear, and even more disturbing, two pink nipples poked at the fabric.

"Oh my God!" She gasped and promptly folded her arms over her chest. Her face flamed. So did a few other parts.

Ric's eyes widened, then darted in another direction. He mumbled something that was probably an apology, but with her mind screaming a few dozen curse words, she didn't hear him. He caught her shoulder in one of his huge hands and pulled. "Come inside. You can wear my jacket. You must be cold."

She could guess where he got that idea from! "Thanks. I'm freezing. Wouldn't you know it? Out of nowhere it just started pouring. I hate this time of year." She stepped into the classroom but hung back by the door, letting him go past her. He pulled a tweed jacket off the back of his chair and handed it to her.

Her heart sank. That wasn't the kind of jacket she was hoping for. That jacket looked like the kind that would get ruined easily. But it did look cozy. "Oh, I don't know. This looks like an expensive jacket. I'll get it all wet—"

"I'm not worried about it. Please." He held the jacket by the shoulders and rounded Sophie. "You look like you're freezing."

"Okay. Thanks." She stuffed her right arm through one sleeve, then twisted slightly to find the other one with her left hand. Her shoulder brushed against Ric as she slid her hand into the opening. She found herself short of breath all over again. This guy had a real talent for stopping all normal biological processes in a girl. She voluntarily sucked in a deep breath and turned, whispering, "Thanks" when she was facing him full front.

His chin tipped down as he regarded her with eyes that seemed more gold than brown, unlike earlier. His fingers skimmed the length of her arms, then caught the collar. "My pleasure." He straightened the collar—must've been lopsided. When he blinked, his eyes shone even more gold, like the color of a cat's eyes.

That warm, velvet sensation fluttered through her head again, setting her heart rate into triple time. She tried to think of something funny and clever to say, something to break the spell that seemed to be tangling itself around her, snarling the impulses charging through her brain. "I . . . I . . ."

His head tipped to the side. His eyelids fell to half-mast, partly obscuring those bizarre gold eyes. His tongue darted out to moisten his lips.

Oh my God, he's going to kiss me!

She closed her eyes, dragged in a deep breath, and waited, knowing it would be the kiss of a lifetime, like none she'd ever experienced.

Unfortunately, no sooner did his warm, moist lips make contact with hers than a voice called from somewhere behind them, "Professor Vogel?"

Interrupted again! Dammit.

That young person's voice acted like a bucket of ice water falling from the sky, completely quenching the spark that brief kiss had just begun to ignite. She twisted her neck to look one way. Ric looked the other. The result was impact between her forehead and his nose.

He yelped in surprise. Both his hands flew to his face. "Yes, yes. Matt?"

"Sorry, Professor Vogel. I came back here to ask you a question about Monday night's assignment." The young man's nervous gaze hip-hopped from Ric to Sophie, then back to Ric again. "I can call your office Monday morning if that would be better."

Apparently checking his nose for a fracture, Ric said, "No, that's okay. What's your question?"

"I was just wondering if we had to answer the questions on the section on sexual reproduction or just asexual?"

Sophie snorted through her nose.

Ric gave her a one-eyebrow-lifted, teary-eyed glance, then turned to Matt and said, "You need to read the entire chapter and answer all the questions at the end of each section."

"Okay. Sorry for, er, interrupting. I didn't think you'd have company."

"We're doing some . . . research," Ric said, motioning toward Sophie.

"Yeah. Sure. If that's what you want to call it." He chuckled, then called over his shoulder as he walked back to the door, "I think I'll put in my application for department student research assistant if this is the kind of research the bio department is doing." He shut the door behind him.

Sophie laughed. "Smart kid. Is it broken?" She pointed at Ric's nose.

"No. Just sore. Maybe we should take this back to my office. It's a little more private. We won't have any more interruptions."

That last word sent a shudder of expectation down her spine. She'd never done *it* in a university professor's office before. Sounded like fun. "Sure. Okay. Say, what's this about sexual reproduction? I thought you were a biology teacher, not sex ed."

He gave her a martyred look tempered with just the slightest smile. "We don't teach sex ed in college. The chapter's on cellular reproduction, not human reproduction." He gathered some things from his desk, including the book from the library, then opened the door for her. "Some people's minds."

"What can I say? I hear the word *sex*, I tend to think in human terms. I'd say that's pretty ordinary," she teased as she fell into step beside him.

Moments later Sophie and Ric made themselves comfortable in his closet-sized office—the size of which was fine by her. The closer she was to the hunky professor the better. She asked, "Can I ask you a stupid question?"

"Fire away." He stretched his arms overhead. What a view! Thanks to the well-fitting, short-sleeved shirt he wore, she could see all the yummy planes and ridges of his sculpted chest and arms. Sure she was about to melt, she fanned herself with the nearest scrap of paper she could get in her hands.

"Are you warm?"

"Just a little."

"You could take off the jacket." His gaze dropped to her chest; then he said, "On second thought, I could open the door." He pressed his palms to the desktop as he started to rise from his chair.

"Oh no!" she said, halting him. "I'm fine. Really. I'll take privacy over creature comforts any day."

"Okay. But you'll let me know if it gets too hot?"

"You betcha."

He settled back into his chair again. She drank in the sight of him, so yummy in so many ways. Perfect hair, perfect face, weirdly wonderful eyes that again looked like molten chocolate. Shoulders, chest, narrow waist and hips. She could hardly believe she was in this room with this man. And even more, she could hardly believe he seemed to be flirting with her! No one who looked like he did ever gave her a second look, let alone a come-hither one.

"You wanted to ask me a question?" he said a few moments later, probably feeling weird being ogled again. She was definitely stuck in ogle mode.

"Oh, yeah. Um. Well, why is a professor of natural science doing research on religious relics? I'd expect that to be appropriate research material for a professor of religious studies or even history. But biology? What would an old spear and shield have to do with cellular reproduction?"

"More than you might think."

She leaned forward, intrigued. When he didn't elaborate, she said, "That's all you're going to say?"

"For now."

"Meanie."

He chuckled as he cracked open the book and thumbed through several pages. She liked the way his voice seemed to frolic with her insides like a bouncy puppy. She also liked the way he moved his fingers. They looked deft and capable of doing some wonderful things to choice parts of her anatomy. She fanned herself again but the bitty scrap of paper did nothing to cool her flaming face.

"This is the only book I've found that refers to the Spear of Joshua, or Romakh Yehowshu'a, and Shield of David, Mawgane Dahveed."

"Do you think they really exist?"

"Yes, I do. But I'm beginning to wonder if they are literally a spear and shield."

"If they aren't, what would they be?"

"Well, the Bible's full of metaphors and symbols. There are those who believe every word is to be taken literally and those who believe none of it should. I'm somewhere in the middle. Some of the historical references have been collaborated by extrabiblical sources."

"I see you've done your homework here. I'm impressed. I can't say I've read the Bible cover to cover. I've read bits and pieces, the popular stories mostly, like the stories of Noah and Adam and Eve."

"Do you know who David and Joshua were?"

She rummaged through the deepest recesses of her mind where she stowed little-used facts learned when she was a kid. "David was the kid who killed the giant Goliath, right?"

"Yes, he did that, among other things." Ric rested his elbows on the desktop and steepled his fingers. His forefingers rested just below his lips. Adorable lips. Kissable lips. "And Joshua?"

"I'm a little rusty on the Bible but, I vaguely remember he was a warrior of some kind, I think," she answered, still staring at his mouth.

"Yes. That's correct."

She already knew he would taste wonderful, sweet and spicy. She wondered if he'd object if she took up where they'd left off in the classroom.

"So, uh." She leaned forward. He leaned back. Guess he wasn't in the mood for a lip-lock now. Bummer! What were they talking about? Oh yeah. David. "Why wouldn't you think they were literal if the guys were real? Didn't David have a shield when he fought Goliath?"

He shook his head. "No."

"Oh." She let her gaze wander for a few. It decided to take a rest on his shoulders for a while. After all, that was some rough terrain, climbing all those bulges and bumps. She fanned herself harder.

Concentrate, you hussy! This is for Dao, the guy who held you together after your sister died. Remember him?

That chastisement cooled her raging hormones considerably, and her foggy head cleared a bit too.

"If you remember the story, David went before the giant with no sword or shield. He had his slingshot and a handful of stones."

"I guess I forgot that part. I feel a little stupid. I should know this stuff, went to Catholic schools for years."

"Don't feel stupid. There are parts of the Bible I know nothing about too."

His confession didn't make her feel a whole lot better but she continued the conversation anyway. Obviously the time of impressing him with her knowledge of all things biblical had passed. It was time to get answers. For Dao. "Didn't Joshua have a spear when he fought with . . . whoever he fought with?"

"Yes."

"And didn't David eventually fight with a shield against somebody?"

"Most likely."

"Then there you go! What makes you think the spear and shield aren't literally an old spear and shield?"

He pursed his lips, then drew them into a long, narrow line. Yet his face was still as sexy and perfect as it had been before. "Tradition for one. The Magen David is the Star of David, the symbol worn by the Jewish. The six-pointed star. According to tradition it has magical powers and appeared on King David's shield and King Solomon's ring."

She struggled to keep from falling back into lust mode again. Parts south of her waist refused to listen. "So we're looking for something with the Star of David on it?"

"Perhaps, and then again, maybe not. I read something once . . ." He shuffled through the stack of papers sitting next to the book. "This was written about thirty years ago. I think the author was ahead of his time." He pulled out a smudgy copy of an article and set it in front of her.

She scanned the page. "This is from that tabloid you see at the grocery store? The one with stories of Mary's likeness burned into roast beef or promises of the Second Coming written in tea leaves?"

He shrugged. "At the time it was probably the only medium that would take this story seriously enough to print it."

"Maybe there's a reason for that."

"You said you had an open mind," he challenged, his gaze drilling hers until she squirmed, for more than one reason. "Read the whole thing before you make a judgment. We must know what we are searching for before we can find it."

"That part I can agree with." She gave him a quick questioning glance, which was answered with a slight shake of his head. Then she dropped her eyes to the article and started reading.

After about two paragraphs, however, Sophie realized she didn't understand a single word the author was saying. She handed the paper back to Ric. "This is way over my head. It should be in a theology textbook, not in a tabloid."

"My point exactly."

"Why would they print this?"

"Because it has a spark of truth yet seems unbelievable as well."

"Want to give me a layman's summary then? I mean, if you've got this all figured out, why don't you have the sword and shield already?"

"Spear. Romakh Yehowshu'a. Joshua's spear. Because I don't have it all figured out yet. But I'm hoping you'll be able to help me; we'll tackle it together. I've been working on this for a long time but haven't been able to make the pieces fit."

She laughed. "You honestly don't expect me to believe that *I*—the one who doesn't know diddly about the Bible, or David or Joshua or Jewish symbols—will be able to help *you*—a superbrilliant college professor? How could I possibly help you? For all practical purposes, I'd say I need you more than you need me."

"That's very kind," he said, his eyes sparkling, his expression full of naughty promises, which had her retracing her words to see if she'd said anything too suggestive.

When she realized the "I need you" thing could be taken at least a couple of ways, she felt her face heating again. Her privates went into party mode. "I'm talking about the research, you understand."

One side of his mouth quirked. "Of course. So was I. In researching this topic, you happen to have one thing going for you that I don't—objectivity."

She felt her still-stinging face screwing up into a mask of confusion. "My friend is possibly near death, his very life being drained by what my boss is telling me is a real-life vampire, and you say I'm objective? I'd say I'm desperate."

"You're objective because you don't have any preconceived notions—"

"Sure I do. I assumed the shield and spear were literal weapons. And I'm still skeptical of your theory that they're not. So why don't you tell me the real reason why you invited me here tonight? I'm dying to know."

He looked at her thoughtfully for a moment, as if he was trying to find a gentle way to break some bad news to her. "Because I sense we both need someone at our side as we travel this road. Am I wrong?"

"You?"

"Yes."

Her heart did a little pitter-pattering. He needed her. Not just because she was brilliant and could solve some riddle for him—which she wasn't and couldn't—but because he wanted her at his side, his partner. "That would be . . . nice."

"But before we shake on this deal, I need to hear it. I need to hear you need me too, and not just because I know more about this subject than you do."

"Wow. Okay." Her gaze brushed over his features—the cute crinkles at the corners of his eyes, the little mole on his left cheek—and felt the warmth of his companionship and friendship in eyes gone all warm and golden seep into her bones. "I need someone whom I can trust, someone who won't laugh when I make a stupid mistake, and some-one who'll cheer me on when I get frustrated. Although I haven't known you but a couple of hours tops, I feel like that person is you. That I've been searching for you, that I've known you a whole lot longer than one day. Is that strange?"

"Not at all."

"Good. Then we have a deal? We're not just going to share this book but we're going to share this journey, help each other, any way we can?"

"You bet." Just like he had in the library, he offered his hand to her, and just like before, she took it. Again, a strange tingle buzzed up her arm, like a current of low-voltage electricity. Not sure what it was, or if it would hurt her, she gave his hand a quick shake, then released it, checking her hand when he let go.

Just like that, with a simple handshake, they formed their partnership.

But only one knew what that handshake really meant.

Chapter 4

"Stay the night."

Sophie took one look at Lisse's face and gave her head a vehement shake. "No. Thanks." It wasn't because Lisse looked particularly bothered by Dao's suggestion, but the opposite, because she looked fairly pleased by it. If—and Sophie admitted this was still a big if—Lisse was a vampire, the fact that she was seemingly thrilled to have another female under her roof for the night didn't bode well for Sophie's health and well-being. What good would she be to Dao if she was dead?

"Please," Dao said. "We have a great deal of catching up to do. We haven't seen each other in such a long time, since before the wedding."

"I was here a few days ago."

"You were not. Don't lie to me."

Now, she was really worried. Never mind the fact that it seemed her already skeletally thin friend looked like he'd lost another few pounds, but now he was confused too. He needed to get to a doctor. Pronto!

"What time's your doctor's appointment tomorrow?"

"His appointment is at eight o'clock and it would be a great help if you could take him," Lisse answered. "I was going to have him drive himself, but I worry about his safety."

"That makes two of us," Sophie said, still not feeling real keen on the idea of staying in the same home with a suspected blood-sucking husband killer.

"And I'm afraid I have a prior appointment I cannot reschedule," Lisse said importantly. "It would be a great help—to both of us—if you'd take him. I know you've been a great friend to my husband in the past."

"I'd be happy to drive by in the morning and pick him up."

"That's foolish!" Dao piped in. "You've stayed here hundreds of times. In morning rush hour it'd take you over an hour to get here. We have a perfectly comfortable spare bedroom. You'll have privacy."

He was systematically killing off every one of her believable excuses. Darn it.

"I don't have any clothes, toothbrush. Can't deny the importance of oral hygiene," she said, frantically working her way through the unbelievable excuses now. She had a feeling in her belly that this was a bad—with a capital *B*—idea. That if she spent the night there, something very terrible would happen. To her, to Dao, maybe to both of them.

"Yes, you do," Dao countered. "You left several things here the last time you spent the night. You have some toiletries in the bathroom and clothes hanging in the closet. And since I know you can wear casual clothes to work, I won't hear the excuse that they're not dressy enough."

"Speaking of work, I'd have to call Tim," Sophie said, pulling one final excuse from her stash, knowing Dao wouldn't have a card to trump that one. "Tell him I'm coming in late tomorrow. Maybe this isn't such a good idea. I can call the doctor's office and reschedule the appointment."

"Very well," Dao said. "You can use our phone. Call him now."

Whew! Disaster averted. "I'll need the doctor's phone number."

"No. I mean your boss," Dao corrected. "Call him."

"He's not in the office on Sundays," Sophie lied, knowing he would be. Tim never took a day off work, not even when he was near death with the flu.

"You can leave a message then," Lisse offered, handing Sophie the cordless. "Please, this would mean so much to both of us."

I bet it would. "Well . . ." Sophie figured her best bet was to call Tim, the boss who expected her to show up as well when she was near death, and let him do the deed for her. There was no way he'd let her come in late on such short notice, at least not without her doing some serious groveling, which she'd been prepared to do if she hadn't been pressured to stay the night. Now, there was no way she'd get on her knees and grovel. "Okay. I'll give it a try but my boss is a real slave driver, let me tell you." She punched the number and when he picked up said, "Hi, Tim. It's Sophie. Wow, what're you doing in the office on a Sunday?"

"You know I always work on Sundays," was his dry response.

"Oh, really?" She tried to look surprised as she gave Dao and Lisse a what-do-you-know look.

"I am talking to Sophie Hahn, my secretary, am I not?" Tim asked.

"Yes, of course. Listen, I need to come in late tomorrow morning."

Naturally, Tim protested with all the bluster he was famous for. She turned apologetic eyes to Dao and Lisse, respectively, as she listened to Tim's lecture about the need for him to be able to count on her to show up for work every day no matter what.

"Actually, it's not me. It's my friend Dao," she explained when he paused to take a breath. "He's ill and his wife can't take him to the doctor tomorrow morning," Sophie continued, figuring that last part would lay the last couple of nails into the proverbial coffin. "They want me to stay with them tonight and take him to the doctor in the morning."

Unfortunately, it had the opposite effect.

"What?" Tim screeched. He then went into Paranormal Geek mode and told her this was the opportunity of a lifetime, one she had to take, no matter the risks. He told her to try to catch the wife by surprise, snap a picture or two when she was in her snakewoman state, and collect any scales or proof she could find, then suggested she sleep with a string of garlic around her neck and wished her luck.

As she punched the button, ending the call, for a few seconds she considered lying to Dao and Lisse but changed her mind. Maybe Tim was right. Maybe this was exactly what she needed, the opportunity to see for herself whether her best friend was married to a grotesque snakewoman. Or just a woman. At least she'd see her friend received the medical care he so desperately needed.

"It's all set. I just need to go pick up a few things at the store." Sophie headed for the front door.

"Wonderful!" Dao said, looking as chipper as he'd been on his wedding day.

Lisse caught Sophie's wrist in ice-cold fingers. "Thank you. You have no idea what this means to me."

Sophie's gaze dropped to the other woman's clammy hand, then climbed up to her face. "No problem. I'll be back in a few." She gently wriggled her hand free of the woman's grip and, fighting a shiver, ran out to her car.

A quick trip to a local Meijer landed her all the goodies she could think to buy for a night spent with a vampire, including plenty of garlic and a throwaway camera. She returned to Dao's house just in time for some dinner.

The only thing that convinced Sophie that it was safe to

eat the delicious-smelling food was the fact that it was served family style, each person helping himself or herself from bowls of steamed rice, stir-fried veggies, and scrumptious garlic chicken. Sophie ate herself into a near coma, then excused herself to the guest room, figuring she'd better get to sleep early if she was going to prowl around in the middle of the night playing vampire slayer.

Dao ate a whole lot more than Sophie expected, considering his weight loss, and then excitedly excused himself to his office to work on his latest project. His office was next door to her room. The distant tap-tapping of his computer keys lulled her to sleep.

"A rare beauty," a decidedly male voice murmured sometime later. The voice was rich and deep, much lower in pitch than Dao's.

"Who's there?" Sophie blinked open her eyes and sat up. The covers slid down, exposing her upper body to the chilly air. Not sure if the room was pitch or her eyelids were still closed, she blinked several times. No, her eyes were definitely open.

"Your skin is smooth as silk," the voice said.

"Who's here? And how can you see a blasted thing in here? It's darker than a bottomless cave."

"Pit. You mean bottomless pit," the voice corrected.

"Whatever." She felt the string of garlic lifting from her chest and swatted at the air, trying to find the hand that was pulling it away. "Hey! What're you doing? Leave that alone. Dammit, why's it so dark in here? Where's the lamp?"

"I can see you just fine. I can see the way your hair falls over your shoulders, how one strand curls around your breast. I can see your pupils, dilated from the dark, and from your fear."

"Now I know you're lying. 'Cause I'm not afraid. Annoyed, yes. Scared, not." She yanked on the strap of her tank top—it had slid down over her shoulder—and tried to pretend her heart wasn't thumping so hard against her breastbone that she swore she could hear it. The voice-in-the-dark thing was plain too weird for words. She scooted to the side of the bed so she could flip on a light, but as she dropped her legs over the side, something pushed against her shoulders, knocking her onto her back. "Okay, deep voice guy. Now things are getting creepy. Get the hell out of here."

"Such fire. Such passion. I can smell your fear. It's the most intoxicating aphrodisiac on earth."

Something brushed across her breast.

"Eep!" Totally blind and not sure where the guy was, she did a log roll on the mattress and then tried to jump up. Again, she was knocked down. And these weren't gentle shoves. They were the kind of blows a woman should never be the victim of. They were the kind of blows that sent Sophie's head spinning and bile up her throat. She screamed but a large, cold hand clapped over her mouth, muffling the sound almost immediately.

"There's no need for that." Cool lips pressed against her temple as fingers traced up her arm. "I'm not going to hurt you. At least not much." His chuckle was empty, evil.

She shuddered and tried to scream again but his hand was still pressed firmly against her mouth. Try as she might, she couldn't even bite it.

Those icky fingers skittered up her arm like spiders, then along her collarbone and down toward her breast. She kicked at the blackness, hoping to strike him by dumb luck, but the only effect her efforts produced was the weight of a body on the tops of her thighs. That left only her arms free. She raised them to the hand pressed so firmly against her mouth that she felt like she might suffocate and dug her nails into the cool skin.

He didn't react, at least not the way she was hoping. Instead of recoiling, he threw his weight on her arms, ripped the front of her tank top off, and with little effort gagged her. Then he tore her sweats down the front and pulled them off. In the darkness, the rending sound of the cotton blend struck terror in her. Certain she was fighting now for her life, she struggled against him as he spread her legs and tied them to the footboard, then bound her hands together.

The fabric he used was pulled so tight her skin burned and her hands went instantly numb.

Her throat stung and she realized she had been screaming, despite the gag. Hot tears ran down her temples and wetted her hair.

A split second later, the room unexpectedly filled with light, forcing her to blink and squint as she struggled to get a look at her assailant.

She was shocked. If not for the fact that the jerk had knocked her from here to tomorrow and torn her clothes off her body, she might've thought he was a stone fox. Almost the opposite of Ric, this guy was dark. He had long, dark hair, a masculine, square-jawed face with intense eyes. The only things they shared in common were their very large, very strong-looking bodies.

She tried to talk through the gag, ask him why he was doing this. Surely this guy, looking the way he did, didn't need to sneak into women's bedrooms in the middle of the night to get some action.

He stood at the foot of the bed, thick, muscular arms crossed over a massive chest, and regarded her with a stern expression. "Look what you made me do. I didn't want it to be this way, love." Still completely clothed—head to toe in black—he crawled on top of her. His gaze was fierce and wild as it met hers, like a dog that was poised for attack.

Her nose burned as another round of tears dribbled from her eyes. She shook her head back and forth, trying to plead with him with her eyes, hoping she might reach a soft part of him, somewhere deep inside. A part of him that could show mercy.

"This your first time?" he asked, nodding his head. His touch was unexpectedly soft as he wiped away the wetness streaming down either side of her face. "She didn't tell me that. I'll make it good for you. I promise." He followed the path of her tears with a trail of soft kisses. "I'm so glad you decided to stay here tonight."

"She? Who? You knew?" she asked around the gag. Naturally, it didn't come out like that and he had no idea what she said.

He nodded, though she knew for a fact he couldn't be responding to her question, and sat up on his knees, wedged tightly against her hips. "The first time is always frightening. But after this, you'll learn to enjoy it. There's nothing like it, or so I've heard. I've been told it's very erotic."

What? What are you going to do to me? Sophie's heart hammered against her ribs, sending adrenaline through her body. Every muscle in her coiled like tight springs, despite the bindings holding her legs straight and apart and her arms up over her head. Over and over, she tested the strength of the fabric holding her, yanking, twisting, tugging, but it didn't give. Not an inch.

Meanwhile, she tried, despite panic so intense she was nearly blind, to study his face. When she went to the police—assuming she lived!—she wanted to be able to describe every inch of this bastard, right down to the mole on his ass if he had one. He would pay! Big-time!

When his hand cupped her breast, she arched her back in a quick thrust, hoping to knock it away. It worked, but only for an instant. He seemed undaunted as he grabbed the center hook of her bra and unfastened it, then squeezed both her breasts, one with each hand. "So lovely. So full and ripe." He leaned lower and she shut her eyes, unable to watch him as he closed his mouth over her nipple. She was scared. Furious. Panic-stricken. Desperate to get away. Pissed off.

Again, she arched her back, hoping to hit the son of a bitch silly with her stomach, not that it was hard or anything. When it came to weapons, her belly was probably one of the lamest, but at the moment it was all she had. That and her head. She pulled at the strips binding her arms and legs, her mind racing, trying to grasp at a solution, an escape from what was becoming more inevitable with every breath she took.

Then, the inevitable became immediate. In a quick motion almost too fast to see, he ripped the front of her panties away, exposing all of her to his feasting eyes.

She gagged and tossed her head to the side, hoping she wouldn't choke from her own vomit.

The man drew in a visible breath, his lips curled into a cruel smile. "The scent of your need. So sweet. Almost as intoxicating as the smell of your fear."

"Go to hell!" she tried to shout.

"I don't need you nude but"—he ran a finger over her sex, then brought it to his nose and inhaled—"I'll enjoy my meal much more when you are completely uncovered. Your scent is so incredibly sweet. I can't wait to taste you. To have your flavor fill my mouth, my throat." When he smiled, a set of long fangs flashed in the dim lamplight. Fangs like she'd seen in the vampire movie she'd watched last month, and on that vampire romance book cover she'd checked out last week at Borders.

They're real? Vampires really exist?

"You'll enjoy the feeding. I promise." He lowered his head, clearly aiming for her inner thigh.

Not fond of an insect bite, let alone the whopper of a chomp Mr. Fangs was about to impart on her, Sophie fought with a frenzy against her bindings. She tossed her head, kicked her feet, thrashed her body from side to side, twisted her wrists until she was breathless and dizzy and worn out. Finally, completely spent, she stilled and tried to psych herself up for more struggling in a minute or two.

"That's it, my love. Relax," he said, watching her dully. "It won't hurt for long." Again, he lowered his head to her thigh, but before his teeth even grazed her skin, she went into fight mode again.

Those teeth were not going to sink into her skin! Nuh-uh! That was bound to hurt like a son of a gun, never mind the whole "Will I become one of them?" question.

This time, he scowled. "You do not want to make me angry, my love. I must feed. I *will* feed." This time he pinned her hips to the mattress with his hands as he lowered his head.

First she felt damp warmth as his tongue laved her skin. And then the fierce, blinding pain of his bite. She felt those teeth sink into her flesh. As he fed, there was a strange sensation of building ripples of heat washing up her body, ripples that traveled out from the point where he fed. Each one was bigger, hotter, fiercer until they were like gigantic tsunamis blasting her with white heat. She shuddered, her body thrown into an unexpected orgasm. Every part of her convulsed, even as he drew more and more of her strength from her body.

Finally, completely exhausted, she lay still. He lifted his head, licked away the blood smeared across his lips, and smiled. His teeth retracted up into his jaw. He kissed her forehead, whispered a promise to return to her, and flipped out the light. Despite her numb hands and feet, the burn at her wrists and ankles, and the throbbing on her right thigh, she fell asleep instantly.

When Sophie woke, the birds outside the window were chirping, the warm light of morning spilling in through the lace curtains. She was lying on her stomach. The bindings were gone but the red burn marks on her wrists gave testimony to what had happened last night. It hadn't been a dream.

She tossed off the blanket to check her leg and found she was still nude. There wasn't even the slightest bruise on her thigh where the vampire had bitten her, yet her ankles were marred with big, ugly red welts.

She couldn't believe it! Vampires did exist and she'd been a snack for some dark-haired bloodsucker! Worse yet, he'd made her come! She wasn't sure which part was the hardest to swallow.

She was still trying to deal with it when she stole a quick glance at the clock, then, shocked by the time, scurried from the bed.

"No way!"

Eleven freaking o'clock? One hour before noon! Not only did she miss Dao's doctor's appointment, but she was also late for work. "Shit!" She gathered her clothes from the closet, raced to the bathroom, showered, and dressed.

No one stirred in the master bedroom. Maybe Dao'd gone to the doctor without her? She hoped he was okay. Damn it, she'd known something bad was going to happen last night. Lisse was behind that little social call she'd received last night. She had no doubt. Probably to keep her from taking Dao to the doctor.

"Dao? Are you in there?" When Sophie received no answer to her knocks, she tried the bedroom door. It was unlocked. She pushed it open and peered into the darkened room. Right away, she saw there were two people in the bed.

One of the heads lifted—Lisse's. "Did you sleep all right?" she asked, with the kind of smile that suggested she already knew the answer.

"I . . . missed the appointment."

"That's all right. I rescheduled. It's just as well," Lisse whispered. "My dear Dao. He's so very tired. I didn't have the heart to wake him this morning. You will lock the door on the way out?"

Was he sleeping or dead? "Yes. Of course," Sophie said, not intending to do any such thing. She needed to see Dao, to make sure that blood-sucking, no-good snake hadn't done something awful to him.

"Very well. Thanks anyway. Your heart was in the right place." Lisse rested her head back on the pillow, effectively ending the conversation.

Not sure what to do, Sophie shut the door. She went back to the spare room; gathered her torn clothes, unused camera, and purse; and went to the living room to place it next to the door. Then, she unwrapped the camera and tiptoed back to the master bedroom door. She'd missed the doctor's office visit but she had to at least make sure Dao would survive until she could get him to a doctor later.

She did everything in her power to turn the doorknob and push open the door swiftly and silently. Lisse was lying on top of Dao, her head tossed back in bliss as she rode him. The covers were thrown off them both.

It was clear Dao was very much alive. But that didn't make Sophie feel any better.

A long serpentine tail coiled under Lisse's torso. The very tip twitched like a rattler's tail.

Breathless with fear, Sophie raised the camera to her eye to snap the picture. The exact moment she pressed the button, Lisse twisted her neck to look at her and bared hooked, white fangs.

"How dare you!" the snakewoman hissed.

Sophie snapped several shots, then made a mad dash for the front door, her heart up in her throat. Tim was right! Poor, poor Dao. He was being drained of life by the woman he thought he loved.

Sophie left her friend's house vowing to do whatever was necessary to get him away from that monster. She was so furious, she didn't even remember driving to work. But, despite her mental gymnastics, she couldn't come up with a single idea on how to save him.

She walked into the office, late as she said she would be, and answered Tim's scowl with a wave of the camera. "I have your proof!"

"You'd better because I was ready to fire you. I've had to sit here all morning answering phones. I missed two appointments."

"It's here. I saw her. She looks like a hairy cobra. Scary." She gave an involuntary shudder. "I never in a million years would've believed it if I hadn't seen it with my own eyes. Vampires are real! Vampires . . . are real." She dropped into her chair and hit the power button on her computer. She caught sight of the red burn marks on her wrists as she moved. "Oh, and there's more."

"More?" Tim grinned gleefully. "What? What?"

"I think one of her evil minions paid me a visit last night too. At first I thought it was a dream but take a look." She held out her wrists for him to inspect. "He tied me up and the marks are still there."

"Do I want to ask what he did after that?"

She felt her cheeks flame. "No, he didn't . . . you know . . . you sicko. But he bit me."

"Where?" Tim's wide-eyed gaze flew to her throat.

"Not there. On the leg. But there's no mark. Not even a little red bump. Nothing."

"Mmmm. That's bad."

"It's bad that there's no mark?" Despite the fact that the bite had been on her leg, her hand flew to her neck.

"No, it's bad that he bit you."

"Why?" she asked, fighting another shudder. "Do real vampires carry some bizarre disease I need to know about? Or am I going to become one of them? I really, really like the sun. I don't think I could live in eternal darkness."

"It's bad because that means he'll have a certain measure of power over you the next time you see him."

"I don't like the sound of that, either. I pride myself in my independence and bullheadedness."

"I've noticed."

Sophie stuck her tongue out. Yes, it was juvenile, but then again, so was Tim's comment. "What kind of power will he have over me? Will he be able to hypnotize me? Will I be like a zombie, unable to think for myself?"

"You've been watching too much late-night TV."

"No, I don't watch any TV at all—outside of *The Apprentice*. I'm addicted to that show, I admit it. I just have an active imagination."

"Let's put it this way, after one bite you might not become a zombie but you'd also find it mighty difficult to resist any commands he might make."

Her heart stopped. "Even if they were to hurt someone I care about?"

Tim nodded gravely. "Even if they were to hurt someone you care about."

"Shit." Was Lisse trying to find a way to use her? To kill her husband? Oh no! "Is there a cure? Please, please tell me there's a cure or I won't be able to trust myself around anyone I care about, especially Dao."

"There're a couple of ways that I know of. One, you have to defeat the one who made him, if you can figure out whom that was."

Defeat? Her stomach turned. She could just imagine what that would involve. "Could it be Lisse?"

"The lamia?"

"Yes. That's the only Lisse I know."

"It's possible but unlikely. There's no record of any progeny from the lamiae."

"Shoot. Then I have no clue where to start. I didn't even get the bloodsucker's name. What's option number two?

I'm assuming there's at least one other way. You said 'couple.' That implies two."

"Yes, two. The other is to get another vampire to bite you. Not just any vampire, a member of another—"

"Not on your life! That hurt like hell. I'm not letting any more vampires near my person, under no circumstances. That option is out. Besides, it's not like I can put an ad in the paper asking for vampire volunteers. Could you just imagine the freaks who would answer that ad? Crazies with a blood fetish. Or nuts who haven't taken their happy pills for a few weeks. I wouldn't know where to hunt down another real vampire."

Tim shrugged. "I don't know what to tell you then."

"In other words, you're saying I'm screwed."

Tim nodded again and patted her shoulder. "Sorry to say it but yes, I think so."

"Shit." How would she help Dao now? She didn't even dare get near him.

"Say, do you mind if I take a few readings from you?" Tim asked, eyeing her like a scientist might a frog stretched out in a tin pan. "If you cooperate, I might be convinced to give you a bonus."

"A bonus? What kind of bonus?" Sophie had a feeling that might come in handy very soon. She had no idea what it was going to take to save Dao and herself from the bloodsuckers, but she figured having Tim owe her a favor or two might be to her advantage. "Tell me your tests don't involve needles? I hate needles. Or pain. And have I told you that blood—"

"Most of them are painless. But I know you'll be a good sport. It's for The Cause. I've never had the recipient of a real vampire bite in my office before."

"Just promise me job stability for the next five years. And any help you can offer regarding vampires would be appreciated too. I'll give you free reign—as long as you don't expect me to strip naked for you. That would be too creepy."

"You got it." He offered his hand, and for the second time in twenty-four hours, she found herself shaking a man's hand in a deal.

"Okay. I'm all yours. But be gentle, will you? I've been through a lot the past twenty-four hours."

"No problem." He raced back to his office and returned with what looked like a medieval torture device.

Chapter 5

"Hello, Sophie." Even on the voice mail, Ric's voice sounded silky. Her girly parts got all warm and happy as Sophie listened to his message. "I've found a local expert on rare biblical artifacts. She's out of a small Catholic university up in Grand Rapids. I'm going out to interview her tomorrow. I'd like to know if you might like to join me. I'm thinking of leaving tonight and getting a hotel room in the Grand Rapids area overnight."

She looked at the ugly purple bruise on the crook of her left arm. After the battery of tests Tim had put her through, he owed her. Big-time. No better time than the present to call in one of the many favors he owed her.

She rang Tim, told him to hire a temp for tomorrow. Much to Sophie's surprise, he didn't give her the usual bluster or threats. Instead, he wished her luck and told her if she needed anything to give him a call.

Next, she called the number Ric had left for her. He didn't answer so she left a message for him, telling him she'd be ready to go, bags packed, by eight.

Finally, she put in a call to Dao, told him she was leaving town for a day or two but would call him later to check up on him. Naturally, Lisse had lied. There was no doctor's appointment later. Then again, how much could a doctor do for a guy who was being drained by a vampire? Dao sounded tired, but reasonably well enough. His spirits were good at least. He was well enough to tease her about not needing a mother. But he was disappointed when she said she couldn't come by and read some more of his latest work in progress. She figured that would be risky, for a number of reasons. One, she might insult him if he pressed her to tell him her honest opinion because she didn't dare lie to her dearest friend. And two, if that vampire showed up and did his vampire-voodoo-hypnotism on her, she might do something to hurt Dao. She couldn't risk either.

It didn't take her long to pack her suitcase. She made sure she had her very best underwear—a girl never knew what might happen on a road trip with a sexy college professor—and appropriate professional attire for their meeting tomorrow with the expert. Her stomach was jumpier than normal, so not wanting to risk upchucking in poor Ric's car, she took a double dose of motion sickness medicine. Ready at last, and feeling the effect of the medicine, she flopped her weary body on the sofa and waited for Ric to show up.

By the time he arrived, ten to eight—she loved a man who was punctual—she was feeling really good. Like had-a-couple-of-Long-Island's good. Who would've thought a couple of little bitter pills would do that to a girl? She knew she had a goofy smile plastered over her face when she opened the door to let him in, but she couldn't seem to shake it off.

"Hi?" Ric half said, half asked as he eyeballed her. "Are you ready?"

"Yeppers, as ready as I'll ever be." She thrust her overnight bag at him, then bent to pick up her suitcase.

"I see you packed like a typical female," he said on a chuckle.

"You know, life isn't fair. You guys can get away with a clean pair of underwear and socks, a little deodorant, and a toothbrush whereas we women have to pack half our bathroom with us when we go anywhere." She swiped a second time at the suitcase, which seemed to be sliding just out of her reach when she moved. "I swear I did the best I could." Not used to wearing heels, she stumbled when her ankle turned. Fortunately, there was a tall, very solid man standing next to her to keep her from falling over.

Sort of leaning against him, she tested her twisted ankle; then when it passed muster, she righted herself.

"Are you sure you're okay? You seem a little . . ." He let his words trail off unfinished.

"A little what? A little nervous? Yes, I'm nervous. Who wouldn't be? I'm going on a three-hour road trip with you, for God's sake. Look at you. You're like a movie star or something." She reached up and combed her fingers through his hair. "Look at this. Soft as silk, with sunny highlights. The color makes you look like a sexy beach bum. I can barely contain myself."

The left side of his mouth curled up into a naughty smile. "I wouldn't have guessed."

"And this body! What can I say about that? Sheesh! It's absolutely perfect. I bet there's a puddle of drool around you wherever you go. Women have to go absolutely gaga for you." She wrapped her hands around a thick bicep and squeezed. "Rock hard. Yummy."

"Can't say I've ever seen any puddles, though I appreciate the compliment. At least none that could be attributed to drooling women. Uh, did you happen to hit the happy sauce a little early today?"

"Oh, heck no. I don't touch the stuff. Hate feeling out of control, if you know what I mean."

"Sure, I understand completely." He caught her chin in his hand and tipped it up until she met his gaze.

"Plus I've been told I act like a complete moron when I'm loaded. . . ." Sophie stared into eyes the color of honey graham crackers. She was hungry. "What're you doing?"

"Checking something. They're a little dilated."

Dilated? "What?"

"Your pupils."

"Oh." That kind of dilated. She giggled. "I was beginning to wonder. Thought maybe you worked a second job in a maternity ward somewhere. I suppose that's a silly thing to think." She giggled some more.

"You're acting a little giddy too." His cute eyebrows marched to the center of his forehead as he lowered his head.

Oh boy! He was going to kiss her! Her girly parts started doing the wave as she closed her eyes and puckered up. But after waiting for several excruciating seconds, she blinked open her eyes. He was still studying her, like a specimen in his lab. "What's wrong?"

"I don't smell anything."

"What did you expect to smell? I brushed my teeth and used mouthwash. Minty fresh, not mediciney. Smell." She blew a gentle stream into his face.

"Yes, I already did. Thanks."

"Since I passed the eye exam and breath test, are we ready to leave?"

"I guess." Ric took the heavy suitcase from Sophie and held the door until she was outside. Her ankle twisted once more when she took the porch steps a little too quick. And this time it smarted something fierce. She let out a little yelp and hobbled to the car.

"I swear I'm not usually this clumsy," she explained to a worried-looking Ric as she flopped into the passenger seat. "I'm not used to walking in heels, would rather wear a pair of tennies any day, but I figured I should look nice for you."

"I appreciate the thought." He shut the door and rounded the rear of the car, tossing her suitcase into the trunk. That minor detail taken care of, he took his seat and started the car. "Okay, off we go."

"Yippee. I feel like I'm back in college again." She rolled down the window a crack. Even though Ric's car was probably twice the size of hers, it still felt mighty cramped in there. Little frissons of awareness skittered over her skin, making her warm. She was thankful for the medicine, which seemed to be working beautifully. "By the way, I figure I can tell you this. I had my very first face-to-face— er, rather face-to-leg—experience with a real-live vampire last night."

"You did?" He looked surprised, maybe even a little alarmed. His gaze flew from where it should be—the road full of traffic—to her face. "When?"

"When I was sleeping. Eyes on the road, please." When he returned his attention to where it belonged, she added, "I spent the night over at Dao's. His icky snakewoman wife sicced some creepy vampire on me while I was sleeping. I'm sure of it."

"What happened?"

"He bit me, that's what happened."

Once again, his gaze flew from the road. "Where?"

"On the leg. It hurt like a son of a gun." She didn't add the other part, the part about her having lost all control and succumbing to a bite-induced orgasm. He didn't need to know about that. No one needed to know about that. Heck, she wished she didn't know about that.

"Shit!" He slammed his flattened palms against the steering wheel. Hard.

"It's okay. I swear. Healed up nicely. Though I'm a little scared I might hurt Dao now and I still have the burn marks from where he tied me—" She cut off the rest of the sentence when Ric glared at her. For some reason, she had the impulse to defend herself. "I swear I didn't enjoy it. Not one little bit. I called him all kinds of bad names but he wouldn't stop. One of the few people I've ever met who actually listened when their mom told them that names don't hurt. I guess real vampires aren't particularly sensitive."

Ric grumbled some incoherent something or other.

"Tim told me I'll be like the guy's zombie or something, won't be able to resist his commands. Do you know anything about that? Do you know anything about vampires?"

"It's possible. Depends upon how much venom he injected."

"Venom? Like a snake?"

"Exactly." He glanced at her again, but only for a split second. "This could explain your erratic behavior tonight."

"That, or the four pills I took for motion sickness. I get awfully sick when I take long car rides."

"Ah . . . so that's it."

"Am I acting that loopy?"

"Loopy, no. Clumsy, yes. And you're being rather . . . blunt. Whatever you took, it seems to act as a truth serum for you."

"Oh dear. I'll have to keep that in mind next time. I don't know what's worse, unloading all my deepest, darkest secrets on you or unloading my lunch."

He grimaced.

"Yeah. I'm with you on that. The lunch is probably more embarrassing and definitely more stinky. Just promise me you won't repeat anything I tell you to anyone."

"You have my word."

"Excellent. Now before I confess anything more embarrassing than my lust for your yummy bod, I think I'd better take a little nappy."

"No way. I'm having fun talking to you like this. Stay awake and keep me company." His words were a demand, but his lighthearted tone tempered them. And the smile that accompanied the words, well, that did her in.

"Okay," she relented on a sigh.

"Let's see how much we can learn about each other in three hours, shall we?"

"I'm game. There's lots of stuff I'd like to know about you." *Like what you look like naked.* "Can I ask the first question?"

He chuckled like he'd heard her thoughts. Good thing he couldn't. "Certainly. Shoot."

She studied his profile for a second. It was a very nice profile. His forehead was neither too heavy like a Neanderthal's nor soft like a woman's. His nose was long and straight, his jaw strong. *He couldn't have heard my thoughts. That's impossible. Then again, I used to think vampires weren't real and now I know better.* "Um . . . okay, for starters, what's your middle name?"

"Middle name?" The one eyebrow she could see jumped up an inch or two.

"Yeah. I think a person's middle name tells a lot about them, sometimes more than their first name."

"My middle name is Grant."

"Ric Grant?" she repeated. The sounds kind of got stuck in her throat. "Nothing personal, but that's a little . . . I don't know . . . short. Hard even. Ric Grant, Ric Grant, Ric Grant."

"Actually, my full name is Alric Grant Vogel. Grant was my grandfather's middle name."

"Alric Grant." The sounds flowed from her tongue nice and smooth, like his silky hair. Silky like his low, rumbly voice too. Silky like the skin on his chest probably felt too . . . "Mmmm. That's better."

"What about yours?"

"Sophie Elizabeth Hahn. I don't think there's an Elizabeth in my family anywhere. Knowing my mother, she picked it because she liked the way it sounded. I'm very different from my mother in most ways, but when it comes to names, the sounds—or specifically how they flow—are most important."

"Very interesting. So, in what ways are you different from her?"

"Uh-uh! My turn again. No fair sneaking in an extra question," she scolded. She made sure her tone remained light and playful, though. "Do you have any brothers and sisters?" She lifted her bottled water to her mouth.

"I was the youngest of twelve."

"Twelve! Ack!" She almost spewed a mouthful of water all over the windshield. "Your poor, poor mother."

He shrugged, so like a man. No respect for what a toll pregnancy took on a woman's body. "I had friends in even larger families."

"Where the heck did you live? Out in the burbs where I grew up, two, three kids tops was the average. My mother had five and we were looked at as the neighborhood freaks."

"I was born and raised in Germany."

"Germany? Oooh! How cool! I've never been to Europe but I'd love to go there someday. I've heard Germany is beautiful."

"It is. I've been there many times. I like to go home a couple times a year."

"A couple times? Each and every year?"

"Sure," he said, like it was no bigger deal than going to the car wash.

"Holy smokes! I'd be happy if I got there once in my lifetime. That's what I get for majoring in psychology in college. Can't do a gosh darn thing with a psychology degree unless you have at least a master's. Do me a favor, would ya, stash me in your suitcase next time you go."

Ric regarded her with those honey-hued eyes of his and said, "Sure." His expression was so serious, she wondered if he didn't mean it. And the way he pursed his lips just so made her wonder a bunch of other things, like what they might feel like skimming along her stomach or inner thigh.

Sophie swallowed a sigh and glanced out the window. It wasn't dark yet. At this time of year it didn't get dark until well past eight o'clock. But the sky to the west was a pretty combination of purple and salmony pink. The freeway was bordered on both sides by flat, green farmland. "Um . . . I lost track. Whose turn is it?" There. The flame burning between her legs was down to a mild simmer. She had a feeling it wouldn't stay that way for long, though.

"I think it's my turn," he said, without looking from the road. "I'd like to change gears. I want to know about your friend Dao."

"Oh, okay. Let's see, we've been friends since childhood but lost touch with each other after high school. He reappeared my senior year in college, briefly dated my roommate. After they broke up, we stayed in touch. He's an only child and his middle name is—"

"No, I want to know why you two were never lovers."

"My, my, you don't beat around the bush, do you? And you called *me* blunt. Did you pop a few pills too?"

Ric glanced her way and gave her a very nonapologetic grin. "What can I say, I'm a guy."

"That you are." Sophie pushed on his cheek until he was facing front again. "As the guy steering the car, you must look forward, please."

He humphed her and grumbled, "I was driving long before you were born."

"How's that possible?" she asked.

"What's possible?"

"Your driving since before I was born. That would make you like fortysomething. You don't look that old."

"Why thanks. But I don't have to answer that question."

"Sure you do."

"No, I don't. You haven't answered mine yet."

"Darn. Okay, Dao and I agreed a long time ago that it would be icky to sleep together so we haven't. There. Now my turn. How old are—"

"But you didn't answer my question; you basically re-stated it. Why did you decide it would be icky? Forgive me, but *icky* isn't a word I'd use to describe becoming intimate with you."

Awww! How sweet! "I don't know. I guess we knew too much about each other."

"Then maybe we should stop the question-and-answer session, yes? I wouldn't want you to decide you know too much about me too."

Does that mean he wants to sleep with me? Whoo-hoo! "No! We can't stop the question-and-answer session yet. Not until you tell me how old you are."

"Take a guess."

Not that game. She hated that game. She was always very wrong. Insultingly wrong. She didn't want to insult Ric. Not when things were going so well. "No, you tell me. I don't want to guess wrong and owe you an apology or something."

"I can't."

"Why not? Do you have an age hang-up?"

"No, I don't."

"Then just fess up." She lifted her water bottle to her mouth again and took a big mouthful.

"You wouldn't believe me if I told you."

"Sure I would. You're a very honest and believable man. I know that already."

"Fine. I'm three hundred eighty-six years old."

This time she did spew the water all over the windshield.

Chapter 6

"Three hundred? Did you say three hundred?" Sophie repeated. "How can that be? That would mean you were born . . . like in the seventeen hundreds." She laughed because what else could she do? "What a joker you are."

"Actually, I'm not joking and your math's a little off. I was born the year of our Lord sixteen hundred nineteen."

"Yeah. Right. And I'm the queen of England."

He bowed his head. "Your Grace."

"Why are you lying to me? I hate liars. I mean, so I was a little pushy. I don't deserve such blatant teasing. I'd be happy to tell you how old I am. I'll be twenty-six this July."

"Hmmm . . . that makes us three hundred forty years apart in age. Do large age differences bother you?" he asked, sounding serious as death.

She scowled. "Shut up."

"I'm not joking. I really am three hundred eighty-six years old. Okay, I'm actually three hundred eighty-five. But my birthday is next month and considering my age, a month doesn't make much of a difference."

"Are you trying to creep me out? Because if you are, it's working. How could you be almost four hundred years old? Huh? How is that possible? It's not. And that's why I know you're lying," she rambled to no one in particular. When he reached out to give her shoulder a reassuring touch, she shrunk away. "No touchy, buster. Like I said, I have a thing against liars."

Ric steered the car off the road. The tires skidded in the gravel at the shoulder as he brought it to a stop. Then he turned his entire upper body to face her. "This shouldn't be too much of a stretch for you to believe, considering the story you told me about last night."

"Are you mocking me?"

"No."

"Then what are you trying to say?" Suddenly feeling very cold, she crossed her arms over her chest.

"I'm trying to tell you that I'm a member of a very rare race."

"Huh? What race?" She scooted closer to the door. Suddenly Alric Grant Vogel, stone fox, was resembling a wolf in fox's clothing. Was he on the bad guy's side too? Or just a nut job?

"A race of people who have their roots in an ancient place that was destroyed a long time ago."

"You're not making any sense. Use some terms I can understand or I'm outta here. This is getting too weird for words."

"Okay. How about vampire? I know you recognize that word, although it's not my first choice of terms. It's really a misnomer. A very general term to describe a number of races, all very different from each other."

"You? A vampire?"

"Yes." He looked dead serious.

"Aw, nuts! No."

"Yes."

"Darn it! I knew you were too good to be real. Gorgeous, intelligent—"

"Thanks." His expression brightened.

She smacked his shoulder. "I didn't mean that as a compliment. There's an unspoken 'but' there."

"What but? But what?"

"But . . . but you're certifiably insane," she mumbled.

"I assure you, I'm perfectly sane."

"I've never met a nut who thought they were nutty." She released the door lock.

"Where are you going?"

"I think I'll take a walk. A long walk."

"And you're calling me the nut? We're sitting in the middle of nowhere, on a long stretch of highway with nothing but miles of farmland all around us."

"That's okay. I could use the exercise. I ate a big dinner." Sophie pushed the door open, but before she could get out of the car, Ric caught her left arm in a grip as tight as a sprung bear trap. She glared at the offending hand, letting anger hide the panic blossoming in her chest. "Let me go."

"Not yet. Please, let me explain."

"Let me go. You can explain in the relative safety of the open space outside the car." She made sure to emphasize the word *outside*.

"Fine." He released her.

She stepped out of the car and slammed the door. Darn it! Now what? She had a friend being drained of blood by his wife, a real vampire. She needed the shield and spear to free him from that sticky situation before his wife drained him dry. She couldn't be trusted anywhere near her friend, now that some other stupid vampire had bitten her. And now she had a traveling companion who was claiming to be a vampire himself—or some such thing. What the heck did he mean by race of people?

We are descendents of the Atlantians, his voice said in her head as he rounded the front of the car. *A small number of our people survived the Great Calamity but our land and history were struck from the pages of history, a great tragedy to humankind. We were successful in curing a great many diseases that still plague humans to this day.*

"You can talk in my head. Does that mean you can hear my thoughts too?"

"Yes."

"Every one of them?"

"Pretty much."

That fact made her more uncomfortable than the part about his people being from some place that supposedly never existed.

"I do try to respect your privacy. I don't strive to hear your every thought."

"Thanks . . . I think." She leaned back against the car, tipped her head until it rested against the car's roof, and stared up at the starry sky. When had it gotten dark outside?

"Then you believe me? You don't doubt my sanity any longer?"

"I'm beginning to doubt my own. Yours? Well, that's yet to be determined, and I admit it's not my place to decide."

"But you do believe you were visited by what you called a vampire last night?"

"Yes. But I saw him with my own eyes. He did things to me, things no man has ever done before."

Ric gave her a wounded look.

Was he jealous? Why did that make her feel all warm and happy inside? "Not pleasant things. Oh no, not the least bit enjoyable."

"I know you're lying." His expression darkening with each step, he walked nearer until his chest was a mere fraction of an inch from hers. She could feel her nipples straining against the silk cups of her bra and thin cotton of her shirt. Traitors!

Down, you two, she scolded. *There won't be any action*

for you—not now. A shame. I had such high hopes. "And he came to me after dark, like a real vampire. You, on the other hand, walk in broad daylight like it's nothing. You can't be a vampire."

"There's an explanation for that." Ric caught her chin between his thumb and forefinger and held it. His eyes dark now, as dark and glum as his expression, he stared into Sophie's eyes. "He'll come back for you."

"Who?"

"The one I see in your memory. The one with the dark hair."

"Why would he do that? I figured he'd been sicced on me to make me sleep in so I'd miss Dao's doctor's appointment and snakewoman could have her way with him. Or to make me hurt Dao somehow. But I figured if I stayed away from Dao's house—"

"No. I can smell his mark on you. Whether he was sent to ruin your plans or not, he has decided you are his."

"Well, I do have some say in that, don't I? Because he wasn't my type, even if he was—" She stared at Ric's lips as he glared at her. So soft, even when twisted into a troubled frown. If only he didn't think he was one of those, a bloodsucker. A vampire. Like snakewoman and the dark man last night. How could she possibly be attracted to him now?

With a slight shift in his weight, he leaned forward and pressed his body against hers. Her knees all but gave out.

Okay, so she was still attracted to him. When it came to chemistry, logic plain didn't prevail.

"There is only one way to save you," he said through those scrumptious lips.

"Oh yeah? More garlic? Come to think of it, why didn't that work?"

"Old wives' tale. Garlic won't keep away a real vampire. No, the real solution's quite simple, actually."

"Simple? For some reason," she said, breathless and

squirming thanks to the brick wall that was his body being so up close and personal with hers, "I'm having a hard time believing that."

He lowered his mouth until those adorable lips were a fraction of an inch from hers. His gaze snared hers. "When will you cease to doubt me?"

"When you start telling me something that's believable," she answered as she struggled to keep her wits about her. They were running for the high hills, taking her willpower with them.

She let her eyelids fall closed and did what every atom in her body longed for—she kissed him. She realized almost immediately that her intended semichaste kiss was going to end up far from harmless.

Even though she was being a good girl and leaving her tongue where it belonged, Ric obviously wasn't going to give her the same respect. Never mind that it was her choice to open her mouth to let him in.

Lip to lip and nipple to chest with the sexiest man on the planet. Well, a girl could resist for only so long.

Sophie figured she'd lasted at least a second or two. That was darn good.

The moment she opened to him, his tongue swooped into her mouth. Lips, tongue, teeth, they all did things that made Sophie's knees buckle. Thankfully, before she slid to the ground, a couple of strong hands caught her by the waist and held her up.

Figuring she owed him a little taste of what he was giving her in retribution, she kissed him back with equal fervor, holding nothing back. And tossing some proverbial gas to the fire, she let her hands roam over his chest. Through the material, she felt the tight nubs of his nipples and teased them with her fingertips. As a reward, she received a throaty groan.

His response only acted to crank up the heat in her own body, specifically to the parts south of her waist. She tipped her hips, literally grinding the aching parts against his thigh. Naturally, that wasn't even close to enough. God help her, she wanted him to touch her there, to stroke away the burn, to fill her. Vampire or not. Imaginary vampire or not.

She moaned into their joined mouths.

He broke the kiss for a split second, stared into her eyes, then pressed the lightest tickly kisses to the corners of her mouth. "Then you are in agreement?"

"Huh?" she asked, running her hands down the center of his flat stomach in search of some lumpier terrain. "Agreement to what?"

"You agree you need to become mine. To save you from a fate worse than death."

"If that isn't the most original pickup line I've ever heard." She gave the firm bulge at the front of his pants a pat.

"I'll take that as a yes." He scooped her up into his arms and she squealed in surprise.

"What are you doing?"

"Taking you away from the road. I assumed you'd prefer a little privacy but if I was wrong . . ." He let the rest of the words trail off, but he didn't exactly leave the sentence incomplete. The rest was spoken by nonverbal means—some waggling eyebrows, a silent suggestion in those golden eyes that practically melted her, and a cockeyed grin.

"No, no. This girl's not into exhibitionism. Sorry to disappoint."

"I will never be disappointed with you." He effortlessly carried her to the rear of the car and with one hand opened the trunk.

"What are you doing? You weren't thinking of . . . of going in there?"

"Heck no." Still holding her, his knee serving as a temporary support for her bottom, he reached down and pulled something from the trunk's dark interior. Then he slammed the trunk closed and turned toward the field. She smiled and wrapped an arm around his neck and nuzzled his chest. He smelled wonderful, his cologne spicy and masculine. Underlying the tangy scent lingered his own more subdued aroma. It wasn't as powerful, but it was far more intoxicating. She practically hyperventilated trying to capture that scent in her nose.

Ric set her on her feet, shook out a blanket on the ground, and then kneeling, pulled her down to him. "My people's process of claiming a wife is a little more complicated than the process humans go through. There are stages of marriage. There are no laws governing how many we must take." He kissed her silly again until she'd almost forgotten her objection to his words. Almost.

"Wife?" she said around his tongue, which wasn't exactly easy.

He reclaimed his tongue from her mouth. "Yes, wife. How else would you become mine?" He pulled off one of her shoes, then the other.

Sophie didn't try to stop him. "I didn't realize . . . I mean, you seem to be a very nice man—er, vampire—but wife? I wasn't planning on making any major life-changing decisions on this trip. We're supposed to be tracking down a shield and spear to save my friend Dao from a bad marriage. Why would I go rushing into a marriage with someone I hardly know—a man who claims to be a vampire, to top it all off?"

"Believe me, you won't be rushing into anything." He removed her other shoe. "We may remain at the first stage indefinitely. That would be okay with me. It will also serve your purpose."

Again, she didn't stop him. Nor did she stop him when he pulled off her socks. Having him see her bare feet was no big deal. Of course, when he started to tug at her top, she had to put up a little resistance. It was only right since she was a respectable woman.

"I do respect you, Sophie," he said, just before he pulled her shirt off.

She crossed her arms over her now nearly bare torso. Only her satin bra remained. "Quit poking around in my thoughts. That's not fair. I can't do the same."

"You will be able to once we've become one, for a few moments. You will see soon."

"I could appreciate that benefit." She caught his hands at her waist, before he'd unbuckled her belt. "Hold up a minute. I'm practically naked and you're still fully clothed. That's not right."

"Oh. Well, far be it for me to be unfair." He yanked off his shoes, then slipped off his socks and stuffed them in his shoes. When he went for the hem of his shirt, Sophie stopped him.

"May I?" she asked.

"Absolutely." He lifted his arms in a show of surrender.

She curled her fingertips around the bottom hem of his pullover and pushed it up, revealing some of the most cut abdominal muscles she'd ever seen. That scrumptious sight was followed by an even better one when she uncovered his chest.

It was smooth, muscular, and covered with only the slightest sprinkling of crisp hair at the center. Two small pink nipples poked out at her, beckoning her touch. She traced each areola with an index finger and received a sharp gasp as her reward.

She smiled at his covered head, then took advantage of the fact that his shirt was inside out covering him from the neck up to tease each pebbled nipple with her tongue and teeth.

He didn't let her get away with that. He yanked the shirt off, tossed it on the blanket, and playfully pushed her onto her back. "That isn't fair," he growled.

"What? I didn't do anything that any other red-blooded American woman wouldn't do."

"That's beside the point. Now, off with your pants."

Sophie shuddered—and not because she was scared. "Are you going to spank me?"

"Not unless you want me to." Ric grappled with her belt for all of three seconds before he had it unfastened. It took even less time for him to unbutton and unzip her pants. They came off before she drew her next breath. Granted, that had to have been a lifetime, since she was struggling mighty hard to make her insides cooperate.

Why was it when she got around Ric her autonomic nervous system shut down? In contrast, the other part, the part that registered sensations, like taste and touch and smell—she inhaled and sighed—seemed to be working just fine, maybe too well. She wondered if, since he was a biology teacher, he'd have an answer to that conundrum. When he slipped her panties down over her hips, she decided she'd have to ask him later. If she wasn't in a coma.

Within a couple of stuttering heartbeats, she found herself lying completely naked under the heated gaze of one hot vampire wannabe and a million, zillion stars.

She was dizzy, hot, and tense. There wasn't a part of her body that didn't scream for his touch, even the soles of her feet. Luckily, he seemed willing to oblige. Still dressed from the waist down, he kneeled before her and lifted one leg. He massaged her foot and she emitted a sigh of contentment.

"You like?" he asked, with one eyebrow quite a bit higher than the other. One side of his mouth quirked too. It seemed he had issues making both sides of his face do the same thing.

"I've never had a foot massage."

"Did you know that according to Eastern medicine, there are points on your feet and ankles that are directly connected to erogenous zones?"

"You're joking."

"Not entirely." He stroked a small area on her big toe. "Like here."

She gasped as a rush of warmth gathered between her legs. Score one for the Eastern medicine guys. Course, she couldn't be positively certain it was his touch that produced that yummy effect or that smoldering gaze of his. Could be both.

His gentle strokes wandered up her ankle and she squirmed as her more delicate parts heated more. By the time he reached her thigh, she was a sweating, trembling ball of gelatinous goo.

No man had ever done that to her. She was practically begging for him to make love to her before he'd even touched her genitals. And when his hand slipped between her thighs, his fingertips grazing her folds, well, that was nearly the end of her.

She cried out into the night. Her voice sounded small and hollow in the open field. He lifted his hands to her knees and gently pulled them apart.

"I want to taste you."

"Like, drink my blood?" she asked without thinking. His face was nowhere near her neck, but then again the real vampire hadn't bitten her on the neck either.

"No, I want to taste you here." He swiped a long, tapered finger down her slit.

Her spine arched automatically at the invasion. Rather than draw closed, her knees parted wider, giving him all the access his heart desired.

And he took it, greedily. His hair tickled her thighs as he tipped his head down and took the first shy taste of her with his warm velvety tongue. That first taste was followed by lots more, and not so shy. His tongue, teeth, lips moved over her, licking, tasting, teasing until every muscle inside her body was tied into tight knotted coils. She trembled all over, writhing under him while he licked, nipped, and kissed her to oblivion and back. Just as she was at the cusp of release he stopped.

She blinked open her eyes. "Why?" she asked between panting breaths.

"It's time now." He unzipped his pants and pushed them down his long legs. He kicked them off, then took care of his snug black underwear.

His erection was something to behold. She burned with the need to feel it deep inside.

"Soon, my love. Very soon."

"Now," she begged, knowing if he made her wait another second, she'd die.

Chapter 7

Ric fought with his body's demand for instant gratification, even though he felt like he'd be engulfed in flames at any second. This was their first time. He owed Sophie more than a quick roll in a field. This was the woman of his dreams, the one he'd waited almost four hundred years to find. There wasn't a single cell in his body that didn't know this for a fact, which was making it doubly hard to go slow, never mind wait until they were in a more suitable setting, like a five-star hotel suite.

"My sweet. So open and willing," he murmured.

"Yes. So, how about getting to the good part here? Before I expire?"

He cringed. She couldn't know how her words ignited his blood. How much he wanted to part her thighs and bury himself deep inside her with a single rough thrust.

She wrapped a soft hand around his erection and he bit back a cry of heated agony. Her hand slid up and down his length as her lush lips pressed against the head. With each swipe of her tongue, he felt his self-control slip. When she opened her mouth and took him inside, it completely snapped.

With a growl, he pushed her onto her back, lifted her thighs, and buried himself in her slick heat. Immediately, his head fell back. He felt his canines elongating as he drove into her over and over. Her smooth, slick walls gripped him tightly, sending him hurling toward climax. Afraid he was going too quickly, he slowed the pace of his thrusting, hoping it would keep him from losing complete control.

Sophie was lying under him, her eyes closed, her beautiful breasts rising and falling with each heavy breath. Her skin had taken on a silver hue in the light of the moon. Silver and perfect. Her body was soft and open and giving, pleasing him in every way. Her skin was like satin, smooth and warm. Her sweet scent lingered in his nose as he inhaled. Her long hair had fallen loose from the ponytail it had been tied into and was fanned out around her head like a halo.

Their bodies working together, moving in the primal rhythm of lovemaking, he bent low and inhaled, catching the scent of her shampoo. Floral. Feminine. As he shifted lower, his chest grazed against her pebbled nipples. Her sharp intake of breath sounded in his ears. He slid his hands between their bodies and closed them over her breasts, kneading them, pulling her nipples and rolling them between his thumbs and forefingers.

Her soft moan drove him crazy. Despite his wish to go slow for her, he couldn't. Once again, his thrusts came fast and hard. She writhed underneath him, pulled his hands from her breasts, moving them lower until they rested on the crisp hair above the point of their joining. His fingertip found the target she intended for him to find and stroked it, while he listened to the silent cries of ecstasy in her head.

She was close and so was he. Their minds were fused, their thoughts one, just as their bodies were. He finally found the closeness he'd hungered for. For that brief instant, he was whole. Mind, body, spirit. And it was bliss, a profound pleasure he wanted to last forever.

Together, they found their release. Their voices melded as they cried out in ecstasy to the stars. When it was over and her spirit was pulled from his grasp, the crisp slap of reality stung him.

This was all he could ever have, fleeting moments of wholeness, of sheer joy, followed by hours, days, years, eons of emptiness. It was the only way it could be. She would never take the final step, become his bride in all ways. He had to make sure of it. He would only allow her to take the first one, to protect her.

It took at least an hour—okay, maybe that was a slight exaggeration—for Sophie's heart rate to slow to the normal pace and the tingles to stop. Finally feeling herself, she propped herself up on one elbow and gazed down at the very yummy nude man lying beside her.

That had been the most incredible sex in her life, way beyond anything she'd ever dreamed of. It wasn't because Ric had used any special techniques or crazy positions. It was because of the unique connection she'd felt with him. Like they'd joined more than bodies.

She'd never experienced anything that intense before in her life and although she'd never been the kind to crave sex, she found herself aching all over for the chance to experience that unbelievable connection again with him. It was as if their minds had melded, their spirits. She didn't just hear his thoughts; she felt his feelings.

She blindly stared at his chest, tracing the lines of his developed muscles as she thought about their lovemaking until she blinked back to the present and actually saw him again. His skin was a cool silver in the light of the moon. Smooth and flawless with the exception of a very large scar on the right side of his abdomen. It cut a jagged line down to his hip. She softly traced it, wondering how he'd gotten it.

She let her head drop onto his chest, realizing after a

minute or two that there was no steady rise and fall with each breath. "Are you okay?" she asked, giving him a little shake. She lifted her head to look at his face.

His eyes were closed but the corners of his mouth were lifted into a contented smile. "Yep. Just fine."

"You aren't breathing."

"I don't have to. Remember?"

"Oh yes. How could I forget? You think you're a vampire. Or would you prefer some other term? You said that was too general a term. Son of Darkness maybe? Bloodsucker? Nightstalker?"

"Mmmm. No. I'm not a big fan of the dark thing. How about Perfect One?"

"Perfect?" *You got that right.* "That's a good one. Ha! I laugh at that. Perfect. Oh, you're funny. I'd say Conceited One fits you better." She laughed and slapped his chest. "What do I call you? I'm serious."

"So am I."

She smacked him a second time. "You know, you don't have to claim to be a vampire because you're jealous or anything. Yeah, when that vampire bit me, something happened. But I swear, I don't like him. Not at all. I don't have a vampire fetish. I swear. You've got to believe me."

"I do believe you." Laughing, he snatched her into the tightest naked bear hug of her life.

"Can't. Breathe."

"If you can talk, you can breathe." He kissed her cheek, her eyes, her jaw, then released her and sat up.

Sitting did some very yummy things to his abs, and lifting his arms to stretch did some very yummy things to his shoulders as well. He smiled down at her as she openly goggled him.

"Shouldn't we get going?" she asked, tipping her head to check the road. It would be her luck that while she'd been getting her jollies in the field their car had been towed. Luckily, by raising up on her knees, she could see it was still there. "Wouldn't want to end up stranded out here in the middle of nowhere."

"Ummm. That might not be such a bad thing."

"You're terrible. My friend's near death and you want to hang out in the cornfields and frolic."

He cringed. "I'm sorry about your friend."

"Thank you. He means everything to me, is the closest I have to family anymore. He's helped me through some tough times. Now it's my turn. But I don't have much time, not if what Tim said is right. It's killing me that we have to wait until tomorrow to meet with that lady. But it's the best we can do."

"You know, we still have the rest of tonight," he teased, evidently trying to lift her suddenly drooping spirits. "Want to frolic a little more before we go?" He gave her a toothy grin that did indeed pull her out of her worry a bit.

"No."

He looked injured.

"I mean, it was great. Beyond great, actually. But I'll feel better when we get to Grand Rapids and know we're ready for tomorrow. I do have one question." She sat up and crawled over the blanket, gathering her clothes. "Um . . ." she said, not sure how to ask the question that was still hanging around the back of her mind. "Are we . . . am I . . . what did this mean tonight?"

His left eyebrow shot to the top of his forehead. "Mean?"

"You know. You said you'd have to make me your wife to keep me safe from that other guy. So, when we . . . you know . . . did that make us . . . make me yours forever?"

"Forever? No. Not at all. But it was good for me too. The best." He patted her knee, then pulled on his underwear.

Her face flamed. She stared at her knee, then glared at him as she yanked on her underwear and jeans. "What the heck was that?"

"Reassurance?" He pulled on his pants and stood to buckle his belt.

"No. That was not reassurance. It sounded . . ." Egotistical. Demeaning. ". . . nothing like reassurance."

"Sorry. Let me try this again. You asked what tonight meant, in reference to my earlier remark about protecting you from the dark one. My clan has a very long, very complicated process for marriage. Mainly because compared to the standard human marriage, ours last a whole lot longer." He pulled his shirt over his head, poked his arms through the sleeves, then pulled it down over his yummy stomach. "Life span, you know. And there is no such thing as divorce. So you can see why we must make sure we don't make any hasty decisions."

"Okay," she drawled, fastening her bra. "You did mention something along those lines earlier but you didn't give me any details."

"You'll get more details if they are required. As I said, we may only take this first step. It will counter his venom without binding either of us in a relationship we aren't ready for. I have no need to go further."

She pulled on her shirt, then pants. "Then neither do I. Sex, eh? That's all it took? I mean, that was amazing. Incredible. Out of this world. But it'll protect me from that other guy? So I don't need to be afraid of becoming that other guy's zombie and turning ax murderer? Why does this sound like some very convoluted way to get a girl into bed?"

"It's not. And I'm glad you enjoyed it."

"Oh, I did. You're still hanging on to that vampire thing, are you?"

"Yes. You'll see I'm telling the truth. Soon enough."

"What's that mean?"

"It means you'll have your proof."

"Tell me then, I'd like to know more about you, about being a vampire."

"No problem. I can tell you anything you like about my clan, my life, my history. What do you want to know?"

Sophie stared at him for a moment. What did a girl ask a guy who believed he'd lived for nearly four hundred years? Should she ask him about what it was really like living so long ago? Or for some obscure historical fact that would prove he was telling the truth? A fact she might later reveal to the world so she might win some kind of award. Unfortunately, only one question came to mind. And it wasn't the stuff of a brilliant mind.

She stated it anyway: "I want to hear about all those things but first I have a silly question."

"Silly? Okay."

"If you're a real vampire, why aren't you all dark and broody like the ones I've read about? In books vampires are always tortured souls."

"Oh yes. Broody." He sighed and tied his shoe. "I've never been good at broodiness. It was the only class I failed in vampire school."

"You're making fun of me."

Ric grinned.

Sophie stuffed her foot into her shoe and pretended to be more insulted than she felt. She liked this playful side of him. A lot. She liked the teasing, the banter. "Don't make fun of me. I didn't make the rules. Those other people did."

"Oh? What other people would that be?" he asked as he tied his other shoe.

"The ones who wrote the vampire books. They must've interviewed some real vampires, right?"

"Maybe. I kind of doubt it, though. If what you believe is any indication of what they've written—garlic, daylight, broodiness—they couldn't have interviewed a member of any of the North American clans. I wonder if I contacted them, they'd appreciate my setting them straight."

"Your ego has to be the size of Texas." She laughed and, for kicks, threw her other shoe at him. As she expected, he ducked and it flew into the grass behind him. She dashed past him to find it. "Stop teasing me. You know I'm right.

North American vampire or whatever, you're supposed to be tortured and brooding because you have no choice but to drink blood to survive." She scooped up her shoe and plopped onto the blanket to put it on.

He leaned over her, nibbled on her neck, giving her a severe case of goose bumps. "And why would that make me tortured? I happen to enjoy blood."

Her gaze shot to his face. He wasn't serious, was he? She leaned away. "Eww! Because . . . eww! How can you say you enjoy drinking blood? Oh my God, that's gross. Have I told you that blood makes me sick? I can't stand to look at even a drop."

"It's easy to say. I enjoy drinking blood." He traced a warm, wet line down the column of her neck, whispering, "It's sweeter than the finest dessert, more satisfying than any food you could ever consume." He nibbled her collarbone. "You have no idea what you're missing."

She shivered because he was driving her crazy. She shuddered because he was making her sick. She scrunched up her shoulder and shook her head because she didn't know what to do about either. "No way. Can't be better than ice cream—nothing is. Don't you miss ice cream? And cake? And chocolate? Then again, if you were alive back in the sixteen hundreds, maybe they didn't have those things back then?"

He answered with a lifted brow.

"There you go. You don't know what you're missing. I know I wouldn't want to live without my Ben & Jerry's. I'd be positively miserable being on a perpetual liquid diet."

"Then it's a good thing you aren't one of my clan." Ric took her hand in his and kissed each fingertip, one at a time. It was such a sweet gesture, such a sexy one too. Sophie reconsidered her stand on leaving right away. "Me. Personally, I find a human's diet disgusting. Think about it for a moment. You consume rotted animal flesh for sustenance."

That made the little tinglies halt midtingle. "Now you're

just getting sick. And to think that a second ago, you almost had me convinced to frolic some more. But not anymore. No way. The mood is gone after that comment. Animal flesh. You're serious? You'd rather bite some poor, unsuspecting person and drain them of their life's blood than eat a little chicken?"

"Yes, but it's not sick and it's not gross. Why can't you see that? I don't kill when I feed. My . . . er, donors . . . give more blood when they go to a blood bank. In contrast . . . what did you eat for dinner?"

"A hamburger."

"Animal flesh," he said, with a smug nod. "And the cow didn't walk to the back pasture for a snack after he donated."

"That's assuming the fast-food joint I bought it from used real meat. You never know. Besides, it's not rotted. At least it'd better not be! So, if you're a real vampire, put on the dark, tortured hero face and quit looking so gosh darned happy," she joked, actually kind of seeing his point. Maybe it wasn't as gross as she thought.

For that retort, she was gently pushed back onto the ground and kissed to heaven and back.

She had to give him one thing: this so-called vampire knew what to do with that mouth of his, not to mention a few other parts.

And that made her happy. Very happy.

Ric stared down at Sophie, his heart slightly tight at the thought of what he was about to do. This was the only way he knew to protect her, yet he knew there were risks. The kind of risks he didn't like to take without good cause.

Her trust in him warmed his cold heart until he almost felt complete. To imagine losing that—it was already too painful to consider.

"I must do one final thing before we can leave," he whispered, watching her eyes for fear.

Her trust continued to pour into him through his fingertips. Like warm water fed into his veins, it trickled up his arms until it filled his chest. "Oh, okay. Well, whatever it is, I'll just be over here waiting. I promise I won't watch."

"No. Not that." He laughed. "We vampires don't have to do those sorts of things."

"Oh. Okay. Then what is it?"

"This . . ." He lifted her top and kissed her stomach. He unfastened her pants, pushed them out of his way and licked and nibbled his way down toward the junction of her thighs, then continued the trail over one hip. "There will be pain, but only a moment."

"Pain?" She stiffened under him.

He sensed her panic and lifted his head to meet her gaze. "Nothing more than a pinprick."

"Are you going to bite me? For real?"

"Yes, for real." He smiled, displaying his lengthening canines.

Her eyes widened. "Oh! Wow! You weren't kidding, were you? You are a real vampire. Aw, man. And here I'd sworn off vampires after the last time. I told you, I didn't like it. Will it feel like it did with that other vampire?"

"Hopefully better." Her reference to the other one, the one who had left his mark on her, left a very sour taste in his mouth. A taste that only the flavor of her blood, of her sweet essence, would kill.

"Okay," she said on a sigh. She covered her face with her hands, her body tight under his touch.

"This is the only way."

"I believe you. Although I would've preferred it if just having nookie had taken care of it."

"Me too." He held her gaze for a moment, then glanced down at her hip. His tongue, eager for the first taste, moistened his dry lips. Yet, even though his body hungered for her, he hesitated, knowing that the other's venom—if powerful enough—could kill him. He hoped she'd attracted a lesser bloodline. Something that would give him little trouble. He knew with the first swallow the other's bloodline would be revealed.

His jaw ached as his teeth finished elongating into their necessary length. When they were in position, he moistened her skin with his tongue, eased his fingers between her thighs to stroke her folds, and when she shuddered, on the brink of orgasm, he bit into her skin.

Her blood was sweeter than any he'd ever tasted. It flowed down his throat, but there the pleasure ended and the agony began. It was like swallowing a great ball of fire. It seared his insides, each swallow increasing the torture. Even so, he forced himself to keep drinking until trembling he nearly collapsed on the ground. Sophie lay below him, writhing in pleasure, her fingers tangled in his hair, the scent of her passion filling his nostrils. His name came from her parted lips just before she fell into a deep sleep.

He had his answer now. Sophie had found an Ancient One. That was both good and bad. Good because the venom wouldn't destroy him—though it would make him suffer for several hours. Bad because it was extremely difficult to counteract. Sophie would need several doses of Ric's venom to protect her from the Ancient One. And if the Ancient One returned to her and injected her with more, there was a good chance he would lose her to him.

He had to protect her, whatever it took. Even if she could never be his in all ways, he owed her that much for giving him what she had already.

Chapter 8

"Wake up, sweet thing. We're here."

Completely disoriented, like when she'd woken up from shoulder surgery a few years back, Sophie blinked open her eyes. She hadn't even remembered falling asleep. Didn't recall dreaming. Didn't remember anything after their little roll in the grass. It was a very strange feeling. "Where are we?" Her voice sounded rough, gravelly, like she'd swallowed a bucket of crushed glass.

"The parking lot of our hotel on the east side of Grand Rapids. I've already checked us in, so we can go straight to the room. Here. Let me help you." Ric took her elbow and gently eased her to her feet.

Her legs felt boneless, soft and wobbly, her head swimmy. She clung to a very strong, thick arm for support as she half walked, half stumbled inside the hotel. Even though her eyeballs bobbed around in her head like beach balls on the surf, she caught the occasional curious stare as she struggled to walk without looking like she'd downed a fifth of tequila. "What's wrong with me? I feel awful."

"Probably a combination of things. You'll feel better in the morning." He slid the card into the lock, then opened the door, and still supporting her with one arm, he flipped on the lights with his free hand. "There you are." He walked her to the bed and then turned to head for the door. "Be right back with your luggage."

"Okay." Afraid to try her rubber legs, she stayed put while she waited for him to return. Thanks to a severe case of hotel room jitters—she always got nervous in hotels, even when she wasn't visiting one with a man who made almost every vital organ in her body stop—she was restless but lacked the strength to pace properly. Instead, she was forced to sit and pick nervously at a thread that had pulled loose from the hem of her top.

Ric returned a few minutes later with both her suitcases. He set them on the bed, unzipped the bigger one, and started rummaging through its contents.

"What are you doing?" she asked, feeling a little invaded. No man—no matter how sexy, or adorable, or scrumptious, look at that tush!—had any business digging through her stuff, not that she had anything to hide. It was a matter of principle.

"Helping you get ready for bed," he said, shuffling through her undies. He inspected one piece with particular interest.

Her cheeks the temperature of asphalt on a July afternoon in Arizona, she yanked the black lace garment out of his fist and wadded it up. "I can dress myself. Thanks." She scooted to the suitcase, her head feeling like it was full of water, sloshing this way and that, and pulled out her cute matching shorts set. When he went for the red panties sitting on top, she gave him a warning glare. "Don't even think about it, buddy. Beat it, so I can get dressed without dying from embarrassment."

He leaned close. So close his breath warmed her neck. He whispered, "Did you forget? I already saw you naked." Looking quite pleased, he nodded.

"Yeah, in dim moonlight. Not the glaring light of three hundred–watt incandescent bulbs that'll illuminate every lump on my rear end like a freaking spotlight." She jabbed a finger at the nearby lamp.

"I happen to like your rear end. Lumps or not." He gave her a playful eyebrow waggle, then a wink. "Please. I need to help you. I'm not trying to get in your pants again . . . well, maybe I am a little bit. But I'm trying to do the heroic thing here and help you out. What kind of guy would I be to leave you to struggle by yourself?"

"A polite one?"

He snatched the red panties when she wasn't ready to stop him and unfolded them. "But I can turn off the light if you insist—"

She lunged for the underwear in his hands but missed when he raised his hand a split second before she could catch them. Then, figuring her only hope of retrieving them was if she could catch him off guard like he'd done to her, she feigned disinterest. "Besides, why should I have to struggle to get dressed? I think I can manage on my own, thank you. Been dressing myself for twenty-some odd years now."

He glanced down at the suitcase, presumably to return the panties, but instead finding the matching bra. "But you don't understand—"

This time she was successful, caught him red-handed, one full of red panties, one full of red bra. She reclaimed both, ignoring his protests. "What is your deal? Are we sharing this room? Are you just trying to find a way to tell me you decided that now that we've slept together, you don't want to pay for a second room?"

"No. I'm next door."

"Oh. Okay. Then leave. Please. My head hurts. My stomach hurts. And I'm getting dizzy from playing monkey in the middle with my underwear."

"Fine. I'll leave. But if you need anything, please call. My room number's one-fifteen. Or you can just shout loud in this general direction and I'll hear you." He pointed at the wall.

"Got it." She gave him a grateful smile, then tried to stand. Mistake. Her legs buckled and she cringed as the floor flew up to meet her face.

Before impact, Ric caught her and laid her back on the bed. "Better not try to walk tonight."

"Why? What's wrong with my legs? And my head? And the rest of me? I really don't like this. Should I go see a doctor, maybe?"

"It's nothing to worry about. Promise. I'll explain it in the morning. For now you need to rest. Do you need to take a trip to the bathroom before I go?"

"No!" There were some things she was simply too proud to do. Peeing in front of a man was one of them.

"Very well. If you feel the urge later—"

"I'll be sure to call you," she finished for him, even though she'd almost rather go in her pants than call him for help. "Thanks."

He leaned down and she prepared for another toe-curling smooch. What she received—a stiff, cold, Hollywood air kiss—was far from what she'd expected.

Puzzled by Ric's lukewarm farewell, Sophie watched him leave the room. Of course, by the time she had herself dressed for bed, which was a challenge, her bladder had decided it did indeed need to be emptied. Plus, she needed to brush her teeth. Figuring her legs had to be stronger by now, she tried standing again.

Her forehead slammed into the side rail of the bed on her way down to the carpeted floor, making her see stars.

"Ow, ow, ow!" she yelled, sitting on the floor, rubbing her swelling forehead. "That hurt, dammit."

"You're stubborn," a familiar voice, a voice that rumbled through her body like earthquake aftershocks, said from the general vicinity of the bathroom.

"Tell me something I don't already know." She blinked several times to clear the stars from her vision and tipped her head to look up at the man standing over her. Even with the world swooping up and down like a carnival ride, she could see his expression was a mixture of amusement and worry.

Crossing his arms over his chest, he said, "I told you to call me."

"I don't like to pee in front of people."

"I promise I won't watch."

When her bladder contracted again, threatening to spill its contents on the floor, she mumbled, "Okay." Humiliated beyond belief, she snatched up her dropped toothbrush and toothpaste and let him scoop her into his very capable arms. He carried her with such ease it amazed her. She was not a slight woman, not by anyone's standards.

He stopped directly in front of the pot, then slowly lowered her to her feet, supporting her weight by holding her under the arms. "Okay. I'm going to close my eyes now. Go ahead. Take down your shorts."

"This is weird." She set her toothbrush and toothpaste on the sink, then tugged down her panties.

"No, being ashamed of a natural process that all humans do is weird," he said to the tile wall.

"I'm not going to comment on that at the moment." Her pants adequately out of range, she said, "Okay. Let go." Grabbing the towel rack, she held her weight up with her arms until she was completely seated on the toilet. Trying hard to forget about the six-foot-something man standing mere inches away, she stared up at the ceiling and tried to relax.

It didn't work.

"Are you done yet?" he asked.

"No."

"Okay," he said on a sigh, giving her a closed-eyed martyred look.

She tried staring at the floor. That didn't work either. Finally, she said, "You're going to have to leave for a couple of minutes. I can't go."

"Okay. Knock on the wall when you're ready for me." He exited and closed the door. No sooner did the latch click than the flow started.

"Chicken," she scolded her bladder. A couple of seconds later, she yanked up her shorts while still sitting on the seat, then rapped on the wall. True to his word, Ric reappeared, his eyes closed. "You can open them. I'm dressed."

He smiled. "Good. Ready to head back to bed?"

"I need to brush first." She motioned toward the items sitting next to the sink.

Like a true gentleman, he silently held her erect while she washed her hands and brushed her teeth, then carted her back to the comfort of the big bed. "Rest well. I'll wake you at seven. Will an hour be enough time to do whatever it is you do in the morning?"

"Depends. If I'm able to stand on my own two feet by then—"

"You should be able to."

"I hope I can. If I don't need you to hold me up in the shower, an hour should be plenty of time. Thanks."

He nodded, then left. Again, with nothing but an air kiss to send her off to dreamland.

Was he regretting what they'd done earlier in the field?

Until now she hadn't. She closed her eyes and tried to push aside the memories of a grassy field, the stars, and one naked Ric.

"What have you done?" a deep voice rumbled through Sophie's dreams. It was familiar but strange at the same time. It both called to her and repulsed her.

Somewhere between being awake and asleep, Sophie rolled over, fluffed the pillow, and settled into a comfy position again.

"You have betrayed me with another," the voice said again. Even asleep, the venom making his words sharp and bitter caused her to shudder. "Where is he? He's close. I won't let him have you. You're mine."

A sharp pain burned up her leg, waking her. Her eyes blinking and bleary, she reached down to see if something sharp had scratched her. She felt warm wetness and lifted her hand to her face.

As expected, the near pitch blackness kept her from seeing more than the slight outline of her hand. She reached up to flip on the reading light mounted to the wall above her head. Also, as expected the light left her momentarily blind, well, nearly blind. She had enough optical abilities to see a couple of vital things—the red blood coating her hand and the dark man standing next to her bed.

What does one do when one's leg is bleeding and there's an angry man standing over one? One screams. Unfortunately, said dark, brooding man seemed to have anticipated her reaction. He clamped a cool hand over her mouth before the sound made it past her vocal cords.

That left her with no option but one—fight like hell. Sophie swung her arms wildly; grabbed his cold, clammy arm and dug her fingernails into the flesh; rolled and thrashed; kicked and jabbed—but none of her quasi–kung fu motions seemed to do a bit of good. He held her with effortless ease, one hand still covering her mouth, the other pressing down on her shoulder, pinning her to the mattress. She briefly thought of biting him but quickly changed her mind. He was a vampire. Who knew what the results of biting him would be? It could make her his drone for all eternity.

Instead, she ceased all fighting and struggled to catch her breath through her narrowed nasal passages.

His gaze pierced hers, drilling into her head and giving her a headache. "You will not scream. You will answer me now. Where is he?" The man lifted his hand from her mouth, and although she had every intention of screaming her lungs out, not a peep came out when she opened her mouth. It was a strange sensation. She could feel the vibrations in her throat yet nothing but a soft whooshing sound actually made it out of her mouth.

Furious, she clamped it closed and swung her fists at his midsection. No man stole her thunder!

His gaze became even sharper. "Tell me."

She tried to force her eyes away from his but they wouldn't move. Her mouth opened. Words sat on her tongue and no matter how hard she tried to wrestle them down, they found their way through her lips. "Next door."

Why had she told him that? What was going on? She lunged from the bed, took a single step toward the door, then fell like a moldy old sack of potatoes to the floor. The impact sent all the air from her lungs in a loud "oof." The result: she lay there struggling to inflate them for at least twenty seconds, which felt more like twenty hours.

"He has poisoned you," the dark man said, pointing at her legs.

"No, he hasn't. They're just . . . asleep. That's all. I was . . . sleeping wrong." She rubbed her numb appendages briskly, trying to get some blood to them. "You're the one who poisoned me."

"Why are you so willing to doubt me and believe him?" The dark man stooped down at her side and stared into her eyes again. His gaze had softened a smidge. It wasn't so scary anymore. In fact, it was somewhat reassuring and warm.

"I . . . I . . . don't know. Because you're so rough, I guess."

"I am sorry for that, cherie." He gathered her into his arms and she had to admit it didn't feel too awful being there. The shivers making her teeth chatter stopped. He set her on the bed, then climbed on top of her. His lips, which she had to admit were okay—not as nice as Ric's but attractive nonetheless—curled into a wry smile. "It's easy to trust him because he looks so normal, isn't it?"

"I . . . suppose."

The man drew in a deep breath. "Let me guess. He is blond?"

"Yes."

"And some sort of scientist?"

"A science professor. How did you know?"

"He is a Wissenschaft," he practically spat. "They are nothing to me. They deny their nature, hiding behind scientific theories and logical explanations. You would never wish to be bound to one of them. If you have not taken the second step, there is still time."

"Second step?"

"He did not tell you?"

"No. . . . Tell me what?"

The dark man scowled. "That should not surprise me."

Still not sure if she could believe this man or the one next door, since they both seemed to be calling the other the enemy, Sophie studied the man's admittedly semihandsome face for any sign of deceit. She found none in his very dark but also very expressive eyes. Or in the sharp but strong line of his jaw. Or the powerful forehead. Or the firm but alluring set of his mouth.

"Will you trust me?" the man asked, leaning closer. He set those deep, dark eyes on hers, which made her already muddy mind get even muddier.

"I . . . I don't know. You haven't even told me your name. You haven't told me why you're here. You haven't told me anything."

"Unlike the Wissenschaft I have never denied my nature. I am what you see. I am an Ancient One. Our bloodline is the oldest, our people the most respected of all the Immortals. We have no reason to hide who or what we are. Our people wield great political power. We have members in political seats all over Europe and Asia."

"That's very . . . impressive. But what would you want with someone like me? I'm nobody. I'm not a European monarch or even a regular voter. I spent the last presidential election at home watching reruns of *Sex and the City*. And I'm not an Immortal . . . I don't think."

He sat next to her and plucked a strand of hair off her shoulder. His nearness didn't stir the kind of reaction Ric's did. Instead of shudders of pleasure, shivers of unease danced up her spine.

"I admit, I first came to you as a favor for a friend," he said in a forlorn voice.

"For whom? What friend? Why? Was it that icky snake? Were you trying to make me kill Dao?" she asked as she watched his thumb stroke her hair. Again, she couldn't help noticing how cold his touches made her feel inside. Frigid. Lifeless.

"That is not important. What's important is that now that I've seen you, tasted you, I know you must be mine." He released the tendril he'd been stroking and sighed. "My body burns for your essence. My very soul cries for you. But as much as it pains me, I must let the choice be yours. I will not deceive you, or call upon my powers to force you." He stood and for the first time in who knew how long, she breathed easy again. "You need time to make your decision. I will return to you tomorrow night."

That sentence put a sudden stop to the free movement of air in her lungs.

"Oh," she said once she'd been able to inhale again. "I was hoping I could give you my answer now."

"Have no fear, my sweeting. As I said, the choice will be yours. I will not do as the Wissenschaft did and inject my poison into your veins, forcing you to do my bidding. My first bite was clean, nearly. I only injected a tiny bit, just enough to make my mark."

"Poison? Ric? But how? He didn't bite me."

"He did. You just have no memory of it. His poison erases all memory." The man traced a line from her earlobe down to her collarbone, then down the side of her torso. "He bit you here." He stopped at the swell of her hip.

Her hand dropped to the place he indicated. Her fingers brushed against his as she gently prodded the area, feeling for tenderness.

"For a Wissenschaft his poison is strong. It is the reason why you cannot walk. He wishes to keep you weak, under his control, though he will deny it. He will no doubt deny your inability to walk has anything to do with him."

Sophie nodded and watched as the man turned toward the window. He glanced out and grimaced. "Sunrise approaches. I must go. Remember, my sweeting, to take care with the Wissenschaft. He will deceive you. He has proven that already." His long legs carried him to the door in a mere three strides. "When you know whom you can trust, you will come to me for help. And I will happily give it."

Before he left, she called to him, "Wait."

His hand on the doorknob, he twisted his neck to look at her. An empty smile spread over his face. "Yes, sweeting?"

"You haven't told me. What's your name?"

"Until I know your blood is clean of the Wissenschaft's poison, I cannot tell you that. Perhaps tomorrow night." With a gust of cool wind, he left.

Suddenly freezing cold, Sophie wrapped herself in the blankets. Shivers racked her, shaking her worse than the time she'd had pneumonia. When the blankets failed to warm her, even a little, she tested her legs again. They were still weak but seemed capable of carrying her weight a short distance. She wobbled to the bathroom, cranked on the hot water, and took a long, scalding-hot shower.

With a couple of hours before Ric was supposed to come and wake her, she dressed and left the room in search of a computer. She needed to do some reading. About the Wissenschaft and the Ancient Ones. Somehow, this little secretary had just found herself at the center of a love triangle, pursued by not one but two vampires.

She was quite sure—though she had no impulse to check for herself—that hell had just seen its first winter.

Chapter 9

"Oh yes. I am quite certain the Magen David and Romakh Yehowshu'a do exist," Margaret Mandel, the very attractive woman seated behind the huge mahogany desk, said. Her gaze, as Sophie had noticed from the moment they had entered the room, clung to Ric's face a whole lot longer than it did to Sophie's. The woman stood to adjust the blinds for the third time, seemingly intent upon shutting out every sliver of sunlight from the room. "Did you tell me, Mr. Vogel, that you're doing research for a book? Are you an author?" she asked in a smooth, cultured voice as she returned to her chair.

"Actually, it's Dr. Vogel. I'm a professor of natural sciences at Midwestern Michigan."

"How interesting," the woman said. "You may call me Maggy. I have no need for formalities, though I hold a PhD as well, in European history."

Ric nodded. "Very well, Maggy. In answer to your question, yes, I am writing a book."

Her eyes lit up like firecrackers. "Oh, I do adore authors. My husband is an author too. Perhaps you've heard of him? Maxwell Mandel. He writes erotic thrillers."

Sophie recognized the name immediately and finally saw an opportunity to join the conversation. Thanks to the looks Margaret was giving Ric, and the subject matter of the conversation, she was feeling more and more like a third wheel. "I loved *Blood Reign*."

"Then you'll love the sequel, *Spirit Reign*. It's releasing next month." Margaret didn't bother to slide even a swift glance Sophie's way.

It wasn't easy to tamp down the unexpected and unwelcome jealousy burning up her insides, especially after reading what she had about Ric's clan, but she did her best. Dangerous vampire or not, she needed him right now. She needed his help. She needed his expertise. She didn't need another dose of his potent poison, however, and would make sure to avoid another injection at all costs.

"Wow! That makes what? Six books in one year? How does he do it?" Sophie said, trying to carry on the conversation when all she really wanted to do was turn around and leave both smooth-talking Margaret and sexy, adorable Ric to their love fest. Dao needed her, pronto. She had no time to worry about love triangles and flirtatious historical specialists. She'd called Dao earlier. He wasn't sounding as energetic as the day before, though he still claimed to be feeling okay.

"He writes morning, noon, and night. I swear he plots his books while he's sleeping." Margaret gave Ric a "cat who's eaten a mouse" kind of smile. "But darned if I can distract him, even for a half hour. Even getting him to take a break to eat a decent meal is a chore. And we're newlyweds. Only been married two months. I hate to think what it'll be like after we've been married for years. I'll be forced to take a lover."

Ric, who seemed to have caught the somewhat obvious suggestion in that last bit, if his red ears were any indication, cleared his throat. "I wish him lots of success. But could we please get back to the spear and shield?"

"Yes, of course. As I was saying, I'm fairly certain the Magen does exist." She leaned forward and in a low voice said, "I shouldn't be telling you this because if you put this in your book before my husband's book releases, years of research will be in vain."

"I promise the information won't be released anytime soon," Ric said in a flat voice that didn't inspire a bit of faith to Sophie. "My research is not directly tied to the existence of the artifacts but more to their history and application."

"Is that so?" One overly tweezed eyebrow rose slightly. "I'm intrigued. Would you care to tell me more?"

"Perhaps another time. I'm afraid our time here is short. I have to get back to teach a class tonight."

"Very well." Sophie noted the slightly put-off tone in the woman's voice. "As I was saying, my husband's research has led him to a collector of biblical antiquities living outside of Chicago. Most recently, this gentleman has donated some very notable artifacts to the Smithsonian, including a fishing knife that has been linked to Apostle Peter."

"Interesting. Has your husband been in contact with the gentleman?" Sophie asked.

"Yes. Unfortunately, he has been out of the country on expeditions and hasn't been able to meet with us. However, he is supposed to be returning at the end of the week."

"Do you think you could share his name with us?" Sophie asked when Ric did not.

"Perhaps I could be . . . persuaded," she said, her gaze practically Super Glued to Ric's face.

Ric stood, ran his beautiful hands down his uncreased trousers, then offered one of them to the woman. "Thank you. We'll be in touch."

Be in touch? That sounded like a blowoff.

Caught by surprise by his somewhat rude and abrupt dismissal, even if Margaret did deserve it, Sophie stood and gave the woman a grateful smile. Why was he cutting her off? They were so close to getting the information they needed! Couldn't he suck it up and flirt a little longer to get the information? Damn it! Dao was counting on her, on them. "It was a pleasure meeting you," she lied as she offered the woman her hand. "Thank you very much for your time."

Margaret accepted her hand and gave it a brief shake before releasing it. "You didn't say, what is your interest in the spear and shield?"

"Personal," Sophie answered, not wanting to disclose any more, despite the friendly smile the other woman was now bestowing on her. "I have a love for anything related to the Bible, specifically David and Joshua."

"Oh yes, so do I. My favorite story of the Bible is the one where David sees Tamar bathing and falls instantly in love with her. He sends her husband into battle, knowing he will be killed. It's such a stirring love story."

"Yes, it is," Sophie agreed, feeling a little out of her league when it came to biblical facts.

The woman's eyes hooded, making Sophie wonder if she'd said something wrong. "I wish you luck with your research, both of you." She sat, gave Ric one last glance and then visibly dismissed them by lowering her head to read something on her desk.

Good luck? Good luck! That was it? That was what she'd traveled hours to hear? What the hell! How was that going to help her find the relics? How was that going to help her kill that stupid snakewoman and save her friend? It wasn't. And Ric's clipped manner hadn't helped. Why hadn't he pushed harder, tried to charm the answers from the woman? He'd started in the right direction. Why'd he stop? Yergh!

Sophie didn't ask Ric about his behavior until they were outside the multistory brick-and-glass building and safe and sound in Ric's car. "What happened in there? Why did you cut her off like that? Why didn't you push harder? She would've given you the man's name in Chicago if you'd asked. I can't believe we came all this way for nothing."

"I don't think it was a wasted trip." Ric said calmly, although he was doing a lot of blinking as he drove. And a lot of sweating, which made her wonder how he was managing to be out in the sunlight without being burned to ash. Didn't real vampires ignite in unholy blazes when exposed to sunlight? "But I do think she was lying. That's why I didn't push for the name. I figured it wouldn't do us any good."

"Why would she lie? Is she worried about her husband's research?"

"No. I'm almost one hundred percent sure she's a lamia. I wouldn't be surprised if she has the spear and shield locked up somewhere—or knows where it's locked up."

"Damn. What do we do now? We've hit a roadblock. My friend's back home having the life drained out of him and we're getting nowhere. What if I don't find the relics in time? What if it takes months and months?"

"Easy, baby." He reached for her hand but she pulled hers away. He gave her a quick questioning glance, then continued, "We're getting somewhere. Faster than you think." He dabbed at his forehead with a paper napkin. "I need to go back to the hotel and get out of the sun. Any chance you could call off work for the rest of the week? I think we need to check out Dr. Margaret Mandel a little more closely, maybe take a trip to the outskirts of Chicago too."

"She sure wanted to check you out more closely," Sophie blurted before she thought better of it. Naturally, she regretted it the moment the words slipped through her lips.

Ric slid her a shocked glance, raised eyebrows and all. "You noticed, did you? I was beginning to think you didn't care."

"I . . . I don't care." *You're a liar. A killer. A monster. Why should I care?*

Another surprised look.

"I mean, I don't have any claims on you and you have none on me, right? We're both free to do whatever, with whomever. Besides, I'm here to help my friend Dao. There's no time to dillydally, as pleasant as a dilly or dally with you might be." Her mind knew this, knew the last thing she needed was to get tangled up with this man, this vampire. Especially right now. Why wouldn't her heart cooperate? Why did merely the thought of Ric touching another woman make her want to scream, even though she now knew the truth about him and his bloodthirsty, lying clansmen? Almost choking on her own words, she added, "I have to admit, I don't see you as the type to sleep with a married woman." *Then again, what do I really know about him, about his heart? Maybe he is the type to sleep with another man's wife. Lie to her. Then kill her. That's what his people do best.*

"I see." Ric didn't speak again. He drove the few miles back to the hotel in silence, which made Sophie nervous and miserable and almost sorry she'd gone on this goose chase. She resisted the urge to fill the big empty void with chatter and instead stared out the window.

Ric walked her up to her room, pushed open the door, then stepped inside behind her, hanging back to block the doorway. His thick arms—the ones she'd been trying to avoid salivating over all morning—crossed over his chest. "Now, want to tell me what's really going on?"

"Going on?" *God, I hope he wasn't reading my thoughts earlier! But if he was, would he have to ask?*

He took one, two, three steps toward her. She took three steps backward in a failing attempt to maintain some space between them. Her steps were about half as long as his. "You're acting funny. Distant, almost scared of me."

"No, I'm not acting scared. I'm acting . . . normal."

Her spine hit the wall behind her and she swallowed a panicked yelp. "I'm just frustrated and upset. I was hoping this woman would give us more than a good-luck wish and a sharky smile. My friend's dying! Quickly. And I can't do a damn thing to help him." Her eyes burned. She blinked the collecting tears away.

He didn't stop moving forward until his chest was mere inches from hers. He looked down into her eyes. He reached for her cheek but she flinched and turned her head. "See? Why won't you let me touch you?" He caught her chin, turned her head. His gaze was dark, sharp, demanding. Still, her traitorous body reacted exactly like it had before. Her nipples reached forward, aching for his touch. Her girly parts burned. Her heart skipped beats at irregular intervals until she was almost dizzy. He caught her upper arms in his fists and squeezed. Hard. Even that didn't ease the celebration going on inside her. "You say you're acting normal? Normal for whom? Since we met at the library you've openly ogled me. You've flirted with me. You've slept with me. You've confided in me. Now you're acting like I'm radioactive."

"That's an apropos term," she murmured, trying to catch her breath, when he let her go and turned away in a huff.

"Huh? What did you say?" He spun on his heel and drilled her with that gaze again.

"Nothing, nothing."

"Bullshit."

"Okay, okay." Still reeling from the effect he had on her body, Sophie scooted along the wall, walking the perimeter of the room until she was well out of reach, and well beyond the distance she was capable of throwing herself. The insane notion of lunging at him and kissing him until they were both senseless ran through her mind at regular intervals, like a jogger running laps. Only when she was way on the opposite side of the room did she consider it safe to continue. "You're right. I *am* acting funny. I've just had some time to think. And well, I think we've been going too fast." *Liar! I hate liars! I hate lies.* "Way, way, way too fast." *No, too slow. Much too slow.* "So, I decided to put on the brakes a bit."

"A bit? You hardly looked at me all morning."

"I'm sorry, have I wounded your vampire pride?" she teased before she thought better of it. She cringed the moment the words came out of her mouth, certain she'd pay for them.

And naturally, she was right.

His expression darkened even more, his eyes the shade of rich earth. He lunged forward, catching her upper arms in his fists before she could get out of reach. "What happened to you? Last night everything was good right up until you went to bed. . . ." He let his sentence kind of hang there as he sniffed the air. "Did he come back for you? I don't smell him."

"Who he?" She squirmed, her body on fire, her brain in meltdown mode, her conscience ablaze.

"The one-who-bit-you he. That's who he. Did he come back last night?" Ric lowered his head to her neck until his breath warmed her skin. Shivers of pleasure skittered down her spine even as shudders of fear quaked her insides.

"No." She blinked twice as his gaze met hers again. She gave a silent groan of frustration. No matter how hard she tried, she couldn't stop it. Whenever she lied, even as a kid, she'd blink. Twice. It was a dead giveaway, had gotten her into so much trouble as a kid. That was, until she'd learned to have her sister do all the lying for her. Unfortunately, her sister wasn't here now. And that was because of a lie, too.

Ric tipped his head. He looked so adorable like that. Sweet, even a little vulnerable. Could he really be the deceiving, bloodthirsty vampire she'd read about?

"What's wrong with your eyes? You've had problems with them since we came back."

"Nothing." Blink, blink. *Darn it!*

"You're blinking an awful lot. Did you get something in them?"

"Uh, maybe. I'm not sure." Blink. Blink. "If you'd kindly release me, I'll go to the bathroom and check."

He freed her immediately but he didn't leave the room when she shut herself in the bathroom for twenty minutes pretending to take care of a troublesome speck of nonexistent dirt in her eye.

She hated what she saw in the mirror—a grown woman hiding in a bathroom because she was too chicken to tell someone the truth. A grown woman who hated lying, who'd learned to despise deception, telling lies left and right.

Lies always led to disaster. To grief and loss. Would her next loss be Dao? Her heart sank at the thought.

Shit!

Rather than spend the rest of the day wasting time, shut in the bathroom, she finally decided to step out of her sanctuary and face the music. If she was going to have any hope of keeping this guy on her side, she supposed she was going to have to be honest with him—or at least mostly honest.

Ric was sitting on the bed when Sophie forced herself from her ceramic-walled haven. His head lifted when she strode into the room.

She halted about three feet away from him, wishing she had at least six more feet between them. "I'm sorry. I'm acting like an ass because I read something today and quite honestly it freaked me out and well . . . I don't want this anymore." She motioned back and forth between them. "You and me. This. Not that I'm not grateful because I know you were doing it for me. But I don't need you to save me from the Ancient One since he's promised not to force me to do anything—"

"Ancient One?" One eyebrow hopped up.

"Yesss."

"You never referred to him as that before," Ric pointed out.

Oops. Stupid slip. "I . . . I . . . didn't? Oh no, I'm pretty sure I have. Or you have. You just don't remember."

Ric jumped to his feet and walked a wide circle around her. "I was right! He was here last night. Damn it. I was . . . I couldn't—"

"Yes, okay, you're right," she admitted on a sigh. "He came here last night but I'm not going to worry about it and neither should you," she said, twisting her upper body to follow him. "He's not going to hurt me, or make me hurt Dao."

Ric stopped directly in front of her and her body went into instant lust mode again. Tingling, pitter-pattering, swooning, the whole nine yards. "He told you that?"

"Yes. Well, sorta." She inhaled and caught a noseful of soap and Ric. Tremors of anticipation skipped up and down her limbs.

"And you believed him?" he challenged.

The sharp tone in his voice and in his gaze did nothing but inflame her body more. It was nearly impossible to keep her mind on the conversation. There were so many more pleasant things to think about, like the way the corners of his mouth curled up when he thought he had her bested. And the sparkle in his eye when he challenged her. She forced her chin up to face his challenge head-on. "Yes, I did. He hasn't lied to me. Not since the first time. And everything I read on the Web site said Ancient Ones are known to keep their word."

"Let me ask you this." He caught her chin in his hand and tilted it up even more. She stared into his eyes. At the moment they were very dark, almost black. Once more pure, unadulterated lust charged through her body like a bolt of electricity. "Does every human being behave the same?"

"No. Of course not." His mouth was so close. Would he kiss her? What would she do if he did? Kiss him back? Oh yes. That sounded nice. Darn it, why wasn't he kissing her yet?

He lowered his head until his mouth was a fraction of an inch from hers, until his breath cyclically heated her lips. "Then what makes you so certain every Ancient One will?"

Her eyelids fell closed for a brief instant, giving her a moment's ability to use rational thought. "I . . . good point. I hadn't thought about it that way."

His gaze softened slightly as he released her chin. His hand dropped to her shoulder. "What you might read on the Internet is not only likely to be inaccurate but also dangerously generalizing. Don't let it give you false security—or false fear. You must learn to trust your instincts or you'll end up trusting the wrong people, fearing the ones you should trust, and being hurt—or worse."

So aware of his touch she wanted to crumple into a pile on the floor, she nodded and whispered, "But you lied to me. What was I supposed to think?"

"Lied?"

Gathering strength from somewhere deep inside, from hurt and confusion and anger, Sophie pushed back from Ric and crossed her arms over her chest. "You told me there was nothing wrong with my legs. That I'd be okay."

"That was the truth. How was that a lie? You're walking fine now, aren't you?"

"Yes, but it was a lie by omission. You didn't tell me you'd bitten me. That you'd injected me with your poison, that the poison was causing my paralysis."

"I didn't want you to be fearful. I knew you'd be okay. That it was a temporary effect. It was necessary to—"

"Necessary for what?" she interrupted, now really burning up with anger. "To keep me under your control? That's why you paralyzed me, isn't it?"

He looked shocked and confused, but she wasn't fooled. "Is that what you read on the Net?"

"No, that's what the Ancient One told me. So, you see, I'm not just believing vague generalizations on the Internet. I've talked to a genuine source on the subject."

"Since you're in the mood to listen to the genuine source, will you at least give me equal time?"

"I . . . suppose," she acquiesced, knowing she'd believe him no matter what he said. Why? Because in her heart, she wanted to believe him.

Ric held his hands out to Sophie, adding a reassuring nod until she took his hands and let him lead her to the bed. "There is venom in every vampire's bite," he said, encouraging her to sit with a tip of his head. She sat. "It happens that the venom in my bite has two properties—one, it is an amnesiac that erases your memory of being bitten, and two, it causes varying degrees of temporary paralysis, depending upon where you are bitten, but only the first time. I have no control over the release of the venom. It happens whenever I bite. However, I can control where I bite you, and thereby lessen the effects. I took mercy and bit you where I knew you'd suffer the least."

"Oh."

"The venom of the Ancient Ones is far more deadly and its effects are more insidious."

"Effects? What kinds of effects?"

"An Ancient One's venom acts as a hypnotic. Even days after a bite, the venom will allow the Ancient One to gain control over your mind and will."

"That's why . . . that's scary. Really, really scary."

"Which is why this is so important." He took both her shoulders in his hands and searched her face with eyes that had gone all warm and brown, like hot cocoa. "You must tell me the truth. Did he bite you again last night?"

She shook her head. "No. Not that I remember."

"That's good. Repeated exposure to the venom amplifies the effects."

"But what about the other part I read? The part about your people torturing humans, killing them for their gain? How do you explain that?"

He dropped his gaze. "Then you have heard what my clan is called and what we are known to do."

She nodded again. "Wise . . . wise and something. They . . . torture people?" She hated the sound of the words, hated the way they felt in her mouth.

"Wissenschaft. We are the ones who seek a cure for our weaknesses through science. However, our research—which does not involve the torturing of innocent humans anymore—has led to rumors of cruelty, nightmarish experiments performed on unwilling victims. But that was a long time ago, hundreds of years. Even humans have been known to do the same, the Nazis, your own government. Just remember, you cannot believe everything you read. It's as good as the reliability of its source. Also, I am an individual, with my own values, my own morals, my own will. What you read on the Internet are not laws but sweeping generalizations. You cannot accurately describe any individual—human or vampire—according to their race, blood, or creed."

She nodded as his words eased the worst of her fears. She knew in her heart he spoke the truth. "I've always felt that way about human beings. I don't know why I was so willing to believe so differently about vampires."

"It's easy to fall victim to prejudice."

"But not me! My best friend is a Chinese American. I never assumed he'd act a certain way because he's Asian. My boss is African American but I don't even see the color of his skin anymore." She sighed and crossed her arms over herself. "I'm sorry."

"Don't be. You're dealing with things that are new and frightening, and yes, extremely dangerous. It's natural for you to react as you have, to question your instincts and fear everyone, including the ones you should trust. Your life is in peril and you must determine who is the real danger—me or the Ancient One. Did he tell you his name?"

"No. He refused."

"He is wise."

Suddenly weary, Sophie flopped onto her back and stared up at the ceiling. "I don't understand why he wants me. Why you want me. I've been alone for so long. No human male has wanted me. Why am I so irresistible to you vampy types?"

"Most human men are blind to true beauty. They wouldn't see it if it was standing before their eyes. Wissenschaft, Ancient Ones, we all see you the same way. We see your heart, your soul, your spirit. That is where your true beauty lies. Humans can only see your outside."

She felt her face flushing red hot. She lifted her hands up to cool her burning cheeks. "I wish I could see the insides of people too, like you. To see their hearts, their souls. Then I would always know whom to trust and whom to fear."

"There is a way, however—"

"Don't tell me I'd have to become a bloodsucker too because I'm not willing to give up my Ben & Jerry's to read people's hearts and minds. Ice cream wins, hands down."

Ric shrugged and sat next to her. "The choice is yours. And I am perfectly content with it."

Her body warmed at his nearness. Her brain confused or not, her body knew which vampire it liked. "Thanks, but no thanks. I'm not sure living four hundred years sounds all that great."

"Immortality has its benefits as well as its drawbacks."

"Will you tell me? What's it like to live for centuries?"

"Both pleasant and difficult, like life is for all beings, mortal included."

"But isn't it exciting? Seeing so many changes, so many advances, right? Cars. Spaceships. Computers. Medicine."

"Things only began to change quickly in the last couple of centuries. Before that, they stayed very much the same. Quite honestly, I preferred life the way it was back then. There are more creature comforts in this day, with air-conditioning and central heat, vehicles that carry one from place to place with little effort, medicines to ease most kinds of sickness and pain. But it's also a time of great gluttony. Young humans have very little drive, especially in this country. So many of them have no regard for education, for hard work, for progress."

"That's very sad."

"I long to return to my time, a time when a man's work had purpose. He toiled for his home, his family, his king. His work gave his life meaning. It's not the same in this day."

"I guess we're all a product of our times. You, the seventeenth-century Europe; me, present-day America. Yet, I feel like we are so alike."

His gaze met hers, warmed her insides. "Me too."

She felt herself smiling as her gaze wandered over his adorable face. His stubborn chin, and straight, aristocratic nose, his slightly mussed hair. She saw no hint of his true age on his face. He looked young and full of life. "It's hard to wrap my mind around the fact that you're that old, that you lived back when Elizabeth the First was queen—she was, wasn't she?—and people talked with all those thous and thines, like characters in Shakespeare. I've always adored Shakespeare, by the way. And I've always sought to live a simple life, strove to live by my principles."

"And now you see the beauty that I see in you." He rested his palm against her cheek and gazed into her eyes. His eyes were now a soft golden brown. Warm and rich and comforting. "And sometimes it's hard to believe I haven't known you since I took my first breath. In so many ways you feel like a part of me that's been missing. A part that I've been seeking."

Sophie searched his face, wanting to believe what he said so bad it burned her up inside. She'd never in a million years expected to find a man who would love her, let alone adore her with the intensity she saw even now in Ric's gaze, after such a short time. He literally looked like he'd move mountains for her. She had to admit it was a smidge overwhelming. "I . . . I . . . don't know what to say."

"Do not speak with your mind. Speak with your heart and I will hear you." He pressed his mouth to hers. At the instant of contact, she felt wave upon wave of warmth rush through her body. And as his tongue slipped into her mouth, twisting around and stroking hers, she sent him all the wonderful thoughts and feelings pulsing through her body, both the physical sensations and the emotions.

She felt his body stiffen against hers. He groaned into their joined mouths. The sound fueled the fire blazing through her body. At that moment, all she could think about was giving back to him. Giving the happiness she found in his arms, the warmth she found in his embrace, the passion she found in his kiss.

She reached around and slipped her hands under his shirt, letting them slide up the silky skin of his back. She relaxed into his arms as he slowly crawled on top of her. The mattress groaned as their combined weight shifted.

His mouth continued to torment her, his tongue, teeth, and lips stirring such intense need for completion that she shook. Her fingernails raked down his back. Her pelvis tipped until the parts that ached the most for his touch ground into his hip. She wrapped her legs around him and clung to him.

"Make love to me," she whispered.

Chapter 10

"I thought you said you didn't want this," Ric said between delightful, goose bump–producing nibbles along her collarbone.

Sophie didn't respond—mostly because at the moment the coordination of brain, tongue, and diaphragm required to produce speech was impossible.

"Hmmm?" he said just before he ran that extremely lithe tongue of his up the column of her neck. "Remember what you said about not needing me?" His naughty tongue dipped into her ear, and she shivered. "Remember?" He caught her earlobe between his teeth and bit oh so gently. His hands slid down the sides of her body until his thumbs teased the outermost parts of her breasts through her clothes. Her spine arched, pushing her chest up against his and she groaned when their bodies made contact.

"I . . . I . . . ohhhh," she said on a moan when his kisses trailed lower, into the valley between her breasts, exposed by the deep vee of her blouse. One of his hands wedged between their bodies and cupped her breasts and she let loose with another moan. Her nipples were tight, sensitive peaks, pressing against the lace cups of her bra. The friction of his touch through the layers of fabric was about to cause her demise. She was sure of it. She'd die right there. In bed. With him on top of her. "Pleasssse," she begged.

"Please, what?" Ric said, laughter in his voice. He shifted his position to free both hands and asked, "Are you particularly fond of this blouse?"

"No, not really. Why?"

Eight tiny buttons sprayed in eight different directions when he ripped the front of her shirt open. She gasped in surprise, then went ahead and gasped again when she caught the hungry look in Ric's eyes as they took in the sight of her almost bare torso. Her tiny demibra barely covered her nipples and the lower half of her breasts. Obviously displeased with any bit of flesh hidden, he shoved his hands under her back, clearly going for the hooks. She shook her head, reached between her bosoms, and unfastened the front clasp, keeping her gaze locked to his face as she let the cups fall away.

Blazing hunger flashed across his golden eyes as his gaze traveled over her body like a smooth caress. The heat she saw simmering in his gaze seeped into her body and sank to her groin, where it swirled round and round like a whirlpool. Already she needed to feel him inside, his glorious rod sliding in and out of her slick folds, filling her, completing her. She lifted her hands to her breasts, and smiling against the hunger threatening to put an end to all vital functions, she caught her nipples between her fingers and thumbs, and pinched.

Ric bit his lower lip and his neck turned the shade of beets. "Dammit, woman." He knocked her hands away and closed his warm mouth over one taut peak, stirring a groan from deep in her chest. His velvet tongue laved the sensitive bud until she trembled all over; then he turned his attention to the other one, giving it equal treatment.

While he drove her crazy, torturing her with tongue, lips, and teeth, she strove to do the same to him—well, as best she could considering her current state. She traced the taut points of his nipples through his shirt until his breathing grew ragged in her ear. Then she slid her hands down, down, down to the bulge front and center in his pants.

He stopped his onslaught on her breasts only long enough to give her a growl of satisfaction. "You said—"

"I don't care what I said." She grabbed his hand and set it between her legs.

"But I don't want to make you—"

"That was a long time ago. At least ten minutes. This is now." She fumbled with the snap of his pants, plunged her hand inside to stroke his warm rod when she got them unfastened. "I'm telling you I want this, I want you. I . . . need you."

She stared into his eyes and pulled her hand free of his pants, lifting both hands to cover her mouth. Had she just said that? Admitted she *needed* him? Oh God!

Needing him was definitely more serious than wanting to be his casual lover, like she'd agreed to be. Needing involved deep feelings, vulnerability . . . risk. Like she needed more of that right now! Heck, she was facing risk even in her sleep these days!

Ric stopped tormenting her, gave her a look she couldn't exactly read, and pulled her into a tight hug. He tenderly palmed her face like it was made of the most delicate crystal and kissed her forehead, both cheeks, eyelids too. She felt special, cherished, reassured. "I need you too," he said.

With oh so much tenderness, he brushed his mouth over hers, teasing her with soft kisses that made her squirm, sigh, moan. His hands remained on her face but hers wandered down over the lumpy terrain of cotton-covered chest. When he slipped his tongue into her mouth and stroked hers, she dug her fingernails into the hard bulk of his shoulders.

"Oh, God," she murmured into their joined mouths. Burning need coiled tight, low in her stomach, when he deepened the kiss. His tongue thrust in and out in time to the throb pulsing between her legs. She rocked her hips back and forth, anxious to rub away the ache, ready to cry out and beg him to fill her. She slid her hand into his pants again and fisted his erection, stroking the ridge circling the head with her thumb.

He sucked in a surprised gasp and broke the kiss. He looked sad, troubled as he sat back and looked down at her. "I . . . I . . . Forgive me."

"Forgive you?" Dizzy, barely able to see, Sophie propped herself up on her elbows.

"Can you trust me?" Ric tipped his head, stroked her cheek with his knuckles.

She captured his hand and twined her fingers through his. "Ye—yes? I believe so. I want to."

His smile filled her soul and spirit with so much happiness she thought she might cry. He unfastened her pants and pushed them down her legs, tugging them off when they reached her feet. Lying there in only her panties, in the bright light of several lamps, she felt exposed, vulnerable again. She reached for the coverlet but he caught her wrist before she could pull it over herself.

"No. Please don't." He released her wrist. "Don't hide from me. I know we haven't known each other long but I want you to trust me. There isn't a more beautiful woman in the world. In all humanity."

"But I'm not skinny."

"You're perfect." He covered her soft belly with tickly kisses.

"And I have cellulite." Giggling, she motioned toward her hips.

"You're perfect." He kissed a path lower, over her hip and down one thigh.

"My rear end looks like cottage cheese."

"You're perfect." Without warning, he flipped her over onto her belly and ran his palms over her lace-covered buttocks. "This is perfect." He squeezed and she gulped. He stroked and she sighed. He pulled down her panties and kissed the small of her back, just above her bottom, and she shook. Her empty sex clenched and unclenched, hot, pulsing.

"Oh."

Off came the panties and there she was, lying there with her rear end exposed, in the glaring light. Yet Ric continued like he wasn't looking at the most grotesque thing on earth. He kneaded her bottom, gently parted her ample cheeks, and ran a probing finger up and down her crack until it found her wet slit. Then he pushed that finger inside.

Sophie dropped her head onto the bed, buried her face in the pillows. Still his words reached her ears, promises of pleasure, rewards for her trust. Reassurances that she was beautiful to him. His fingers slowly plunging in and out, almost but not quite rubbing away the ache deep inside her, he positioned his other hand lower, under her mound, where it could rub against her sensitive nub.

She was in heaven! And hell. Her body had marched itself right up to the point of completion but was refusing to budge from its spot just shy of the pinnacle, despite Ric's very thorough touches to her most sensitive parts. "Ric." She groaned, hardly able to breathe. "Please. Now. It's been long enough."

"Okay." He stopped stroking and, while she struggled to inflate her lungs, removed the final pieces of clothing acting as a barrier between them. Then he caught her hips in his hands and pulled until she was propped up on her knees, her rear end high in the air. His penis probed at her crack, sliding up and down from anus to vagina, and spreading cool, slick juices with it. "Can you trust me?" The head of his erection pressed against the delicate tissues between her anus and slit. They burned as he increased the pressure.

"I . . . I want to."

"Do you like to be screwed in the bottom?"

"Never tried it. But it sounds terribly painful." His penis pushed again, this time moving up, closer to her anus rather than back toward her sex. "Oh . . . is that what you want to do? Now?"

"I was thinking about it."

"I . . . I really want you inside the other part."

"Where?" His penis slid lower again, prodding at the proper opening, and she let out a sigh of relief. "Here?" With a single, smooth stroke, he buried his rod to the hilt, filling her at last, and she shouted out his name, so grateful, so overwhelmed by the pleasure their joining brought. He held her hips still for a handful of seconds, allowing her to really relish the fullness.

She opened her mind to him again, shared the waves of bliss that crashed through her body, one after the other, faster, faster, until she couldn't tell when one ended and the next began.

Ric pushed on her hips until only the very tip of his member breached her opening, then swiftly pulled back, meeting her backward thrust with a forward thrust of his hips, over and over. Her buttocks struck his thighs when their bodies met, adding an erotic slap-slap to the already overwhelming horde of sensations swirling around her. The scents of their arousal, the sound of his groans, the swirls of colors behind her tightly clamped eyelids. The sensation of tight, trembling need building, building until it drove her every move, every breath, every thought.

And then she felt her chest heating, her breathing quicken. Her legs trembled. Her arms shook with the effort of holding herself up. She rocked backward, eager to feel him deep inside, when that first delightful spasm gripped her.

He shouted her name as she came, her sex rhythmically milking him. He slowed his pace, which amplified her pleasure a hundred times. The orgasm lasted, and lasted, and lasted. It had a grip on her, wouldn't let her go. It was wonderful. It was horrible. She wanted it to last forever but wanted it to stop too.

"Oh my God!" she cried out.

He withdrew from her, teased her anus while she still spasmed. "Trust me."

"Stop it, please!"

"Trust me."

"Yes."

He pushed slowly, allowing her tight hole time to stretch. The burn didn't stop her orgasm but only intensified it until tears streamed down her cheeks. He stopped moving the second he was deep inside, shouted out with his release, and dug his blunt-tipped fingernails into her hips.

His thoughts swirled around in her head. His emotions— the kind of joy she only knew with him and the soul-shattering sorrow of hundreds of years of loneliness—filled her heart, pummeling her spirit. She felt every emotion, good and bad. Triumph and defeat. Hope and despair. They gripped her like an iron fist, squeezing the life from her spirit.

And only when he'd spilled his seed deep within her bottom was she finally released from his thoughts, feelings. Peace at last. But also a distance she hated. Their connection was so intense it almost drove her mad, but when it was gone, she felt so empty and lost she ached from head to toe.

Moments later, he pulled out, eased her onto her back, and cradled her in his arms. One finger ran up and down her arm, from shoulder to wrist and back again. With the other hand, he rubbed away the last of the tears clinging to her eyelashes, her cheeks.

"You trusted me."

She tipped her head to glance at him and her heart swelled at the look she saw on his face. So sweet, tender. His mouth curled into a warm smile, his eyes the shade of golden oak. "Yeah."

"You know what this means?" He kissed her forehead, brushed away a strand of hair that had worked itself over her eyes.

"No."

"It means we can take the second step if you want."

Sophie's heart leaped. What did this mean? She sat up and twisted, to face him. "But I thought we weren't going to go any further. That the first step was as far as we needed to take it."

Semireclined, his shoulders and head propped up on a pile of pillows, Ric ran his hands up and down her arms in a familiar comforting motion. "We don't have to go any further if you don't want to."

"I'm not sure. I don't know what it means. Will you tell me? Will it keep me from the Ancient One? Is that why you want to now? Or is there another reason?"

Did she dare hope? Could he need to feel close to her too? As much as she did him? Did he want to be fused to her like they were when they made love?

"No," he said softly.

Her heart sank to her toes.

He cleared his throat. "I want to because my heart aches the moment our connection is broken."

Her spirit took flight. He did crave that connection too! Just as much as she did! She briefly considered jumping up and doing a little naked happy dance but changed her mind when she took in his very grave expression. Wasn't he happy?

"I'm weak. I'm selfish," he said, yanking his hands from her. "I can't be content with mere moments with you, with our souls joined. I thought I would be. I know it's not what you want." He sat up fully, mussed his hair by dragging his fingers through it, then turned his pleading eyes toward her. "You have no idea, do you?"

"No idea about what?" she asked, almost too thrilled to speak. He wanted her! She wanted him, like she'd never wanted a man before. Who cared if she'd known him only a couple of days? Some things a person just knew, right? And so what if he drank a little blood? As long as she didn't have to watch, what did it matter?

"How beautiful you are. And how rare the kind of beauty you possess is."

"It is?" Her cheeks flamed and she pressed her fingers to them in a feeble attempt to cool them. "I . . . wow. This can't be happening. Pinch me. Pinch me now." When he didn't do as she asked, she pinched herself, half expecting to wake up alone in her bed. These days she could never be too sure. Dreams, reality, they'd sort of mushed together, the lines between them blurring. She pinched again, just to be sure.

But by golly, she didn't wake up! She wasn't dreaming. Ric was there, her adorable, sexy Ric. With her, looking flustered and confused. And she was happy. Oh, so happy.

"Does this mean you're glad to take the next step then?" he asked.

"Tell me." She traced the line between his pecs with her forefinger. "Will that wonderful connection last if I do? Will I hear your thoughts all the time? Feel your emotions? Share your joy, your pain? Will that empty spot in my heart be filled for always?"

He mashed her hand against his chest, sandwiched it between his palm and scrumptious golden skin with just a sprinkling of blond hair. "Not completely, not just after the second step. But we would become closer."

"Closer?" she whispered.

"Yes."

"I'd like that."

His lips curled into a soft smile. "Me too."

"Yeah?" Her face heated more. "Okay. I'm game. But please tell me step two doesn't involve blood. Have I told you that blood absolutely grosses me out?" She felt her nose wrinkling.

"No, no blood. That's later."

"And I'll still be able to eat food. Right? 'Cause I'm fond of my rotting animal flesh."

"Yes." He mirrored her disgusted look.

She clapped her hands. "Sounds like a piece of cake then."

"I wouldn't take it too lightly," he warned. "The second step involves something that can be very difficult for some people, something foreign, frightening even."

"Which is?" she prodded when he didn't explain.

"I can't tell you until the step has been completed."

"Then how will I know what to do? How will I know when I'm taking the step even?"

"I hope you will know when the time comes. If not, then maybe it isn't right for us to continue."

"Oh, how I hate these blasted vampire mysteries. Why can't you people make it simple? A couple of blood tests, a vow before a magistrate and be done with it?" Despite the fact that she knew he wouldn't give with the information, she gave him an intimidating glare anyway.

Naturally, it didn't work.

Ric knew Sophie was annoyed and frustrated but he was powerless to tell her more. It was the way it was, the way it had always been. And he knew that if he took shortcuts, there were too many consequences to pay.

Although he was overjoyed by the fact that she wanted to take the second step, which up until this very moment he hadn't thought he wanted, he was worried about her, about the dangers she would face with each step, the risks she would be forced to take.

There were reasons for those risks but he still regretted having to put her through such grueling tests. Failure would cost her more than she could afford to lose, more than they both could afford to lose.

Still, he couldn't ignore the calling any longer. Her spirit spoke to him, pulling him closer, snaring him in its grasp until he knew he was powerless to break free. He didn't want to be freed any longer.

They were bound even before they'd taken the first step. He knew that now. And he feared they were destined to complete all five steps, despite the risks.

He stood.

"Where are you going?"

"We're going to get you something to eat before you collapse from starvation, and then I have some work to do if we're going to find those relics and save your friend."

"Excellent plan. But how about me? How can I help?" She scrambled to reclaim her clothes and put them on. "I can't sit around and do nothing. I'll go crazy."

"We'll . . . er, talk about it later." He hated to see her cover her body. But they were close to finding the relics; he could feel it. His people's suffering would end soon. He had to stay focused. Somehow. And keep Sophie out of his way.

He had the perfect solution.

Chapter 11

Like both times before, Sophie knew her Ancient One was in the room before she'd fully awakened. What she didn't know was who else was in the room with them both.

She could swear it was the crisp sting of testosterone flooding the room that made her pull herself from the incredibly amusing dream she'd been enjoying. It couldn't be anything else. The room was silent and dark. Noise hadn't awakened her. Light hadn't either. Nope. Had to be male hormones. She wondered what she'd done to deserve such a glorious awakening.

Her eyelids fluttered open at the sound of a low, threatening growl, like the warning rumble of a dog.

"Ric?" she said, spying him first. Speaking of dogs, his stiff stance reminded her of the posture her childhood dog took when she spied a cat on the loose. Her dog, Daisy, had been nothing like her name suggested. She was no pansy, either; never took mercy on a stray cat once she had hold of it.

Sophie's gut instinct told her Ric would be no less vicious once he had his hands wrapped around his prey. In a way, that thought made her warm and tingly inside. The combination of sex appeal and danger was something she'd never tasted before in a man. It was a very spicy, intoxicating flavor.

"What's wrong?" she asked.

His answer was in the form of a continuing glare in the general direction of the bathroom. Naturally, Sophie let her gaze follow the line of his unwavering one.

"Oh," was about all she could think to say for a second or two. "Hello, there," she said to the familiar Ancient One, his stiff pose mirroring Ric's, as he stood frozen just inside the doorway. Her gaze ping-ponged between the two men a few times, then, slightly dizzy, she said, "I feel like I should make some introductions. Ric, this is the Ancient One. Ancient One—by the way, it's getting real old calling you that so I think I'll call you . . . Andy—this is Ric."

Both men flinched. Muscles bunched, teeth gnashed, cockles raised. Oh boy. Seeing an old-fashioned vampire rumble coming on, she climbed from the bed, grabbed the two-ton book she'd picked up during her earlier trip to the library off the nightstand, and positioned herself between the two glaring men.

Whew baby, now that was a position to be in. The testosterone floating about the room was almost enough to knock a girl out. Sophie practically fell over—undoubtedly overdosed on the stuff—then recovered by musing on the wonder of having both men making love to her at once. Oh, wouldn't that be heaven? One to pleasure her above the waist, one below? Or front and back? The options were endless.

When neither man spoke, she said, brandishing her book like a raised sword, "I don't suppose there's any hope we can settle our differences and all be friends?"

"She's mine. I found her first," Ric growled like a Neanderthal man . . . bedecked in Ralph Lauren.

"Uh, hello? Found her?" Sophie turned to give him a good dose of ugly eyes. "First, have we forgotten I'm still in the room? And second, I'd appreciate it if you didn't treat me like someone's misplaced . . . er, basketball. Last I read, that finders-keepers expression didn't apply to people."

"You do not deserve her," Andy retorted, giving Ric his own dose of ugly eyes. "You're not telling her everything. As I am sure you know, the law states your lies make her free to make her own choice."

Sophie waved her book in front of Andy's face in an effort to get him to look at her. If they were going to fight over her, they'd better at least look at her! "Excuse me, I appreciate your thought process here, but his lies have nothing to do with my choices. And I have no idea what law you're referring to, but as an American citizen, I've always been free to make my own decisions—men, homes, cars, jobs, the whole nine yards." She poked him in the chest. Her knuckle popped and she yelped, shaking it. "I never even let my sister have a say when it came to men. That was probably stupid. No, I admit that was absolutely stupid. My sister could spot a loser from five hundred feet, but still, you get the point. No one tells me who I sleep with and whom I don't."

It looked like neither man was about to listen to a word she said—typical. Like a couple of children, they continued glaring at each other and hurling insults. Ric stiffened at Andy's questioning of his breeding and hurled back a stinger of his own, topping it off with, "Why don't you go find a nice cool mausoleum to cozy up in? No one here has an interest in cozying up with the likes of you."

"Hey, speak for yourself," Sophie said, not so much because she was even considering making kissy faces with Andy—though the thought had crossed her mind once or twice—but more because if there was one thing a man could do to really piss her off, it was speak for her. She gave Ric a shove, which didn't budge him even a fraction of an inch. That made her even madder. "I have my own mouth, tongue, and vocal cords, Ric!" she shouted, like that would do any good. "And I'm quite capable of using them, thank you. But I'll keep you in mind as a standby if I ever get laryngitis. And you—" She whirled around to address Andy again.

"I'm giving you exactly ten seconds to leave," Ric growled from behind her. She could imagine his dark-eyed stare still focused on Andy.

"—you behave yourself," she scolded Andy, feeling like she was dealing with a couple of toddlers fighting over a favorite toy. "I appreciate the fact that you offered to help us, but *please*, this isn't helping."

"Ooh, ten whole seconds." Andy, again ignoring what she said, despite the fact that she was standing in front of him waving her arm like a deranged chicken, chuckled at Ric's bravado. He checked his fingernails, glanced at his wristwatch until the full ten seconds had passed, and a few extras—Sophie counted them in heartbeats—then grinned. "I appreciate the offer but I think I'll stick around a while longer. Sophie and I have some things to discuss."

"Now we're getting somewhere." Sophie nodded.

"Don't believe a word this man tells you. He doesn't care about you," Ric said, finally addressing her but his gaze still firmly fixed on Andy.

That set off another round of insult volleys. The language flying between the two was enough to make a sailor blush. Sophie was tempted to take notes, just in case she needed some colorful insults later. Instead, she stood between them, watching the action and musing about the crazy twist her life had taken recently.

Well, this was interesting, if a little bit scary. Sophie had never been fought over by two men, let alone two amazingly gorgeous, incredibly powerful men. Except for the fact that she was slightly leery of the second one, didn't know how much she could trust him, she might've been giggling like a schoolgirl. The fact that she had no clue how powerful either was, or how much damage they could do to each other, also dimmed the giggle factor a bit. Plus, the fact that both of them were essential to her search for a couple of moldy old artifacts that she needed to kill the stupid snakewoman married to her best friend brought the potential glee factor down even a few more notches.

Somehow, she had to diffuse this situation. Pronto! Before the bodies started flying. As it was, the two men were slowly inching their way closer to each other. Their puffed-up chests and thrust-up chins were no more than a couple of feet apart now. And she was still wedged in the middle, but losing breathing space fast.

She dropped the book on the floor and put both arms out, to keep the men apart, at least enough to allow her an occasional deep breath, and shouted at the top of her lungs, "Enough!"

For the first time in close to a half hour, the room was swallowed up in complete silence. She could actually hear herself breathing.

"Ric, Andy, you both say you want to help me but all you're doing is making things worse! Stop acting like a couple of children, shut up, and let's figure out what we need to do to find the stupid spear and shield. I have a lamia to kill! And I intend to do it with you or without you. Both of you!" She turned to Ric first and was pleased to see he seemed to have simmered down a bit. It wasn't more than a degree or two, but it was something. "Please, Ric. You don't know what this means to me. My best friend is dying, being sucked dry by his wife, a woman I introduced him to! Darn it, it's my fault. I'm going to cause the death of yet another person—"

Ric began, "You're not responsible—"

"Just like my poor little sister. I caused her death too. It was all my fault. I knew she was in danger but she was doing it for me . . . and . . ." Sophie swallowed several times as rage, regret, guilt burned a hole in her belly. "I couldn't tell. . . . She died because of me, because of a lie."

Both men stood silent, looking at her with wide, un-blinking eyes.

Finally, an eon or so later, "How does he think he's going to help us?" Ric grumbled, pointing at Andy.

She began, "He says—"

Andy interrupted, "I know where to find the items you need. The harp and the sword."

"Harp?" Sophie repeated. "We aren't looking for a harp. We're looking for the shield. The Magen."

"See?" Andy gave her a doleful shake of his head. "That Wissenschaft has led you astray already."

"I have not!" Ric said. His chest muscles flexed under Sophie's fingertips as she pressed her hand against his shirt, with the misguided but hopeful intention of holding him back. "I have brought her this far."

"Into the hands of the one who would see her fail," Andy challenged.

"I know Margaret Mandel is a lamia," Ric said.

"Not only a lamia but also Lisse's sister," Andy corrected.

"Her sister. What's that matter?" Ric shrugged his shoulders. "We know she was lying about the shield and spear. And we had no intention of searching out the gentleman in Chicago."

"A poor decision," Andy said, also looking like he was cooling down. "He is a Guardian."

"Guardian of what?" Sophie asked, finally feeling like they were getting some useful information.

Andy took a seat in a chair that was almost too small to hold his bulk. "Since the lamiae do not procreate, they must protect their population. They pay anyone; humans, dragons—"

"Dragons?" Sophie interrupted, disappointed. So much for her hopes of getting useful information out of this one. "Like the fire-breathing, scaly monster, overgrown reptile variety?" She stole a glance at Ric and noticed he looked as surprised as she did. Or was that something else? Fear, maybe? She turned back to Andy and chuckled, even though the last thing she felt like doing at the moment was laughing. "Real-live dragons. That's funny."

"You laugh?" Andy raised one ebony eyebrow.

"Surely you don't expect me to believe there are real dragons prowling around the earth," Sophie said, hoping he was kidding, hoping this whole conversation was a joke. Fighting a half woman, half snake was scary enough. Dealing with a dragon—big teeth, fire, scales . . . big teeth!— that was another thing altogether.

"Yet you believe in vampires, the Wissenschaft, Ancient Ones, and lamiae," Ric pointed out.

What was this? Were those two joining forces? She was beginning to wonder if that was such a good thing. "You're standing here." She poked at Ric's chest. "See? Solid, firm. Real. And him too." She poked at Andy's chest to illustrate. "And in case you've forgotten, I've been bitten by both of you bloodsuckers, so I know your fangs are real too. How can I not believe in you? But I can state unequivocally that I've never, ever seen a fire-breathing dragon . . . that is, outside of the movies. In particular, the one in *Shrek* was frightening. And a girl dragon to top it off. She was tough. Whew. That fire breath was something. Wouldn't want to mess with her. Poor Donkey!"

"Take my word for it, she was a pussycat compared to the real thing," Andy warned.

"I have no experience with dragons myself," Ric said. "But I've heard of those who have dared tangle with them. Not pretty."

Ric believed him?

"There's no way around it, you'll have to face a Guardian sooner or later if you're going to get the harp and spear," Andy said. "He might not have what you're looking for yet, but he'll fight you for it or try to steal it from you once you've found it. Those guys mean business."

"Yeah. So I've heard." Ric didn't sound pleased.

"I can't tell you how to beat them, since I haven't defeated one personally, but I can tell you about their weaknesses. Those are well known among the Ancient Ones," Andy offered.

Ric took a seat in the chair next to Andy, rested his foot on his opposite knee, and looking like they were long-lost chums, gave him an encouraging nod. "Tell me. As men of science, my clan has no use for them and thus has no information on them in our annals."

"As I expected," Andy said, with a solemn nod. "I will tell you everything I know."

And just like that, a new and unlikely friendship was born, between one gorgeous but pigheaded Wissenschaft and an equally stubborn but not quite as yummy Ancient One.

As both of the men's gazes found her, their brows raised in a collective gaze of assessment, Sophie again wondered if their new partnership was a good thing or a bad thing. She figured it was probably both.

In the meantime, the shower was calling and she was in no position to refuse. To put it mildly, she reeked. Plus she was anxious to do something useful. When she emerged from the bathroom, smelling Zestfully clean, and feeling fresh and energized and ready to go spear hunting, Andy was gone. Ric was reclining in the bed, his head turned so his face was to the wall. His chest wasn't moving. Even ten or so feet away, she could tell he wasn't breathing; then again, he'd proven once already that that didn't mean much.

Just to reassure herself, she called his name.

He didn't respond.

Now she was worried. She called louder. Nothing. A million possibilities hopped around inside her head like Ping-Pong balls in a rubber-walled room. Had something terrible happened while she was in the shower? Had Andy been pretending to befriend Ric only to attack him once she'd left the room?

A whole lot more freaked out than she ever thought she would be, she ran to the bed, took one good breath to fill her deflating lungs, and grabbed his arm, figuring she'd roll him onto his back and take a look. What she would do after that was beyond her.

Did CPR work on the undead? Would a guy who rarely breathed need CPR? How would she know if there was something truly wrong with him?

It took a great deal of effort, strained muscles in places she hadn't even known she had muscles, grunting and groaning, to get Ric over onto his back.

Dead weight. Dead . . .

Shoving that thought aside, she shook him. "Ric?"

He didn't respond. Not an eyelash flutter, or a nose flare. Nothing.

"Ric, come on! Yeah, I gave you a hard time about being all manly and protective about Andy or whatever his name is, but you got over it . . . right? Ric? This. Isn't. Funny!" She shook him harder, slapped his cheek lightly, then again with a whole lot more force. Even with her practically punching him he remained deathly still. "Oh, God! He's dead? How? Oh, God! What happened? Did Andy do something?" she shouted to no one, because there was no one there to answer her. She ran around, shaking her hands, wanting to do something, anything, to bring Ric back but having no idea what to do. She paced. "Dead. My vampire sweetie's dead? Was it garlic? A silver bullet? I didn't see a stake in his heart. Surely I would've seen that." She did a quick check for obvious injuries—bullet holes, burnmarks—and then for garlic and holy water. "Nothing? Did he starve to death? Does he need blood? Oh, man. I hope that isn't it, because if it is, that means I'll have to supply it to him and I can't do that."

She adjusted the collar of her pullover and leaned over

him until her neck was pressed against his closed mouth. "Come on, baby. I know you want some. Drinky-drinky."

He didn't bite, slurp, or even lick.

"Darn it!" She glanced at her wrist, then pried his lips open—he looked a little bit like a horse with his lips curled back like that—and rubbed her wrist against the front of his teeth.

That did nothing either. Didn't inspire even a twitch. Frustrated, near panic-stricken, she smacked his chest. "What the heck am I supposed to do? Huh? Damn it, if this is step two of the big plan, you could've given me a warning, a hint or two. A study guide. Something."

She paced some more.

"Okay. What do I know about vampires?" She stopped pacing. "Not much. They need blood. But Ric knows I'm ignorant of the ways of the vamp. So if this is a test, he wouldn't expect me to know something he knows I don't know. . . . Jeez, I sound like Abbott and Costello."

Sophie turned around and looked at Ric again. "Blood. That's the only thing I can think of. It's the only thing I know. That has to be it. But where do I get it from?" She looked around the room. Like there was going to be a ready supply of fresh blood in the hotel room. "Oh, man, he wouldn't expect me to actually supply the blood, as in cut myself, would he? Why couldn't he have passed out at a blood bank? I could just order up a unit or two of O-neg and be done with it."

She stared at his pale face, wishing he would answer her.

"Shit! It's a little thing. Right? I just need to make a small scratch. A poke, like the doctor does when he checks for iron. I have to try. I just hope I can supply what he needs before I pass out cold." Determined to do what she could, she marched to the bathroom, found her pink Lady Schick, closed her eyes, and ran her fingertip along the blade. It stung like heck, had to have sliced clear down to the bone. She yelped and opened her eyes after bracing herself for what had to be a virtual river of blood gushing from the wound.

There wasn't even a single drop. She could see the narrow slice in the skin but evidently it didn't go deep enough to cause bleeding. "Darn it! I nick myself every freaking morning while shaving and now I can't produce a single drop of blood when I need to?" Her heart racing, her hands shaking, stars twinkling before her eyes, she counted to three and tried again. Once again pain shot through her hand. This time it was so bad she dropped the razor in surprise. "Owwww! What I do for you, bloodsucker!"

This had to have worked. There had to be blood pouring from the wound, gushing, pulsing. . . . Her stomach turned. She blinked open her eyes but could barely see, thanks to the stars shutting out most of her field of vision. She thought she caught sight of some red and hoped it was good enough. At a near swoon, her head spinning, she went over to the bed, wormed her finger into his mouth and rubbed her fingertip along his teeth, the inside of his cheek.

"Wake up, dammit!" she said, tears now making it even harder to see. She felt breathless, near unconscious, like after she'd woken up from surgery and had had a reaction to the painkillers. "I can't . . . do . . . any . . . more." Giving in to the darkness that had slowly pulled her, she fell over, landing next to him on the mattress.

Chapter 12

"Wakey-wakey, sweetheart," Ric said, shaking her shoulder.

Sophie rolled over, burying her head under the pillow. Her head felt like a block of cement and her stomach hurt. "Noooo. Tired. Leave me alone."

"But, sweetcheeks, I'm in the mood to celebrate," he said, sounding much too happy for a dead undead guy.

Sweetcheeks? What kind of name was that to call her? "Celebrate what?" she grumbled into the darkness. "You're dead. Remember? A ghost. That doesn't sound like something worth celebrating to me. How am I going to help Dao now? All by myself? I can't fight a dragon. Dao's gonna die, just like you did."

"I'm not dead." He sat next to her. The bed creaked as his weight tested the worn springs. Ghosts didn't make springs creak, did they? "You saved me."

"I did?" Nursing a major migraine all of a sudden, she blinked open her eyes, squinting against the glare of the lamp behind Ric. "You're not dead?"

"Nope."

Shielding her eyes from the lamplight so her head wouldn't explode, she sat up and shifted her position so she could look at his face. It looked healthy and handsome and so very alive. She was thrilled! She was overjoyed! She was . . . pissed! She smacked him. When he didn't look adequately chastised, she hit him again, and again, and again, punctuating each strike with a single word. "How. Could. You. Do. That. To. Me!"

"It was the second step. I said you'd know what to do when the time came. See? Nothing to worry about."

"Nothing to worry about?" Despite the fact that the world spun like a Tilt-A-Whirl whenever she moved, she jumped up and smacked him some more. "Nothing to worry about? You were dead and I almost didn't save you. I passed out! What if I'd failed? What would've happened to Dao?" This time, her strikes were harder, as her fear and anger worked their way out of her system. Each smack thumped dully against his chest. "Huh? What would've you done then, big, bad bloodsucker? What if I'd fainted before I stuck my freaking bloody finger in your mouth? What if I'd been too chicken to cut myself? What if my razor'd been too dull . . . ?" She stomped away, stared blindly out the window. "Men! Gah!" She heard him follow her to the window. Despite the fact that she was fuming, awareness and longing shimmied up her spine.

"Doesn't matter. I knew you were ready. You didn't fail."

Not happy with his answer, Sophie slumped forward, pressing her forehead against the cool glass and crossed her arms over her chest, shooting him "that wasn't nice" barbs from her eyes as she tipped her head. She could see he wasn't sorry, not at all. Sure, he didn't go as far as beaming a smile at her, but he wasn't doing a very good job at hiding one either. Infuriating man! Sexy, hunky, infuriating man.

Ric gently uncurled her fingers from around her upper arm. Clearly trying to cool her anger, he kissed each fingertip. It wasn't working. Nuh-uh! Neither was that pitiful look he had on his face, the one that said, "Don't be mad, I adore you." She'd be good and angry for a long time. He flipped her hand over and traced a wet line down her palm, then up her wrist. Little tickles did the cha-cha along her nerve endings.

Mad. She was mad. Very mad. Seething mad.

"I checked on your friend, Dao. Found the phone number in your purse. He's okay. Sounds a little shaky but he's still alive. Your Ancient One says as long as Dao's not confused, still knows who you are, who he is, you still have time." His expression changed from all business to seductive; his eyes shifted from a warm brown to a soft gold. Her hand still cradled in his left hand, he lifted his other to her face, palmed her cheek, traced her lower lip with his thumb. "You're so sexy when you're mad."

"No, I'm not. I'm intimidating. I'm damn scary."

He called Dao? Wasn't that sweet? Her heart did a happy little pitter-patter but she forced it to return to normal rhythm.

Mad. She had to stay mad. At least another thirty seconds, if she was going to have any hope of teaching the lughead not to do something so stupid ever again.

"Oh, yes." He nodded. "Sexy *and* intimidating. Most definitely."

"Quit humoring me," she said flatly. "I hate that. Makes me madder . . ." She noted the pleased look on his face. ". . . which is what you want? You masochist! Grrr! Men! Vampires! You're all crazy."

"Yes, we are. That's why we can't stay away from adorable, sexy, amazing, infuriating, stubborn women like you."

"Humph. I should be insulted."

"No, you shouldn't. I said infuriating and stubborn." He flashed a grin that nearly brought her to her infuriating, stubborn knees. "Come." He flattened her hand to his forearm, encouraging her to grip it. "Let's go celebrate. My treat. You must be starving. How about some dinner? I'll tell you what I found out while you were taking your nap—"

"Dinner? I don't think I could eat. I'm too mad at you right now for almost dying—wait! Did you say dinner? What happened to breakfast? What day of the week is it?" She glanced at the clock. "Six in the morning? You woke me at six A.M.? That's plain not right." She let go of his arm, marched back to the bed, and made herself comfy-cozy. She knew they couldn't go anywhere during the day. Why would he wake her up so early? "You vampire types keep some crazy hours. Wake me at eight, no earlier. My head's about to explode like an atom bomb and I need to recover from the shock of your almost dying, never mind the insult of your humoring me when I was genuinely upset. . . ."

"I'm so sorry, baby." He completely obliterated every one of her defenses when he sat on the bed and pulled her into a warm hug. She sagged against him, grateful for his warmth, his support. Him. She was grateful for him. "I wished I could've warned you but the second step is a test of trust. I had to trust you would know what to do. And I had to trust that you'd have the strength to do it. You did."

"But I was scared."

"And very brave and smart. I'm proud of how quickly you figured out what to do. Look at me. I'm good as new. Because of you, because you're so intelligent and brave and giving," Ric consoled. "Now come on, it's six P.M.," he corrected. "You've been out for a while. You're dehydrated, which is why your head hurts, and you need to eat before we get going." He rubbed her shoulder; then when she refused to move, he gave her thigh a smack. "Get up! You're not going to feel better until you drink and eat. Remember? You're here for your friend. What good will you be to him if you collapse?"

"Fine, fine! You'd better be right because I swear I'm dying from meningitis. Maybe that razor blade was dirty and I got blood poisoning. Oh my God! I didn't think about sterilizing it." Sophie reluctantly let Ric go so he could stand, and she stared at the glaring red numbers on the clock. "Six at night? See? I'm sick, dying. I never sleep more than eight hours. I'd have to be near death to have slept that long. That's like twenty hours. Shit! I can't believe I wasted so much time."

"It's okay. I promise." Ric didn't look too impressed or worried. "And you're not sick. I would know."

"How would you know?"

"I would feel it too. The second step has brought us closer and although we are not completely joined, if something is wrong with either of us, the other will know. You slept for so long because you were simply worn out, exhausted."

"But I should be helping—"

"I've been working while you slept. I'll fill you in later."

"Yeah, yeah. You keep saying that but you never tell me anything. I'm beginning to wonder if you're keeping me in the dark on purpose—forgive the pun."

"This time I promise I'll tell you everything. Let's get you dressed." While she dragged herself across the room to check herself for signs of infection in the bathroom mirror—like a rash, a flush from fever—he went to her suitcase, which was sitting on top of the dresser, her clothes a disorganized heap on top. He picked out her sexy black teddy. "Oooh. Nice. How about you wear this?" He held it up to get a better look.

She flipped on the bathroom light, wincing at the jackhammers drilling her skull from the inside. "I think I'll need to wear more than that if I'm going to stay out of jail—that is, if I don't end up in the hospital first. Owwwww."

"Fine, fine." He sighed melodramatically. "I guess you'd better wear some more conservative clothes." He chose a pair of cropped jeans and a knit top, handed them to her, along with the toothbrush he found in the pocket of her suitcase, next to her other female necessities.

"That's better." She brushed her teeth, found some clean underwear, then plopped her bottom back on the bed again, her pounding head sandwiched between her hands. "Speaking of better, do you have any drugs? I can't eat like this. I can't think like this. I can't even walk like this."

"Nope. Sorry, sweetie. Want me to go down to the lobby and get something? They probably have aspirin in the vending machine."

"Yes. That would be wonderful. Thank you. It'll give me time to get myself pretty for you, take a quick shower. Who knows, maybe some scalding water'll ease the pounding."

"Fair enough. I'll be back in a few." He brushed his mouth over hers in a soft kiss that momentarily had her thinking about much more pleasant ways to cure an excruciating headache. Didn't she read somewhere that nookie cured headaches? "While you're dressing, you might want to pack up. Once we've made sure you've had enough to eat, we've got to hit the road. It's a long drive to Chicago."

More surprises? She didn't want any more surprises. She was tired of surprises. Weary of them. Eager for a boring, humdrum day. But at least they were getting somewhere! That made her breathe a little easier. "Chicago? I thought we weren't going to meet that man. He's a dragon."

"He is. But Julian says it's the only way we'll find the spear and shield."

"Julian? Who's Julian?"

"Julian Tsiaris. Your Ancient One. That's his real name. He's coming too, is meeting us in an hour. So hustle up. We're planning on hitting the road by seven. We vampire types prefer traveling after dark. It's a little easier on the skin, if you know what I mean."

"You mean I'm going to spend the next who knows how many hours trapped in a car with the both of you?" she asked, dragging herself back into the bathroom.

"Yep."

"Oh, man." The pain in her head increased tenfold. "You'd better hurry up with those drugs, then. A double dose of vamp testosterone? I can just imagine what kind of hell that'll be." She smiled. "We're really getting closer to finding the artifacts?"

"Yes, we are."

"Thank God!"

"What'll it be? Fries, cheeseburger?" Ric twisted his neck to glance at Julian, who sat beside him in the passenger seat.

Julian lifted his brows in response. "I don't consume human food. You do? And I have seen you travel by day as well. Have you begun the Second Death?"

Great. Now that was all he needed, one small piece of information the Ancient One could use against him. Fortunately, it wouldn't do the Ancient One much good, yet. While Ric hadn't started the Second Death, he was close enough to begin feeling a few of the effects. His power wasn't what it had been a few decades ago. He was paying the price for living with the humans. Blending in with the mortals—walking in daylight, eating, drinking, mimicking breathing and a pulse—they all came with a price for his people. A very dear price.

"Second Death? What—Second—Death?" Sophie asked behind him, nudging his shoulder once for each word. When he didn't respond, because he knew it would only make her more fearful, she turned to Julian and sighed. "Tell me. Please. Mr. Can'tsharemysecrets won't talk."

"I'm sorry I brought it up," Julian mumbled. "Did I say death? I meant Second *Debt*."

"Nice try, Julius Caesar." Sophie said, using the nickname she'd bestowed upon him since they'd left the hotel.

"My name's Julian, not Julius. Caesar was a spineless—"

"Hold up!" Sophie said, from the backseat. "You knew

Julius Caesar? Like the real Caesar? The guy with the leaves on his head? Exactly how old are you?"

"A man never divulges his true age," Julian rebutted, sounding injured. "And he didn't wear leaves—"

"Sweetcheeks!" Ric interrupted, his arm hanging out the window, the buzzing voice on the restaurant's drive-through intercom grating on his nerves. All he wanted to do was get their food and get back on the road. Why was that so difficult?

"What? Have I told you how much I hate that nick-name? I don't have sweet cheeks."

"That's a matter of opinion. What do you want to eat? I think the woman in there is either going to fall asleep waiting for us to finish placing our order or kill me with annoying feedback from her microphone. Please, forget about that other thing. Give me your order."

"I'd like the truth, please. With a side of patience."

"Funny. Now what do you really want? You're the only one here who needs to eat this stuff. Do you want me to leave?"

"No, no. I'm starving—thanks to having to be the food source for the likes of you. I'll have a burger, fries, milk-shake. Do they sell strings of garlic, by any chance?"

Two not-so-amused vampires scoffed at her joke. Ric shouted her order into the metal box serving as a speaker, then made several corrections to their messed-up order—how hard could it be to get two burgers, a couple orders of fries, one milkshake, and one soda correct?

Once their order was confirmed, he pulled up to the second window to pay and collect the paper bags full of food.

"If you want to pull over, I'll take over the wheel while you eat," Julian offered, sending Ric's suspicions to the fore again. Was it an innocent offer, or an underhanded at-tempt to either delay their arrival in Chicago or make sure they arrived at just the right time to be greeted by the lamiae welcome wagon?

Although Julian hadn't done anything all night to prove he was a threat, Ric wasn't about to just accept his seemingly new friendship with open arms. Put on an act? Sure. But he had too much at stake to completely trust the Ancient One, even if they were known for always speaking the truth. There were lies by commission and omission. There was nothing stopping the reportedly 2,100-year-old vampire from committing the latter.

He just needed to keep any vital information from reaching Julian's ear, not easy with Sophie asking questions.

"I'll be fine. Thanks anyway." He steered the car back into traffic, heading toward the freeway entrance ramp. Once on the highway, it was no problem eating and driving. That was what a knee was for.

The food didn't keep Sophie quiet for long, ten minutes tops, and then she was back to asking the kinds of questions he knew she wasn't ready to hear the answers to—and questions he definitely didn't want Julian to hear the answers to either.

"What's the Second Death?" she asked again.

Julian gave Ric a guilty shrug. Was that honest guilt or feigned? "Sorry. Wasn't thinking."

After swallowing a sigh of irritation, Ric said, "It's the final death."

"What made Julian ask you if you were dying?"

"Because I can eat food and walk in sunlight," he explained.

"Interesting. Let's talk about that eating thing," Sophie said, wedging her body between the two front seats. "This is the first time I've seen you eat and it raises some interesting questions. For instance, I thought you said if I turned into one of you vampy types, I wouldn't be able to eat food anymore."

"You won't," Julian said.

"Why not? If he can eat, why couldn't I? That doesn't seem fair." Sophie sounded sulky.

Ric peered in the rearview mirror. Oh, yeah. She was pouting. He adored the way her bottom lip protruded just enough to be tempting when she pouted. He could imagine the effect it must have had on her parents when she was a child. He knew for a fact that if they had a beautiful little girl with her glistening mahogany hair, expressive eyes, and full lips he'd be powerless to do anything but give her her heart's desire.

Good thing they weren't going to be producing any children. They'd have to complete all the steps of the marriage ritual before they could do that. And that was not going to happen. The second step was as far as he would let them go, if he had any control over it.

No marriage. No children.

"You wouldn't be able to eat because you would be a young Wissenschaft and as a young Wissenschaft you would lack the power to do so," Ric explained.

The bottom lip slipped back into place. What a shame.

"Okay. But eventually, I'd be able to eat again, right? Like in a few months or so?"

"No, not months. Many, many years." He wadded up the wrapper for his sandwich and crushed it into the bag. "Remember, I'm no infant. I'm several hundred years old."

"And don't look a day over thirty," Sophie said, leaning over to nibble on his earlobe. The French fry that was halfway down his throat stopped at midchest level, and one certain part south of the waist went rock hard in two seconds flat, putting thought of anything but sliding it into her slick canal from his mind. He swallowed. Hard.

"Just wait until I get you alone," he growled, trying to make some adjustments down below while driving—no easy task. "I'll make you pay for that."

"For what?" she whispered in his ear. "This?" Her

tongue rimmed his outer ear, then plunged inside, making his body rigid from scalp to big toe.

"Hmmm. Does this mean you're finished being angry with me for earlier?" he asked.

"Not on your life, buddy. I'll be furious for at least another ten seconds." She giggled, letting him know she wasn't even remotely close to being furious. "Actually, it means I'm trying to use my feminine wiles to get what I want."

"Ah, I see."

Giggling again, she sat back and resumed her line of questioning. "So, eating real food leads to death?"

"No, not exactly," Ric said, wishing she'd be distracted by something, anything. Wishing he was in a position to distract her. He could think of a thing or two that would take all thought of eating and clear it from her mind.

"That's all you're going to say?" She sat forward again and ran her tongue down the side of his neck, and he sucked in an audible gulp of air.

"Yes," he said, his voice wavering. His will, too.

"Nothing more?" she asked, now nibbling on his neck. Nipping, licking, driving him crazy. His erection pushed against the front of his pants. His testicles became heavy.

"No," he half spoke, half ground out through gritted teeth. "It's very complicated and I don't think now is the best time to talk about it."

"Nothing like a vague answer to annoy me. I hate it when people won't say what they mean. Julian?"

"Don't ask me to explain. I'm no good at explaining anything."

"Coward," she taunted.

"I'd be an idiot to get in the middle of this," Julian countered.

Sophie let loose with a sharp "Ha!" then added, "You weren't afraid to get in the middle of things earlier—when you snuck into my room."

"Yeah, well, that was before," Julian said.

"Before what? Before we left? Before we slept? Before we what?" she asked.

"Before you took the second step with Ric."

"What's that have to do with answering a question?" Sophie pushed.

"A lot." Julian looked out the window, stabbing out at the dark. "Oh, look. Pretty cows."

"Chicken," Sophie grumbled.

"No," Julian said, with a shake of his head. "Those are much too big to be chickens. Yep, they're definitely cows. Or steer. Hard to tell from so far away."

Ric smiled at the grunt of frustration that blasted from the backseat.

His dear, sweet, sexy, annoying, delightful—and did he say sexy?—Sophie. He knew she wasn't the kind to keep up her silence long, had proven it by spending the past several hours questioning him about some very intimate details of his existence as a vampire, right down to the most sensitive ones, things he couldn't afford for Julian to hear. If only he could get her alone, even for a second, he'd be able to explain, tell her he'd answer her questions when they had more time. And had more privacy.

Sun Tsu had coined the phrase *"Keep your friends close and your enemies closer."* Ric hadn't been given the chance to explain that that was what he was doing there, inviting Julian along as they searched for the shield and spear; he wasn't yet convinced of Julian's unspoken suggestion that the shield was King David's harp. He kicked himself for not taking the time to explain before they left the hotel, but he'd been anxious to get going, wanted to have several hours after they reached Chicago to find the dragon before sunrise. With all the bathroom and food stops Sophie kept initiating, they'd be lucky to get there by three. That would only give him about three hours to search.

As if she read his thoughts, Sophie chose that moment to announce, "I need to take a potty break. Was that a rest stop sign I saw back there?"

Humans! They had to eliminate every few minutes, especially female humans. Ric bit back a groan. "Are you sure you can't hold it?"

"No, I can't hold it. That's bad for my innards. Causes bladder infections and then it feels like I'm peeing acid whenever I go. You don't want to be around me when I have a bladder infection. Believe me. I'm miserable. My doctor said I should never hold it."

"Okay, okay." He surrendered with a lift of his hands. "I would never forgive myself if I were to cause you any sort of physical discomfort, at least if I can help it. We'll stop. Again. But promise me you won't get another giant-sized fountain drink?"

"Hey, first off, you're the one who told me I was dehydrated and need to drink more. Plus, I'm so gosh darned thirsty all the time all of a sudden. What happened? Did that second step make me a diabetic or something? I only donated a drop of blood. Or did you take another drinky-drinky and wipe out my memory again? Because if you did, there'll be hell to pay."

Julian laughed, and Ric, unable to help himself, laughed too. Hell to pay was all too appropriate an expression. He followed the winding exit to the freeway rest area and parked, taking advantage of the stop to get out and stretch his legs. He watched Julian very carefully, waiting to see if he'd excuse himself, to go off and find a phone to contact someone in Chicago. He knew they could be walking into a trap going to the dragon's lair. He guessed the dragon didn't have either of the artifacts they were looking for. And expected they were being led astray, probably to keep them from defeating the lamia who'd sent Julian to visit Sophie in the first place. But lacking any information to confirm his suspicions, he wouldn't ignore the possibility that Julian was telling the truth.

"By the way," Julian said, looking innocent as ever, "I went ahead and reserved three rooms for us at the Marriott."

"Perfect." Ric figured he'd know which it was, very soon. Was Julian a friend or foe?

Chapter 13

"Let me help you with those, and then I'll go find my own room." Ric yanked Sophie's carry-on from her and slung it over his shoulder, then picked up her suitcase with the other hand. He lifted it like it was light as feathers and trailed behind her to the elevator. As they waited for the car to descend from the fifth floor, she glanced around the lobby.

"Where'd Julius Caesar go?"

"Don't know. Probably to his room. Since it's approaching dawn, he's probably anxious to get out of the sunlight."

"Oh, yeah. Why is it you can walk around in daylight and he can't?"

He looked nervous as he glanced around. "I'll explain it later."

"So many secrets." A soft "ding" signaled the elevator's arrival and Sophie instinctively stepped to the right to allow any passengers to pass. After watching several, including a few men in business suits, a couple with a toddler, and a woman, wearing a scowl and a bad case of bed head, she stepped inside and continued, "Have I told you how much I can't stand secrets?"

"Maybe. I can't remember for sure," he said all

nonchalant-like as he reached around her to push the number five. The cozy, albeit brief, contact between her shoulder and his chest made her knees a little wobbly.

The doors slid shut and the car lurched, climbing slowly to the fifth floor. She gripped the metal handrail on the wall for stability. "We've taken the second step. Doesn't that entitle me to a little bit of insider information?"

"Yes. But here and now is not the place or time, neither is in a car with an Ancient One who'd tried to steal you away from me the night before."

Sophie's cheeks burned. Duh! Why was she so witless sometimes? And so willing to believe the worst about people? Ric wasn't trying to keep secrets from her. He was trying to keep secrets from Julian. "Ohhhh. I didn't think . . . I mean, I thought you and Julius Caesar were best pals. You two seemed to be hitting it off so well. And I didn't know the stuff I was asking would be harmful. Sorry." The elevator came to a bumping, stomach-jarring halt and the doors slid open. She stepped out of the car and glanced at the signs with numbers and arrows, searching for room five-twenty-two.

"Don't worry about it. This way," Ric said, turning right down a narrow passageway. "I'm guessing it's down here at the end."

He was right. It was way down there, the last room on the left. Good thing he hadn't allowed her to carry a single thing, not that she wasn't capable of lugging her own suitcases. She could. But her arms would be falling off by now. It was nice being treated with a little bit of respect, even if he'd been tight-lipped and stubborn about sharing information. At least now she had some notion of why he'd been acting that way.

Sophie swiped the card in the lock and pushed open the door. The curtains were drawn, the lights out. The room was completely dark. She made a beeline for the lamp she'd spied sitting on top of the dresser, but Ric stopped her.

"Wait." The door closed behind her, shutting out the light from the hallway. There was a thud, some soft shuffling and then two hands gripped her shoulders from behind.

Instantly in the grip of illogical fear, she gave a shocked gasp and jerked. Her heart pounded in her ears like a bass drum. "What the he—?"

"It's just me, sweetcheeks." Ric's deep voice cut through her fear and soothed her frazzled nerves instantly. He gently eased her around, then gathered her into a warm hug. "It's safe. I just wanted to check the room first."

She sighed, and even though she couldn't see much in the inky blackness but a vague outline of his face, she tipped her head to him in a glare. "You can actually see in here? That is so unfair. Anyway, what's the next step in our relic hunt? Are we going to pay a visit to that Guardian umm-mmph . . ."

He slanted his mouth over hers in a hungry kiss. His teeth nipped at her lower lip; then he suckled it, pulling it inside. His tongue teased with shy, fleeting swipes.

Ready to throw herself mind, body, and soul into the kiss, she opened her mouth, inviting that naughty tongue inside for a party. It accepted the invitation, made itself at home by lounging on the right side of her mouth, then paid a visit to the left. After a second or two there, it grew restless and decided to dance a little sexy tango. Her tongue joined the festivities, giving his a caress or two that had her rubbing against him like a cat in heat. She even purred, for which she received a rumbly chuckle and a pat on the rear end.

Now, seemingly on a mission to conquer, rather than merely pay a friendly visit, his tongue abandoned its gentle caressing motions for a rhythmic stabbing one instead. The change of pace awakened her desire, stirring it from its short nap until it had spread throughout her body like a fever. Parts tingled, her heart rate doubled, tripled, quadrupled. Her breathing quickened until she became breathless.

"You have no idea how much I want you right now," Ric

murmured as he nibbled a path along her jaw and then down her neck. "I'm burning up."

"Me too." She pressed herself against him as snugly as she could, molding her body to his. Her pubic bone ground against his thigh, creating a welcome friction. Her sex spasmed, wetness slicking her panties.

"We should get going sometime soon but . . . damn it . . ." His hands ran down her shoulders, then slid around to her back, where they found her buttocks. He pressed her into him, increasing the friction between her mound and his leg until she was sure she'd drop. Her knees turned to rubber. Her brain lost its struggle to remain afloat amid the desire flooding it and sent up its last warning flare before sinking like the *Titanic*. Her body tensed as the promise of what was about to happen reached her ears.

"To hell with the dragon. He can wait a little longer. I'm going to take you very shortly. Just a quickie."

Sophie shuddered against him, then let him lift her off her feet. He turned, somehow found the bed, and laid her on it. She kicked off her shoes, then scrambled to blindly shuck off her top and jeans.

"I want to share everything with you," he said, pressing his weight on top of her. "I don't want to keep secrets from you any longer. And I don't want you to keep secrets from me either."

Those words made her smile into the darkness like a goon. Finally! No more secrets. Complete honesty. Naturally, she could wait until . . . after they were through . . . to get all her answers. "You have no idea how much that means to me." She reached up, found his neck, hooked her hand around the back and pulled, ready to give him the kiss of a lifetime to show him how grateful she was. He accepted her tongue's forceful intrusion into his mouth, accepted her hands' thorough exploration of all parts south of his neck, and accepted her unspoken invitation to touch her anywhere he liked.

He found her nipples somehow—it couldn't have been because they were as hard as titanium—and pinched first one, then the other until she couldn't drag in a single heavy breath. Then his hand traveled lower, down her stomach to her sodden panties. She just about cried when his weight lifted off her as he sat back. But her sorrow quickly morphed to glee when he pulled her knees apart and traced a line down the center of her moist underpants.

"Mmmm. You're wet."

"Yeah. Imagine that. Want to check under the panties?"

"You bet I do." He stripped her of both underwear and bra. Breathless and burning up, her skin practically on fire, desire bubbling through her veins, Sophie lay there, waiting for his touch in the dark.

He started with her breasts, closed a warm mouth over one aching peak and suckled. Waves of need crashed through her, battering her body, washing away every thought before it reached the surface of her mind. She was left with only sensations. The soft smack of his mouth as he kissed, lapped at her nipple. The scent of her own arousal mixed with the unique combinations of soap and man and something spicy and dangerous that always surrounded Ric. The feeling of his velvet tongue as it alternately laved at her nipple and teased it with quick flicks.

Her growing need took the form of a tightness that started deep in her belly. As Ric abandoned one nipple for the other, that need grew. Heat joined the tension, creating a burning knot deep inside her. It slid lower, between her legs, and she groaned, fisted the coverlet, and opened her legs wider, silently begging for him to soothe the fierce blaze burning there.

She found his shoulder and swiped her tongue along the bulge of a muscle, devouring the wonderful flavor of salt and man. Her fingers followed the line of corded muscles stretching down to his elbows. *"Please,"* she begged.

Even though she couldn't see him, she could see his

smile in her mind, could feel his joy, his hunger and need. They magnified her own, sending spikes of sharp wanting, jagged and painful, through her body. She cried out, called his name until his mouth pressed to hers and he drank in all her cries. One finger slipped between her slick folds, rimmed the outside of her sex, dragging wet warmth up to her clitoris. He drew tight circles over her nub. Round and round.

Her inner thigh muscles stretched and burned as she parted her legs wider, wider. She needed him inside, needed to be filled, needed to be joined with him again. Completed. Whole.

"Ric. Now. Oh, please."

She felt him settle between her thighs, touch her knees with his hands. His erection pushed at her and she arched her back to take him inside. He entered her in one swift, mind-blowing stroke. Instantly, her body was ablaze. So full. Complete. Whole. She wanted to cry. She wanted to laugh. She did both, arched to meet his thrusts, and rode upon the waves of bliss his body gave her.

When he reached down to stroke her clitoris, she was driven to new heights of paradise, to a place where there was no division between them, where she was a part of him and he, her, and their minds and spirits were fused. His emotions blasted through her being, making her heart heavy and light at the same time. His thoughts filled her head. His cries sounded in her ears.

With the first spasm of her climax, he stiffened against her and whispered her name into her head. And the words, *I'm falling in love with you.* The moment he found his release, she confessed as well, "And I'm falling in love with you, too." After a final stroke, he pulled out of her.

Then there was a thud, a shout, and wild jumping all around her.

Confused, Sophie scooted up to the head of the bed and fumbled for the light. It snapped on, flooding the room with blinding white light. She blinked and squinted, struck dumb by what she saw. It didn't make sense.

How could he? What was happening?

Ric was nude, standing at the foot of the bed, Julian's wrist caught in his raised fist, every muscle in Ric's body flexed tight, hard as steel.

Clearly they weren't dancing.

In Julian's hand was a knife. A very large knife with a silver, hooked blade that flashed brightly when Julian's hand twitched.

"What the heck?!" Sophie shouted.

"It's not what you think. I swear," Julian said, his eyes full of surprise, fixed on Ric's red, rage-filled face.

"Not what I think?" Ric said so low Sophie could hardly hear him. "Why don't you tell me what I think?"

Julian's fingers uncurled. The knife fell onto the bed. Sophie stared at it in horror. "I wasn't . . . I mean there was someone . . ." He shook his head. "It doesn't matter. You aren't going to believe me."

"What's to doubt? I felt the blade. I turned around. You're in the midst of a full backswing sure to drive that silver through my ribs and into my heart." Ric shoved at Julian, but Julian barely budged. The worst kind of rage played over Ric's features, the kind that made men do crazy things, things like kill other men.

Sophie's gaze jumped back and forth between the two men. Confused, wanting to believe Julian for some reason but having a hard time ignoring the facts, she wrapped a sheet around herself and stood mute, tense, ready to jump if either man did anything foolish—not that it wouldn't be foolish of her to jump into the middle of a fight between two vampires.

But a girl had to do what a girl had to do when it involved the man she was falling in love with.

"Please, Ric," she said. "Don't do anything stupid—"

"Like murder the bastard? Sneak up on him in the dark

while he's making love and drive a fucking silver stake into his black heart?"

"Yeah. That." Sophie nodded, knowing her feeble attempt at trying to lighten the mood would probably fail. "You know what the sight of blood does to me."

"I swear, I don't know how I got here. But when I figured out where I was, I saw another guy here," Julian insisted, pointing at an empty spot next to where Ric was currently fuming. "He was right there and I . . . I swung the knife at him just before he tried to kill you."

"Nice try, asshole. I know it's not in your disposition to lie, but I'm not buying this story. Was that other guy by any chance a pal of yours? A convenient scapegoat to get you off the hook? Get out of here before I do something we both regret."

Sophie let out a heavy sigh of relief. No dead vampires. Ric was still alive. Alive, not lying in a pool of blood on the bed. To think she'd almost lost him. Had come so close. Instantly, she caught a case of the shivers.

"Thanks for not doing anything crazy," she said, trying hard not to let on how bothered by all this she was. And bothered was a misnomer, actually. Scared poopless, out of her wits, in shock. Those were more appropriate expressions for what she was feeling. She resisted the urge to hurl herself on him and cling to him like a baby. She was not the hurling type. She was not the clinging type. And she was no baby.

She was strong. She was capable. She was independent . . . and she was not fooling anyone, herself included.

She adored this man and even the thought of losing him made her sick. As if on cue, her insides twisted into a double knot.

She received a grunt for an answer to her thanks, a disgusted grunt that suggested he wasn't particularly happy with the way things had gone.

She smoothed her palm down Ric's arm, wishing she could cast away the anger she saw in his eyes. He was furious. Still. And she bet it would take him a long, long time to settle down. "I admire the fact that you took the high road and walked away from the fight," she said. "I've always admired men who have the strength to do that."

"It wasn't my first choice," he said through gritted teeth.

"I know." She coaxed him to sit, then climbed up on the bed behind him and attempted to rub away the knots in his shoulders. It was like massaging a pile of granite. Her knuckles cracked. "I never in a million years expected Julian to do something so . . . evil," she admitted.

"I did."

"Really?"

"Don't trust anyone. That's always been my motto. I knew he was up to something. No one makes a one-eighty overnight. He's on the other team. And he'll try to stop us again, too. I have no doubt he's still taking orders from that lamia. Even so, this was a very bold step to take. He had to believe he'd succeed to dare even try it. He didn't try to conceal his face. Nothing. Either he was so convinced he couldn't fail or he's a lot stupider than I thought. I expected him to be more underhanded, lead us astray, deliver us into a trap. I hate to see what his next attempt will be."

"Oh, God." She sort of regretted the fact that Ric hadn't killed him now. She wrapped her arms around Ric's neck and rested her chin on his shoulder, pressing her upper body against his back. His clean scent filled her nostrils and she nuzzled into his neck, inhaling, wanting to store his scent, to remember it forever.

What if he was right? What if Julian did try again? And what if he succeeded?

"What can we do to stop him?" Sophie asked, fighting against the quakes building inside. Now she knew what a volcano felt like just before it got ready to blow. She was gonna blow and blow bad. Tremors started in her belly.

"Be ready for his next move."

"And then what?" she whispered.

"Stop him."

A boulder of concrete formed in her throat. Stop him. She could guess how. "Why . . . why didn't you stop him tonight if that's what you intend to do?"

"I wasn't ready yet." Ric rested his elbows on his knees and steepled his fingers. "I had to wait and see what his next move was. What if he was telling the truth? I know it's unlikely. I saw no signs of another man in the room with us, but if what he said was true, then I'd find out about it eventually. And I would've realized I'd killed an innocent guy for nothing. I wouldn't be able to live with the guilt. No. It was too soon. We wait."

"What about the dragonman? I really don't want to go there. It sounds too dangerous."

"We're going. On our own. To hell with Julian."

"You think it's safe?"

"Probably."

"Probably?"

"Can't say for sure. You never know with Guardians. The hotel has a computer room downstairs. I'll look up the Guardian in the phone book and we'll pay him a visit this morning, while Julian's sleeping. That ought to reduce the danger factor a bit."

"Okay. That sounds like a plan." Still not over the thought that she could've lost Ric, just like that, Sophie squeezed him again. The realization that she might still lose him made her stomach leap up her throat. Yes, at first he'd been nothing more than a cute sidekick, someone to help her find the artifacts and save Dao. But now, now he was so much more. He was everything to her now. He was her future—she hoped. "I'm so glad you're here with me. I mean, I don't know how I would've managed if I'd had to do this alone. I wouldn't have wanted to."

"Yeah, um"—he stood up, strode across the room to the door—"I'm going downstairs to find the computer."

"Sure. Okay," she said, noting the stiffness in his voice, in his posture. Was he still upset about Julian? Or was there something else going on? "I should check on Dao while you're gone." She peered at the clock. It was awfully early. She figured she'd better give him a call anyway. Who knew when she'd get the chance again.

She settled onto the bed, reclined on a stack of pillows, dialed the number, and prepared to talk to a sleepy, grumpy Dao. He hated being wakened.

The phone rang, and rang, and rang. Not home? Odd. Just as she pulled the receiver from her ear, her finger poised over the button, ready to cut off the call, she heard his gravelly, sleep-thickened voice.

"Uh, hello?"

"Dao?"

"Yes. Who's calling?"

"It's me, Sophie. I just wanted to call, see how you're feeling—"

"Sophie? Sophie who?"

Her belly slid to her toes. What had Ric said about confusion? Dao wasn't confused. No. He was . . . half asleep. That's all. "Your friend Sophie. Sophie Hahn."

"I'm sorry. You must have the wrong number."

"Huh?" She forced a chuckle. Laughing was the last thing she felt like doing at the moment. "You're joking, right? Oh, you're such a crazy guy."

"No, I'm not joking. But I agree, if this is your idea of a joke, it isn't funny. Good-bye."

Her heart stopped. "What? Wait! Don't hang up." The phone to her ear, she yelled, "Wake up, buddy! This is Sophie. Your best woman, the one who stood by your side at your wedding."

"Sorry. I don't know anyone named Sophie and my

friend Bill was my best *man*. Best woman? What the hell is that? You have the wrong number."

Click.

"Oh my God. He doesn't remember me anymore? He doesn't remember his wedding? He doesn't fucking remember I exist, and I'm in Chicago, too far away to help him. It's too late." She let her head fall forward. Her forehead landed in her palms. "He's worse. The witch stole his memory. Damn."

She cried. The tears ran like rivers down her cheeks. It was too much, all of it. Dao's sickness, and the dueling vampires, and the snakewoman, and Julian's attempt to kill Ric while he was making love to her, and the dragon guy, and, and . . . she wasn't fucking Buffy the vampire slayer. She wasn't strong enough. She wasn't brave enough and she wasn't smart enough. "I want to go home."

Someone knocked on her door. Three soft raps.

"Oh, God, what now?" Figuring she'd probably regret going to the door, Sophie rubbed the tears from her burning eyes with the bedsheet, then staggered to the door and peered out the peephole.

Ric.

She opened the door and he swept past her with long, purposeful strides.

"I found him, and lucky for us, he doesn't live far from here. But I want you to stay put while I go have a little chat—"

"Over my dead body. And I mean that literally."

One eyebrow lifted. "Really," he said flatly. "You know, I could've—and probably should've—gone without telling you where I was heading. But I thought I'd do the right thing and come here and explain. No secrets. Remember?" He shook his head, raked his fingers through his hair. "You see what we men have to deal with? We try to give you what you want and you give us grief anyway. And what's wrong? Why are your eyes so red?"

"I just talked to Dao and he doesn't know who I am anymore. What's that mean?"

"Shit." Ric shook his head. "It means you have probably twenty-four, maybe thirty-six hours tops if what Julian implied is true."

"Then that settles it. I'm going with you. I'll go insane with worry if you leave me here to stare at these four walls. I have to do something. Up to this point, you've been doing all the work." When he didn't agree to let her go, she threw in an argument she figured couldn't fail. "Besides, what if Julian comes back while you're gone? Are we sure he was trying to kill you and not me?"

Surprise touched his features. "You have a point. I hadn't thought of that, just assumed he was after me so that he could have you and more easily distract you from the lamia . . . but he might . . . he could . . . bastard!" He crossed his thick arms over his chest. "You're coming with me but you have to promise to do what I say. We don't have time to waste arguing. Got it?"

Got it? Despite the fact that she'd won the battle, she saw red. "Don't talk to me like a defiant child! No one talks to me like that."

"Sorry! I swear I didn't mean it to come out like that." He pulled her to him, held her tightly. He kissed the top of her head and she sighed into his chest. Safe, warm, secure. "Sorry, sweetcheeks. But the thought of you being hurt or worse . . . makes me crazy. I don't know what I'd do if something happened to you. I'd love to just put you away somewhere safe but I know I can't."

"No, you can't lock me in a tower like a princess. This isn't a fairy tale. It's an action adventure. You're Indiana Jones and I'm Willie Scott. We're in this together. Remember? Partners. You watch my back and I'll watch yours. I admit, I haven't felt in control or brave or strong since we left, but I can't leave you now, hide here like a chickenshit. Not when someone's trying to kill you, or me . . . or both of us. And not when Dao's getting worse. I let one person down once and it cost more than I ever wanted to pay. It cost her life. No way. I can't let you down too. I can't let Dao down. I can't let myself down."

"Yeah. I remember we originally said we'd help each other. But since we left Detroit, things have changed. A lot's happened—"

"Tell me about it." She smiled up at him, despite the fear and uncertainty making her heart heavy. "I care about you. I didn't see that coming—okay, maybe I did. Sort of. But I didn't expect to care so much."

His eyes were dark, his face a mask of tension, worry. "I care about you too. More than I ever thought I could. More than I wanted to."

Her smile faded. "I don't know whether to say thank you or I'm sorry."

"Neither. It wasn't anything you did." He kissed her nose. "But you'd better move back a bit or things are going to start happening again." He nodded down in the general direction of their bodies and she instantly recognized the hard bulge pressing against her belly.

"Fair enough." She reluctantly stepped out of his embrace. "But promise me that when all this is through we'll have some quiet time, just you and me. I want to laze around, soak in the bathtub, watch a movie on TV, eat a meal that doesn't come in waxed paper."

"You bet we will."

"Good. So, what do we need to defeat a dragon? Do we need to collect some supplies? Holy water? Garlic?"

"We need a miracle." He took her hand in his, kissed her knuckles, and squeezed gently.

"Great," she said, following him into the hall. "I don't suppose they're on special at Meijers, and I'm pretty sure I'd completely exhausted my lifetime's supply when I met you."

Chapter 14

Sophie wasn't sure what she'd expected a dragon's lair to look like, but she knew for a fact that the little white bungalow with tidy flower beds filled to capacity with petunias was a far cry from what she'd imagined. Where was the forbidding castle? The moat? The rickety wooden bridge and "Danger, stay away" signs?

When they stepped on the front porch and heard a young child's playful shriek through the closed door, she asked Ric, "Are you absolutely positive we're at the right place? Do dragons have flowers? And babies? And garden signs with butterflies on them? We're not even out in the boonies. We're in the heart of suburbia. Frankly, I'd expect someone's grandma to live here."

"If this is the Guardian's house, he's no one's grandma, or grandpa. Don't let appearances fool you."

"Sure. Okay," she said, not at all convinced.

Ric adjusted his badge holder nervously and flipped the pages of paper they'd filled with fake names and arranged on a clipboard. "I just hope he buys our cover."

"Sure he will. You're an expert liar."

He grimaced. "Not anymore, at least not to you."

"I hope you mean that." She checked her own name badge—which displayed the name Sheila Potts—and went through what they'd rehearsed on the way over. The wig she was wearing to hide her hair itched. She poked a finger at her scalp and tried to scratch without knocking the wig off her head or setting it off kilter so she looked like her grandma after being caught in a windstorm. "Why aren't you wearing a wig? This is terrible," she grumbled. "Why aren't you sharing my misery?"

"Because they don't make wigs for men. I wish they did." He smoothed his fake beard, which matched his new hair color, deep brown. The new color looked great on him, gave him a dark mysterious look instead of the sun god, beach bum one. Both looks suited her just fine. "This is the best I could come up with. I'm not convinced it's good enough but what can I do now? Ready?"

Sophie nodded and Ric poked the doorbell. She heard the faint chime sound inside, then the not-so-faint bark of at least a dozen dogs. "Uh-oh."

"Don't worry." Ric donned a smile that made her weaker in the knees than she already was.

She followed suit but guessed her smile looked a lot less convincing than his. "You don't understand. I'm scared to death of dogs."

"I doubt they'll come to the door."

A split second later, it sounded like all bazillion dogs in the house were digging at the inside of the door, trying to bust through to make her their lunch. Sophie backed up one, two, three steps until she was literally teetering on the edge of the porch.

"Don't you go anywhere. I need you here so they don't get a good look at me." Ric caught her sleeve and yanked at the precise moment the front door swung open, revealing a young, pretty woman with an armload of baby and surrounded by the hounds of hell. He gently shoved Sophie in front of him.

The woman eyed them both with suspicion and said through the glass storm door, "Yes?"

Sure those dogs would bust through that single pane of very thin glass at any moment, Sophie cleared her throat. "Hello, madam. We're with the Humane Society collecting signatures to have a law recently passed allowing the shooting of innocent mourning doves to be rescinded. Would you care to sign?"

The woman's eyes went from Sophie's face to some point behind her—Ric's face, she assumed. He pressed the clipboard into Sophie's hand. She offered it to the woman.

"Okay. I guess I can do that," the woman said. Balanced on her hip was the baby, a toothless grin and drool dripping down his chin. She swapped hips, settling him on the opposite side and pushed open the door a couple of inches to allow Sophie to pass the clipboard through.

She set the baby on the floor, signed, and then, smiling, reached for the door, but before she had it opened, Ric said, "Is your husband home too? We could use all the signatures we can get. It's for a good cause."

"Oh." One of the dogs gave the baby's face a tongue bath and the child laughed gleefully. "That's enough, Goliath." The woman shook a scolding finger at the mammoth dog, now working at cleaning the infant's hair, and scooped up the baby. "Sure. Just a moment." She turned to take the clipboard into the interior of the house.

Ric poked Sophie's back. She glanced over her shoulder. "Huh? What?"

Ric shook his head. "Wait!" he said to the woman. "We can't let you to take that out of our sight," he explained. "Sorry, it has personal information on it about the other signers. Phone numbers, addresses. I'm sure you understand."

"Oh. Yeah. I understand." As the woman passed the clipboard back to Sophie, several noses poked out, sniffing her fingers. Instinctively, Sophie jerked her hand away. The woman looked shocked at Sophie's reaction. The dog that had groomed the baby growled and bared its very sharp, very long, very intimidating teeth. After giving Sophie a cautious once-over, the woman slammed the glass door shut and scowled at the beast. "Goliath, what's your problem?" She held up her index finger to Ric and Sophie and disappeared.

The dogs remained. An eighth inch of glass or so the only thing between their teeth and Sophie's delicate skin.

"They hate me. They want to eat me. Look at that one, he's so hungry he's drooling," she whispered, pointing at the one with the smashed-looking face and strings of slime hanging from his loose lips. She gave Ric a nervous glance, but before he could respond, the woman returned, sans the baby, but with a very nice-looking man; a man, Sophie might add, who looked nothing like a dragon. He looked more like a movie star.

"Hello, sir," she said, prepared to recite the spiel she'd just given his wife, but she stopped at that point, distracted by the way he was staring at Ric. And the way Ric was staring at him.

It was that "guy sizing up the foe" type of look. Not good.

Ric glanced down at his name badge, breaking eye contact first.

Clearing her throat, Sophie said, "Hello, we're collecting signatures to send to our . . . local . . . representatives. . . ." She stopped when the movie star shut the door in her face. "He knew?"

"He knows something's up." Ric turned, walked down the front porch stairs, reading the wife's signature. "For one, someone who works for the Humane Society isn't usually scared to death of animals."

"Oh," she said guiltily, following him. "Sorry."

"That's okay. You can't help it. Though if I'd known, I would've picked a different cover for us." Continuing down the front walk to the shaded street, he added, "Hmmm. The last name's right. We have the right guy. I tried to block him from my mind but he's too powerful. I think he got a few things. I couldn't get into his. It's locked up tighter than Fort Knox. But he's definitely an Immortal. He knows I'm one too. We've got to get into that house. Today. Before he moves his cache, or contacts some of his fellow Guardians and invites them to a party."

"How are we supposed to get in there? Those dogs'll tear any unwelcome visitors to shreds before they get more than a foot in the door. Did you see them? They were vicious. Man killers."

"They were grooming the baby. How vicious could they be?"

"That's only because they know the baby. We're strangers."

"I'm not worried about them." He stopped in the street in front of the tree sitting dead center in front of the house.

"I am."

"They probably have an alarm system." He turned around. She watched his dark-eyed gaze travel around the front of the house. "Maybe cameras too."

Admiring his profile—he had such a cute nose and there was this sexy little mole on his cheek—she circled him. "Do we really need to get in there? You're not even sure if this Guardian guy has what we're looking for. Think about it—a lamia sent us here, and an Ancient One tried to kill you. Why would they do that, other than to stop you from getting the shield and spear? It makes no sense."

"True. But if *they* know that we know who and what they are, then they would assume we wouldn't go." He started walking down the street. Long, purposeful strides carried him swiftly.

"Huh?" She jogged to catch up, snagged one of his arms, and gave it a sharp yank. "Slow down! I don't have five-foot-long legs like some people."

"True. But they're oh so perfect." He gave her a glittery-eyed grin that made her blush. "If Maggy knows we know she's a lamia, then she might've sent us here on purpose, banking on the assumption we wouldn't come check it out. And if she also knows—because she'd told Julian to let us in on the big secret—that this gentleman is a Guardian, then she might've been even more inclined to send us here, figuring we'd run the other way rather than take on a Guardian."

"Maybe. But why risk it? Why point us in the right direction at all? Why not lie and send us on a wild goose chase if the lamiae are trying to buy time?"

"I don't know. This may be a wild goose chase. There's no way to find out if we don't get inside. We came all this way. We should check it out."

"I was afraid you'd say that. But if we're wrong, we may not find out where the relics are before . . . before our time is up."

He clasped his hand around hers and continued down the street, this time at a much more comfortable pace. "Remember, the Ancient One doesn't like to tell a lie. He can conveniently forget to tell us something important but he's not likely to tell a lie. And he told us what?"

"That this guy's a Guardian," she said, shuddering when his thumb stroked her palm.

"What else?"

"That Margaret Mandel is a lamia?"

"And?"

Sophie rummaged around in her brain, searching her memory banks. It wasn't easy thinking with Ric giving her that look again—the one that melted her insides, made her all warm and wet and willing. "Oh, yeah. He said that we'd have to face a Guardian sooner or later if you're going to get the harp and spear, and that the Guardian will fight us for it or try to steal it from us once we've found it."

"You see now? We need to know what he has, who his contacts are, and how powerful he is. Julian told me all

Guardians have a weakness. Each one's different. We need to find what this guy's is," he said. Then, tossing an arm over her shoulder, he added, "Don't worry, sweetcheeks. I won't put you on dog duty."

Sinking into him, and falling into step as they rounded a corner, she said, "Why does that not make me feel any better?"

"Because you know me so well. Now let's go make some plans. Your friend needs us."

"There's a strange man at the door." Sophie backed away from the hotel room's peephole and turned to Ric.

"What's he look like?" Ric was sitting on the bed, a pile of papers spread out in front of him, printouts from the library.

She took a second peek. Nice looking. Blond hair. Same weird browny-gold eyes. Same stubborn set of his mouth. "You. Kinda. No, a lot like you, before you dyed your hair, that is. Do you have a twin?"

"Twin? No. Brother? Yes. You can let him in," he said, not looking up from his reading. "He's one of the good guys. I know that for a fact."

"Okay." She unfastened the dead bolt and pulled open the door, stepping aside to greet the visitor with a friendly smile. "Hello there. Welcome to the insanity."

"Hi," Ric's brother said, looking down at her. His eyebrows were bunched together in puzzlement. "Um, do I have the wrong room? I'm looking for—"

"Hey, Barrett. Get your little scrawny butt in here," Ric bellowed from behind Sophie.

Scrawny butt? Not!

Barrett was every bit as big and bulky as Ric. Wide chest that would make most women drool. Tall, solid frame that looked like it belonged on a football field.

Ric slung an arm over Barrett's shoulder and poked him

in the ribs. "This is my baby brother, Barrett," he said, by way of introduction. "Barrett, this is Sophie."

Recognition dawned over Barrett's handsome face. "Ahhh. Yes. Sophie."

"Whatever he told you, ignore it, unless he told you that I'm as beautiful as Angelina Jolie, with Anna Kournikova's body and Albert Einstein's brilliant mind."

"Actually, that's exactly what he said." Barrett flashed her a brilliant smile that told her he was lying through his vampire teeth.

"Ric! What have you told this man?" She spun around to give him a scowl.

He answered with a "who, me? I'm innocent" bat of the eyes.

"Nice to meet you." Barrett gave Sophie a shake of the head, then turned his attention to his brother. "What's all this stuff about taking on a Guardian? You're crazy. Besides, what do you care about a couple of crusty antiques? Your research is about the biological—"

Ric interrupted him with an elbow in the gut. "Later."

Barrett eyed Sophie. "Got it. Sure."

Sophie felt her blood boil. What was that all about? More secrets? Always secrets! Secret research. Secret, secret, secret. She hated secrets!

Two people who were facing life-and-death battles with dragons and lamiae and Ancient Ones had no business keeping secrets from each other. Two people who said they cared about each other, were falling in love with each other, had no business keeping secrets either.

"Got a minute?" she asked Ric. Not willing to wait for his answer, she grabbed whatever body part she could get her hands on first and pulled, hard, toward the bathroom.

Unfortunately, the part she grabbed—the waist of his unsnapped jeans—gave him the wrong impression.

"You sexy little vixen," he whispered, following her. "I

don't have time for this right now. Barrett and I need to make some plans. . . ."

"You'd better make time. Sit." Trying to sound authoritative, so that he'd realize his assumption was wrong, she frowned and pointed toward the toilet.

Why couldn't he be honest with her? What was he hiding now?

"There? Why?" he asked, looking confused. "I don't need to go. Remember? I don't do those things. And even if I did, I wouldn't do it in front of you."

"Just sit down!" It took every ounce of self-control she possessed to keep her voice below shouting level. "I'm getting a stiff neck from looking up at you."

"Sorry," he said, looking somewhat apologetic. He dropped to his knees, which left his head down around her midchest region. "Better?"

"Yes. Thank you." Damn it, he looked so adorable from this vantage, all wide-eyed and sweet. And sexy. She felt her anger fading already. *Secrets! Remember, he's keeping things from you. Now is not the time to go all soft and girly. Be strong!*

"Hmmm. I'm liking this position." He reached around, grabbed her butt and pulled until her pelvis was pressing against his face.

Strong!

He rubbed his chin back and forth over her mound.

Ssstronnng . . .

He slid his hand between her legs and rubbed her through her clothes. She felt her temperature spike. Had to be at least 110 about now. Her knees melted. Her brain was melting too, turning into a blob of gray goo.

Ssssstronnng . . . Oh, hell. Screw strong. I'm weak and proud of it.

She decided to embrace her weakness for a moment and started rocking her hips back and forth, back and forth.

Her sex rubbed against his hand, creating delightful friction. Little jolts of desire blazed through her body. It was a delightful reward. Weak was good. This was great.

She glanced down at his face, peered into his shuttered eyes. Eyes that were hiding things from her.

No, this was not good. Not at all.

Summoning up the very last bit of strength she possessed, she pushed against his shoulders, attempted to put some distance between her body—which was ready to throw Ric to the floor so she could have her way with him—and the wicked, secret-keeping man in front of her. Unfortunately, Ric refused to let her go.

"Oh, yes. This is perfect." His eyes focused up at her face, he opened his mouth and bit down on her crotch through her clothes. Even with a thick pair of jeans and a flimsy bit of lace between her delicate parts and his mouth, the sensation was so intense she was ready to drop down next to him on the tile and invite him on board.

Mad! You're mad. Remember?

"No, Ric." She shoved again. "We need to talk."

"Oh." He unfastened the button on her jeans. "Okay. Go ahead." Her button open, he yanked down the zipper. "Oh, look! Black lace. Nice." He pulled the crotch aside and said, "Hello, sweet thing. How about I have a taste? Mind a visitor? My tongue might like to come in and play."

Mad. Really, really . . . really . . . maaaad . . . She was losing control. Fast. She shut her eyes, dropped her head back, and grabbed a fistful of his shirt. "I can't talk when you're doing that. You're having a chat with my privates, for heaven's sake."

He pulled at her jeans, tugging them down over her hips, down her thighs. "I like your privates. They're sweet. And I think they like me too."

Dizzy, not sure how much longer she could remain standing, Sophie released Ric's shirt, lifted her arms, and braced them against the tile wall behind him. Ric continued tormenting her, rubbing her sex through her panties. "They do. But that's not what we're in here to discusssss . . . ohhhh." Her knees gave.

He caught her as she fell and laid her gently on the cool tile floor. The chill felt wonderful against her burning skin.

"Ric?" she said, making herself comfy. She lifted her hips to let him remove her panties.

"Hmmm?" he said to her thigh. He nibbled. He licked. He laved. He did all things that could be done to a thigh, then did the same things to the other leg.

"I'm seriously pissed at you," she said on a sigh. Even she had to admit, she didn't sound the least bit angry.

"Is that so?" he said to her other thigh. He moved his attention north, to her sex. "What about you, sweet thing? Are you mad at me too?" He pressed a finger inside and Sophie bucked against him, taking his finger as deep inside as it would go. "Mmmm. I'd say she's in a fine mood."

"We are going to . . . talk. About. It."

"Yes, love. We'll talk about anything you like. Whenever you like." He pushed her top up under her chin and unhooked her bra, filling his palms with her breasts. He kneaded her soft flesh, rolled her nipples between his fingers until they were stiff, painful peaks. "Damn it, I can't help myself. I want you all the time."

"I want you all the time too," she said breathlessly.

"No, you don't understand." He crawled on top of her, feathered soft kisses over her mouth until she could think of nothing but the way he tasted, and the way his weight felt, warm and reassuring, on top of her. The way her vagina burned to be filled. "I've never felt like this. God help me, I want to forget about the spear and shield and just stay in here with you making love until the end of time."

She blinked open her eyes, which she hadn't even known she'd closed, and searched his face. She saw the truth in his soft gold eyes. The need. The desire. The passion. And she mentally sent him all the desire she felt for him in return. Sent all her emotions, all her fears and doubts, too. She gave them to him with a kiss. When their mouths joined, their spirits joined as well, fused together like steel in a kiln.

His tongue dipped inside her mouth, sipping, tasting, taking. Hers stroked his, welcoming it inside, begging it for more.

As he shifted his weight, taking it off her, she caught his hands and placed them over her breasts in a silent plea for a caress. He answered her plea with light tickling touches, little circles around her nipples that made them tight and hard. Her blood pounded hot and fast through her body. Her need twisted and turned inside, tugging her muscles and tying them into tight knots. Her breathing sounded hoarse and fast in her ears.

She needed him. Now. "Ric," she croaked.

A soft knock sounded at the door.

"Hey, Ric?" Barrett's muffled voice sifted through the wooden door, putting an instant damper on the fire blazing through Sophie's body. "Hate to . . . er, interrupt. But there's a guy at the door. Says he's a friend of yours."

"Shit." Ric shook his head, his shaggy hair brushing against Sophie's belly, giving her goose bumps. "Sorry, sweetcheeks. Later, okay?" He helped her sit up, found her underpants and jeans; and, looking as sorry as she felt, handed them to her. "After we tackle the dragon."

Quickly shimmying into her jeans—and intentionally forgetting to put on the panties—she said, "But we still need to talk. I was . . . um, I am . . . still mad at you. You're still keeping secrets from me—"

Barrett knocked again. "Ric? He's not going away."

Ric pressed an index finger to Sophie's lips, shushing her. "Later. I promise. I need to see who this is. I didn't call anyone but Barrett."

"Fine," she grumbled. "If you don't, I'll make you pay."

He opened the bathroom door. Sophie gave Barrett a guilty, fleeting look, as they exited the bathroom then took a seat at the small round table at the back of the bedroom, hoping the telltale blush on her face would fade soon.

No man had affected her like Ric had. She wasn't sure she was so thrilled about that fact at the moment.

Ric went to the door, opened it a couple of inches, then said in a low, warning growl, "Julian? I told you to leave. What the hell are you doing back here?"

"What are you talking about?" Julian said, standing outside the doorway. "I've been sleeping for hours, since we arrived this morning."

Puzzled by Julian's seeming confusion, Sophie watched the men with keen interest. Ric looked like he was ready to strangle the Ancient One. The muscles in his arms strained into tight cords.

In a show of brotherly support, Barrett stepped up behind Ric and the two created a rock-hard vampire wall, blocking Julian from coming inside.

Because Sophie could no longer see Julian's face, she was forced to wander closer. She tiptoed up behind the brothers and peered between them.

Julian was speaking in an earnest voice, explaining how he couldn't have been in the room when the attempt on Ric's life had been made. And Ric was shaking his head and throwing icy glares back. Clearly, he wasn't buying the story that Julian was telling now any more than he'd bought the one he'd tried to foist on them earlier.

But Sophie had to give Julian credit—he was a convincing liar. Although she'd been told Ancient Ones were not fond of telling an untruth, she knew he was lying. He had to be this time. She'd seen him earlier, with her own eyes. And he had no valid explanation for how that could be.

Finally, clearly having heard enough, Ric shoved Julian

back out into the hallway and slammed the door. He turned, facing Sophie, and paced the small area of floor between the foot of the bed and the dresser.

Whew, that was one red face. He was beyond pissed and it was obvious Barrett knew it too. Barrett was trying to reassure Ric that they'd find out the truth and get whoever'd tried to slice him up like deli meat.

Sophie's heart ached for him. Yes, there was fury and his anger was intimidating. But there was also vulnerability. And fear. And frustration.

And perhaps that was why she was so confused. Because despite everything, in her heart she wanted to believe Julian. His stuttered, lame explanations made him look more guilty than innocent, yet there was something in his eyes that spoke of his innocence.

Regardless, she trusted Ric and more than anything she wanted to give him her unquestioning faith and support. Urgh! What a mess! If Julian was speaking the truth, why wouldn't he remember being in the room with them earlier? And if he was guilty, why would he come back, knowing how furious Ric was?

Something didn't add up.

"Ric?" She had to ask him, see what he thought.

"Forget about that dumb shit for now," Barrett said in a cool tone. He sat in the sole chair in the room and crossed his ankle over his knee. "We've got to take care of that dragon first. And since you don't know squat about dragons, that's going to take all your attention. Shut up and listen. I'll give you a crash course in Guardians."

"Yeah, yeah." Looking anxious, Ric sat on the bed, waved at his brother. "Go ahead, I'm all ears. Tell me everything you know and don't leave a single thing out, even the most insignificant detail."

"Okay. But this is going to take a while."

"That's fine. We've got all afternoon."

Chapter 15

"Why did I know I'd get dog duty?" Sophie asked, scowling at the raw steak hanging from her pinched fingers.

"All you have to do is wave that steak and toss it into the dog run," Ric said, pulling the black ski mask over his face. "Then, when all the dogs are in the pen, close the gate. I know you can handle it. You're a brave, capable woman." He gave her shoulders a quick rub, which she assumed was meant to reassure her. It didn't. But she wasn't about to tell him that.

"No, that's what I'm trying to tell you. I'm not brave. We've covered this subject already. I'm a chicken. Grade A. Can't you see my feathers? The little red rubbery thing hanging from my chin?" She pinched at the skin under her chin. "What's that thing called?"

"A wattle," Barrett said, pulling an identical mask over his face. With both of them dressed in the same head-to-toe black, faces covered, hair concealed, it was almost impossible to tell them apart.

"A what'll?" Sophie asked, dropping the steak into foil and wrapping it up. Her hands were slimy. Ick.

"No, wattle," Barrett repeated, shaking his head. She glared at him when he started an eye roll.

"Don't you dare." She went to the bathroom, washed

184 / Tawny Taylor

her hands, then secured her hair into a tight, low ponytail. That done, she returned to the room, tucked the meat under her black sweatshirt, and pulled on her ski cap. But unlike the guys, she left her face uncovered. "Don't you think those getups are going to set off a few alarms when you go walking through the hotel lobby?" she asked. "It's bad enough you're wearing all black. But a ski cap in this weather is a bit lame."

"We aren't going through the lobby," Ric said. He pointed at the window. "We want the hotel staff to think we're still here, just in case something . . . unfortunate . . . happens, like a dragon dies tonight and it's somehow traced to us. Claiming we were in our room all night by ourselves is not much of an alibi, but it's better than nothing."

She followed him to the window. The very hard asphalt parking lot below was a long, long way down. She felt sick. She felt dizzy. The world started spinning and she had to back away from the window. Way, way back. "You've got to be kidding. I'm not Spiderman. I can't scale walls with my supersticky spidey web. And I can't jump. If I lived—which is a big if—my leg bones would be splinters. And that's assuming I landed on my feet. Imagine what my head would look like if I landed on that instead. Ever seen that comedian who smashes watermelons on stage for kicks? What's that guy's name?"

"Gallagher," Ric said.

"Huh? Who's Gallagher?" Barrett asked.

"The guy who used to smash watermelons. You have your meat?" Ric asked, taking a step closer to her.

She saw a sparkle in his eye and wished she could see the rest of his face. It was, after all, a very adorable face. Especially when he was sporting a "fuck me now" look. She guessed that was the expression he was wearing at the moment.

Then the sparkle dimmed when he took a second step.

"Yesss." She took a step backward. What was he up to?

She wasn't liking the gleam she saw in his eyes now. Cold determination.

"Good." He lunged forward, caught her by the waist, and crushed her against him. That wasn't so bad. In fact, it was mighty nice. She tipped her head, hoping for a kiss. Unfortunately, he didn't remove his mask.

She motioned toward his face. "Um, this might be better if A, you took that thing off, and B, you sent your brother on a little walky-walky for a few minutes. She glanced over her shoulder at Barrett and gave him an apologetic smile. "Give us maybe fifteen, twenty minutes? You don't mind, do you?"

Barrett didn't respond.

Then, taking her by complete surprise, Ric got all cavemanish, tossed her over his shoulder like a barbarian, and jumped up on the window ledge.

"What the? Oh, God! I'm going to die. Ric! Stop!" Her fingers closed around the cool aluminum window frame and she hung on for life as he pushed the sliding window open. Cool, damp night air brushed her face like invisible feathers. "Ric? What are you doing? Are you going to throw me?" While she was grilling Ric the caveman, Barrett pried each finger free. "Ric!" she shouted, too afraid to fight. They were, after all, on a narrow ledge five stories above the ground. She swatted at Barrett and tried to get a hold on the window frame again, but Ric shimmied out away from the window on the narrow ledge outside. "Ric!"

"Shhh! Trust me?" Ric asked.

"No! Not when you're standing on a window ledge holding me like a sack of potatoes."

"Trust me?" he repeated, setting her on her feet next to him. Instinctively, she wound her limbs around him like a grapevine around a wooden stake. He felt stable and strong, even standing on a five-inch ledge.

She hesitantly glanced down. The parking lot was a long way down. Surely he was just testing her, to see if she was really capable of trusting him. "Okay. I'll trust you. A little. Later. Like when we're back safe and sound inside. But—"

"Trust me," he repeated, firmer, wrapping his arm around her waist and hauling her against his side.

"Okay. Okay." She let her head fall to the side, rest against his bulky upper arm. "You made your point. Now let's go back inside—"

Ric jumped, taking her with him.

"Ric!" Sophie clung to him like a drowning woman to a life preserver. Midair, she gritted her teeth, tensed every muscle in her body, and clamped her eyelids shut, waiting for the impact of her body against rock-hard concrete.

It was taking a long time getting to the ground. She took those precious moments to pray for forgiveness for everything she'd ever done wrong in her life and then listed all the sins she hadn't had the chance to commit yet.

Life was so unfair!

Their landing was tooth jarring, but surprisingly lacking in the pain department. It was as if Ric's legs had been made of rubber, or the concrete had turned to a big foam mattress. They bounced slightly and then Ric set her on her feet.

Naturally, as always the case when she'd had a near-death experience, her knees were like butter. They gave way and she landed on her butt. She gaped up at the caveman and struggled to catch her breath. She swore her lungs had completely collapsed somewhere on their descent. She guessed between the third and second floors. "How?" was all she could say.

"I'll explain later. We need to get going."

Sophie double-checked to make sure she was really as okay as she thought she was—she'd heard shock did crazy things to a body, like make a person walk around with missing limbs and such.

No blood. No protruding bones. All parts checked out okay. Another miracle. Miracle?

Maybe there was hope they'd defeat the dragon tonight after all.

She stood and turned around, just in time to watch Barrett fall from the sky behind her and land lightly on his feet like a freaking ballet dancer. "Oh my God, I want to know how you guys do that!"

"It's a vampire thing," Barrett explained as he headed toward a black Suburban parked only a few feet away. He opened the rear passenger door for her, then slammed it shut after she climbed in.

Ric and Barrett took their seats in the front and off they went, to the dragon's little bungalow on the quiet tree-lined street a mile or two down the road. For the second time in the last twenty minutes, Sophie was glad her stomach was empty.

Ric's mind worked over every piece of information his brother had given him about the Guardians. As it looked now, he'd be lucky to get in and out of that house with his hide intact. His brother, a member of an elite Immortal police force, was his only hope of making it out alive.

But he had no choice. This was it, his chance of getting the spear and shield. A once-in-a-lifetime chance. If he failed, he had no doubt the relics would vanish. The Guardian would send them off to another Guardian through the underground system of couriers they used. Impossible to trace. He'd never get this close again.

During their earlier visit, he hadn't been able to breach the dragon's mental defenses, but he had been able to intercept bits and pieces of what the Guardian had mentally said to his mate: "That's the Wissenschaft and his woman. They're here for the items we talked about."

That was enough for Ric. No doubt thanks to either Maggy or Julian, the Guardian not only knew who Ric and Sophie were, but also what they were after.

But most important, the Guardian knew where the spear and shield were. He had to. Despite the fact that wisdom would dictate the relics needed to be moved, Ric felt in his gut they were still in that house. Somewhere. The Guardian was not threatened, which meant he was prepared.

What sort of defenses would the dragon use to keep them from it? Kingsley was a red dragon. His element was fire, heat. Thus, Ric fully expected to be blasted with flame. Not a particularly pleasant way to spend the night, especially since as a vampire, fire was not something he could easily defend himself from.

Adrenaline was coursing through his body, making him tense, his senses focused and alert as they parked the car. Sophie looked scared and the need to ease her fears burned in his heart. Unfortunately, there were good reasons to be afraid and he didn't want her going into this without knowing how grave the situation was. Fear wasn't always a bad thing.

Her gaze sought his. "Ric?"

He pulled the ski mask up and gave her a serious look. "Sweetcheeks, this is it, our only chance. And I'll be honest with you, we're not prepared. This Guardian is a red dragon, a fire dragon. The most dangerous."

"Why don't we wait then? Call for more help?"

"There's no one I can call. If I knew a mage, that would help. . . ." He didn't hold back the sigh sitting in his throat. "If we don't do this tonight, the Guardian will move the relics."

"You know he has them?"

"I have a good feeling. But if we don't get them tonight, we won't find them again. You know what that means for your friend?"

She dropped her gaze to her feet. "But you're risking your life to save his. If you fail, you'll be gone. Dao will die. I'll . . . lose everything that matters."

Guilt pricked at his heart. She didn't know his true intentions yet. He hoped when she learned what they were, she'd understand.

"Then I won't fail." He pulled her into his arms, crushing her soft body against his. In his mind, he tried to prepare himself for the possibility that he might never hold her again. He listened to her quick, panting breaths, inhaled the bitter scent of her fear, and almost told Barrett to forget it.

And then he reminded himself of his reason for finding the spear and shield.

There were few things that were worth risking life and limb for. There were few things that were worth risking the life of his dearest brother for, and of Sophie, a human who had no idea the true power of the relics she sought. A lovely, kind, intelligent, sexy, delightful human he adored.

But the chance to find a cure for millions of tormented souls was worth all that, and more. Surely Sophie would understand when the time came—if the time came—to explain it to her.

He brushed his mouth over hers in a soul-deep kiss that left him wanting more, so much more. Then he pulled his mask back into place and turned to Barrett, took the fire extinguisher in one fist, the bag of battle supplies in the other—if the assorted bathroom and kitchen products (the most useful weapons they could assemble on such short notice) qualified as battle supplies.

"Ready?" Barrett whispered, his hands full as well.

"Yeah." Ric watched Sophie pull her ski mask over her face. "Let's go."

They walked down the quiet street. Outside of the flickering fireflies and the occasional stray cat, there wasn't any movement around them, no sign of life. They reached the house quickly. Ric and Barrett took their positions at the front and side doors. Sophie tiptoed around to the back, the raw meat in her hand.

Ric looked at his watch, waited for the precise moment they'd agreed on, then drew back to batter the door.

On a whim, he tried it first. Unlocked?

Not a good sign.

He opened it just enough to slip inside, then closed it behind his back. His eyes swept the house's dark interior. He stood in a small entryway, a three-by-three-foot area that led to the living room. There was no sign of movement. He looked up and down. No sign of a trap.

He hesitantly took a single step into the living room and flinched.

Nothing flared, barked, or blew up. Was the Guardian hoping he'd come closer? Where were the dogs? No traps? No defenses?

Barrett's voice sounded in his earpiece. "Found something in the basement."

"Any sign of the dogs?" he said into the microphone clipped to his chest.

"Nope. Not down here."

"Sophie?" Ric said.

"I'm here." Her voice was shaky. "No dogs back here. Nothing."

"This isn't right. It's got to be a trap," Ric said, creeping through the living room, alert for signs of trouble. "No Guardian would leave his lair unprotected."

"I've seen it once or twice," Barrett said. "Some of them get so cocky, thinking their reputation is enough to keep people away. Where are you? Get down here."

"Fine, fine. Coming." Ric passed through a small dining room into the kitchen. The basement stairs were at the rear. He took them very slowly. "Where are you?" he asked Barrett.

"Way in the back. Follow the furnace ducts."

"Okay." When he reached the bottom of the stairs, he said, "Sophie, you still with me?"

"Yes. What's going on in there?" she asked. "I'm scared."

"Nothing. We're okay. It's dead quiet." Ric glanced up, caught sight of the furnace ductwork, and started following it to the left.

"Ric?" Sophie's soft voice was like a soothing caress.

"Yes?"

"Please be careful."

"I will be. Promise."

"I don't want to live without you," she said. "I . . . love you."

Her words tore his insides to shreds. She didn't know what she'd done by saying those words just then. She'd taken the third step by confessing her love for him in the presence of his brother, a fellow clan member.

"I love you too. And I promise I'll do everything in my power to make sure you won't have to live another minute without me, if that's what you really want. But you need to be sure about this. You know what I am. As a man and as an Immortal. Are you sure you want me?"

"Yes. I'm sure."

He wanted to sweep her into his arms and crush her to him. Then again, he wanted to step back and knock some sense into her too. He'd started the process of the Joining in an effort to protect her from the Ancient One. Now, thanks to her willingness to take both the second and third steps, he faced the endless agony of wanting to complete it. His soul cried out for her. His spirit, mind. It would be like an eternal hunger that couldn't be sated, a fire that couldn't be doused. A thirst that could never be quenched.

Completing the Joining was not an option. He would never again Join with another human. He was a scientist who'd spent the last several centuries searching for a cure to his people's disease. Why would he choose to pass it on to another human being? A human being he loved?

He passed through a storage room, full of unmarked cardboard boxes stacked on metal shelves. "Barrett?"

"Getting bored waiting for you. What's the holdup?"

"I'm almost there." He paused at the door in the back of the storeroom. "I see a door."

"Yeah. Come on. I'm back here. Let's hurry up and get this over with."

"Okay." He turned the knob, pushed. The room was enveloped in pitch blackness so thick even his sensitive eyes couldn't find Barrett. "Where are you? It's too damn dark in here—"

A set of hands clamped around both his arms.

Sophie's scream shot into his ear through his earpiece.

A roar of rage rumbled up from his chest and bellowed from his mouth. "Barrett!"

Chapter 16

They burst through the back door like a pack of rabid wolves. One, two, three, four, five . . . six. Six teeth-baring, growling, snarling, people-eating beasts.

"Oh shit!" Taken by surprise, Sophie dropped the steak at her feet and stared, gape mouthed, stunned into a state similar to that of a deer caught in the headlights of an oncoming car.

Teeth flashed in the moonlight. The dogs formed a line and crept closer. She had no doubt they'd be on top of her in about a second flat. She could see their muscles rippling under their fur as they readied to pounce like wild dogs on injured prey.

It was too late. She couldn't run. She knew she couldn't fight them all off. She was a goner.

"Ric," she whispered. Her voice shook. "I love you." Then, as the pack lunged forward, she turned and sprinted for the shed.

She got the door open, but before she could close herself inside, the first animal caught her ankle in his jaws.

The pain stole her breath away. It razored up her leg, charged along her spine, then exploded in her head. Out of instinct, she started kicking her free foot at the biting animal. But a second one caught that ankle and down she went, on her butt.

Within a heartbeat, there were mouths everywhere. Teeth. Pain. The terrifying sounds of clothes ripping, teeth chomping, and dogs growling. Her own screams.

She smelled the sickly sweet scent of blood. The pungent, sulfurous odor of their breath. Wet animal and earth.

Her vision was blurred by her movement, arms flailing, thrashing in a frantic, fruitless effort to find relief from the pain.

She could feel her strength waning. Her limbs were getting heavy and it was getting harder and harder to lift them. Her will to fight was fading as she began to accept her fate. She was dog food.

"Please, just let it be fast. Let one of them bite me in the neck or something, end it quickly." She stilled, then realized the beasts had stopped biting.

She forced her heavy eyelids up and gasped. The dogs were gone.

There were now six enormous, naked men standing in a circle around her, looking down. They were all dark haired and gorgeous. Perfect bodies. Perfect faces. Perfect . . . other parts. Outside of the fact that their eyes glowed red, it was like being stared at by the Chippendales.

Hell spawn or angels?

As she mulled that question over, one of the Chippendales reached down and raked a fingernail over her partially exposed nipple, igniting an unwelcome chain reaction in her body. A great ball of fire burst inside her belly. White-hot need blazed a path down to her sex, where it churned round and round, like thunderclouds over the ocean. Storms were brewing. She dragged in a deep breath and tried to will away the lust threatening to carry her away like a tsunami.

She felt like she was outside of herself, like her body was no longer connected to her mind. She knew she loved Ric, knew these oversexed boy toys were not appealing to her. Yet wanting crashed through her body, carried on the waves of pleasure the strange man's touches stirred.

"This way," the one who had touched her said. He reached a hand down to help her stand. She accepted his help, but the instant she was upright, black and white flashes cut through her vision. Tired. So tired.

She felt the ground smack her in the face.

Her final thought before she let go was of Ric and Dao. She'd let them both down. "I'm . . . sorry."

The dark and quiet was welcome relief from her fear, confusion, pain . . . and lust.

Stripped of his clothes, as well as his lifeline to Sophie, the two-way radio, and tied spread-eagle in the center of a circle painted on the basement's concrete floor, Ric glared up at his brother. His brother! The one person on the planet whom he'd ever trusted. What the fuck?

Barrett was standing next to the Guardian, looking smug.

Speaking of smug, on the dragon's other side stood none other than Margaret Mandel. She looked very pleased as she rubbed her hands together. "Look who we have here. My sweet little Wissenschaft, Ric Vogel. So nice to see you again," she purred.

Ric didn't respond. Instead he looked at the Guardian. "And here I thought you would be my biggest problem."

The Guardian smiled. "From the look of things, I'd say I'm the least of your problems."

Margaret clicked her tongue and shook her head. "You know, you had a choice. I offered the option of becoming my lover but you turned that once-in-a-lifetime opportunity down. Now I'm forced to use you for a much less pleasing purpose—at least from your point of view. A shame, since your body is absolutely exquisite. I would've worshipped it daily." She crouched down, spreading her knees to reveal a pair of black lace panties under her short skirt, and gave him a long, hot sweeping gaze.

Rage piggybacked on confusion charged through his veins, heating them. He trembled with the need to grab hold of the lamia's neck and snap it in two. Her gaze found his face, snared his. Knowing what she'd do, he fought to break his free. It was too dangerous. He would lose the battle if she tried to charm him.

Too late. He felt the velvet touch of her mind to his and instantly the fight left him. He felt his body reacting, warming. His mind slipping away.

He was weakening, falling under her glamour.

"No," he heard himself mumble. He tried to fight back, to resist the lamia's song, calling, calling to him. So sweet and tempting. She was too strong, her will, her mind, her spirit. Then she knelt next to him, pressed her warm, wet mouth over his, and kissed him.

He couldn't stop her.

He hated the fact that he was a male at that point, hated the fact that his body had a mind of its own and didn't give a flying fuck who or what was kissing him. His brain told his traitorous body this was wrong. The danger of falling under the lamia's seduction aside, he loved Sophie. Loved her more than anything, more than he ever expected to. If Sophie saw this, if she knew, it would kill her. Still, his body heated. Wanting coursed through his body on slow ripples.

He bit back a growl, knowing his anger would only encourage the lamia, and instead thought of the most boring, mundane things he could think of, knowing that was the only way to best his aching, lust-filled body. Waiting at the secretary of state's office. Or spending eons in line to collect an unemployment check. Or sitting in rush-hour traffic during the height of summer road-construction season on I-75. Oh yeah, that was a good one. He felt his expression relax into one of complete and utter boredom, despite the vigorous oral attention the lamia was currently giving his neck.

It got to her. When she tried to kiss him again but he refused, she shrieked in anger, "That human couldn't possibly have that much of a hold on you yet!"

He tried not to smile but it was hard. Feeling a little smug, since that was the first time he'd ever won a battle with his single-minded hormones, he just looked at her with raised eyebrows.

"I know why you want the shield and spear." Rising up to a squat, she pulled on her skirt until the hem was up around her waist. She parted her knees and fingered her panties. "Look at me. Don't you want me? Why are you fighting this? I know what you want to do for your people."

Black lace. Wet. Slick. His body warmed again. His brain started to melt, overheated by the unwelcome lust pulsing through his body. It was the glamour, the lamia's most potent weapon. He turned his gaze to the ceiling.

Wood beams. Furnace ductwork. Cobwebs. Much better. At least his brain worked when he stared at those. "Yeah, so what?" he said.

"You weren't thinking of letting that human have the spear and shield, were you."

Was that a question or a statement? He wasn't sure. But he decided not to respond anyway, partly because he wanted to piss the lamia off, partly because he didn't want her knowing anything, and partly because he didn't know the answer himself. When he'd first stumbled into Sophie at the library, he'd expected to continue his search, expected to find the relics and deliver them to the mage. Expected to receive the spell that would free his race from the damnation of a slow, painful death.

Even when he'd taken Sophie as his lover, he'd still expected to carry out his plans. He figured she'd be angry at first, hurt. But he'd help her find another way to defeat the lamia. Divorce was an option, granted almost impossible, and sometimes deadly. But it was something. It was the choice between two good deeds: the salvation of an entire race versus the salvation of a single human being.

Such a simple choice, or so he'd thought until today.

But now . . . now he wasn't so sure he could go through with it. He knew Sophie would hate him for lying to her. Despise him for taking the relics for his purpose, no matter how honorable it was.

That would kill him faster than a day spent sunbathing at the equator.

He would tolerate the most horrid torture easier than he would handle seeing hatred in her eyes, turned on him. He would endure hundreds of years of agony to avoid seeing pain in her eyes, for even a minute.

He cleared his throat. "You just hope I'll take the relics because then your sister's safe from Sophie," he said, turning his gaze back to Margaret.

She shrugged. "No, not really. She wouldn't be safe for long; none of us would. Once Ysgawyn gets the relics, he would have the power to exterminate our entire race, me included."

"You lie. He's a sworn mage, powerless to hurt anyone with his magic."

She shook her head and tsked through her teeth. With slow, deliberate movements she removed her skirt, her blouse, her bra. She stood proud, her brown-tipped breasts high and firm, her waist narrow, her hips full enough to be tempting. The musky-sweet scent of her arousal filled his nostrils. Smiling, her eyes glittering with passionate promise, she reached up to loosen her hair from the tight bun at the back of her head. It fell in heavy waves over her shoulders, framing her siren's face. "Didn't anyone tell you, you can't believe the words of Ysgawyn? He's no longer sworn. And he's not above using any form of deceit to get what he wants. The spell that will bring the destruction of the lamiae will give him power beyond your wildest imaginings. Power like no mage has had in centuries."

Ric closed his eyes against the distraction of her standing nude before him and tried to concentrate on what she'd said. Ysgawyn casting a spell to destroy all the lamiae? Impossible! Or was it? He'd seemed mighty eager to get his hands on those relics. If they didn't serve him in some manner, what could he possibly want with them? "Who am I to believe—"

"Believe Margaret, Ric," Barrett interrupted. "She speaks the truth."

Ric opened his eyes to glare at his brother. The brother who stood by the lamia's side. The brother who seemed to have led him into this trap. "You want me to believe her?" He squinted at the lamia, who had taken a step behind Barrett, the coward. "I'm having a hard time trusting you after this. You lied to me, pretended to be here to help me. Then led me straight into the lamia's trap. And now you have the balls to tell me to believe her? How could I possibly do that? You know what she is. What she and her clan have done to humans. To our people. How could you stomach standing by her side watching this?"

"Yes, I know what she is. But I couldn't let you go through with it," Barrett explained. "I couldn't let you give Ysgawyn the shield and spear. It's against the law of the Immortals."

"You prize the law over the blood we share? We're brothers. Remember? Or has the lamia already worked her glamour on you too? Are you under her spell?"

"No." Barrett shook his head. "I have all my mental capacities intact—"

"That's up for debate."

"Shut up, you bastard, and listen for once." Barrett was gritting his teeth. His face practically glowed it was so red. "You want to know how much you mean to me? I prize your pathetic ass over the law. Your life over my own, even. My freedom. My career. My future." He held out his wrist, showing the mark of the Bond. A deep purple stain forming a full circle around his wrist.

Ric didn't often have to inhale, being a vampire. But at that moment, his lungs burned for air. He sucked in the deepest breath he'd taken in centuries, then fought against the metal cuffs securing his wrists and ankles to the ground. "What. Have. You. Done!"

"I went to the Judicial. Signed a promissory note. My life for yours. I had to. What you were about to do would've cost you your life if you'd succeeded—what you would've done if I hadn't let Margaret stop you. Lamia or not, she's spared you the mistake of an eternity. Please, don't be a fool! Don't go through with it. We both have too much to lose if you do; we all do."

"Went to the Judicial? Why would you do that?" Ric wanted to roar out his rage, shout long and loud until the walls around him tumbled to the ground. His brother had taken The Bond to protect him? For what? Barrett had promised to give up everything, had volunteered to pay the price for his transgressions. Would never again be able to make a decision freely if Ric went through with his plans. Why had Barrett done such a thing? No part of Ric's plan was illegal. "I didn't ask you to. I would never ask you to."

"What choice did I have? After I found out what you were doing, that you'd made a pact with Ysgawyn—"

"To save our people!", Ric hollered. "To spare them the agony of the Second Death. Why should that be against the law? We've sought other ways, spent eons searching for a medical cure, but there is none. Magic is the only answer. And if turning to magic is illegal, then the law has bound us, kept our people from the cure they deserve."

"It's not the magic that the law forbids. It's the end results that would bring judgment to you. Your plan to save our people will ultimately cost the lives of a whole race of Immortals," Barrett explained in a cool voice. "And so many more if that mage is able to complete the spell harnessing the power of the Fury. Forget about the mage for a minute and the disaster he could bring to the Immortals and the humans both. You can't save one race by destroying another."

"But why would I be held responsible for another man's actions? I didn't know what he was going to do with the relics. He didn't tell me. I only knew the price for the spell I needed was the shield and spear. I thought no mage could use them—"

"It doesn't matter. Whether you knew or not, the guilt would be yours." Barrett knelt next to Ric and looked at him with pleading eyes. He unfastened each of Ric's wrists, then ankles. "Please. Complete the spell with Margaret. The relics must be destroyed to bring our people and the lamiae back to harmony, and keep Ysgawyn from completing his spell. It's the only way." He took Margaret's hand and pulled until she was on her knees next to Ric.

Hundreds of years of searching had led to this moment, to a decision so difficult and complex. How could he possibly sort through it all in the space of a heartbeat? Ric knew the agony of watching his brother sentenced to death by the Supreme Immortal Council would likely destroy him. He'd probably not survive to see the freeing of his people from the bonds of the Second Death.

Still, there was Sophie. And her friend. Maybe he couldn't save a race but he could save a single human being. But were there unknown risks involved in that quest too? He had no idea what was involved in the freeing spell. Would that cause more innocent deaths? Would his brother still be forced to pay with his life? Ric's gaze zigzagged between Barrett and Margaret. Was one human life worth the risk?

Barrett stood and took several steps back until he was out of the circle. Margaret pressed gently on Ric's shoulders until he was sitting up on his bent elbows. She traced a circle on his chest and chanted the first lines of the spell. "No," Ric interrupted before she'd completed the first verse. A flare of guilt and anger shot through his spirit as scalding fury pulsed through his veins. He pushed on Margaret's shoulder. Forced her away from him. "I can't. Sophie . . ."

"She has made her own choice. There is nothing you can do for her now." Barrett motioned toward the wall behind him. The Guardian blew a stream of air at the wall and a tiny pinpoint of light glowed in the center, then spread out until the entire wall looked like it was consumed by fire. The flame flared for several seconds, then dimmed, leaving a transparent circle in the center.

"Sophie?" Ric said on a gasp. "Sophie!"

She didn't hear him but he could see her. As clear as if she were right next to him. She was lying on a bed. Her glossy hair was fanned out about her head. Her spine was arched, her breasts pushed high into the air. His mouth watered. His body ached to feel her beneath him.

Why couldn't he be there with her right now? All their worries gone. Their loved ones safe. Why couldn't those be her fingers stroking his stomach, making the muscles tighten?

Sophie's face turned to the side facing him. She stared blindly for a moment, obviously unable to see him. Then she blinked her eyes and shuttered them closed. Peace touched each of her features. Her lovely lips pursed, the corners lifted into a shadow of a smile.

He remembered seeing her react that way to his touches, his kisses. Only this time it was another man whispering in her ear, gliding his hands up her cotton-sheathed thighs.

Julian stood beside her running his hand up her leg. Her stomach. Her breast. He knelt on the bed and lowered his head to kiss her.

For a moment, Ric simply shook his head in disbelief. "It's a trick. Sophie would never—"

"It's no trick." Barrett motioned toward the Ancient One. "You see? They're performing the binding ritual."

Ric looked again, saw the shimmering, translucent rope in Julian's fist. "No." For the third time in the past hour, white-hot rage blasted through his body. Why would Sophie bind herself to another Immortal? It made no sense. Surely she wasn't doing it just to get the spear and shield? She wouldn't do something so foolish. So dangerous.

"She's not binding herself. She's binding you," Barrett said.

Ric shook his head. "No!" He couldn't believe that. Wouldn't believe it. Sophie wouldn't bind him for eternity just to be able to destroy one lamia. She loved him. She trusted him to help her. He knew it; he'd felt her love and faith, had heard her thoughts whispering through his soul like a soft breeze through a forest.

They'd tricked her somehow. That had to be it. But goddess help him, if it wasn't a trick, he needed to stop her before she completed the ritual.

"The human is no longer your concern," Margaret said, sounding impatient. "She has chosen another path. You never completed the Joining with her." She traced a long, slick path up his stomach with her tongue. "It's time. We need to complete the abolition spell. We must destroy the spear and shield. Now."

"This is what you've wanted all along, isn't it," he growled, glaring at her with such hatred his mouth burned with acid. "That's why you told us about the Guardian. You wanted us to find the relics, to get this far so you would be able to convince Barrett that the shield and spear had to be destroyed. That way none of your people will ever again face the threat of death."

"Perhaps." She shrugged. "It doesn't matter. What's done is done. It's no longer safe with the Guardian. If you give the spear and shield to Ysgawyn, your brother will pay the price with his death. And untold millions will pay when the mage summons the Fury. You can forget about helping Sophie's friend too. You don't know the price to be paid for using the relics to destroy my sister. Do you really wish to risk your brother's life? Or Sophie's?"

"You must complete the spell," Barrett echoed.

Margaret smiled triumphantly. "You have no other choice."

This time Ric didn't hold back. He roared, releasing the frustration, anger, and powerlessness boiling and churning inside like hot magma deep in the belly of the earth.

Chapter 17

"No. This is wrong. I can't go through with it." Sophie shoved Julian's head away seconds before it found its target—her mouth. "I love Ric."

"Which is why you must continue," the dark-haired Ancient One explained for the umpteenth time. She was getting really tired of hearing his explanation. For some reason, it wasn't making any sense to her. She loved Ric. Ric loved her. Ric was in danger. So she had to do the nasty with this strange—albeit attractive—man to save him? How was that again? Maybe it was the shock of nearly being torn apart by those hounds from hell, but her brain wasn't able to wrap itself around that concept.

Didn't these Immortal people use any form of logic?

Feeling very . . . dirty, she sat up and wrapped the sheet around herself. "Sorry, bud. But I'm not buying your line. I have a feeling you could explain it to me another thousand times and I still wouldn't get it. I see no way that sleeping with you will save Ric from death or eternal damnation or whatever. Sex is just . . . sex. It doesn't have any power to save people. I'm sure a number of people wish it did. Just think how powerful a porn star would be—"

"You must believe me," he said, looking damn earnest.

"I wouldn't lie to you. For the Immortals, the act of sex is the greatest source of power. It enables us to complete spells. Binding spells to keep people from doing things we don't wish them to. Abolition spells to destroy certain items—"

"Sounds like a pile of cow dung to me. And if sex is such a source of power, like you say, why didn't Ric perform any spells while we . . . you know?"

"Because he cannot. Wissenschafts possess no powers of magic. They are beings of science. Logic and natural law. To complete any spell, he would need another, either a human or an Immortal, to join with him."

"So, bring him in. I'll make love to him and cast the spell."

"It won't work. You can't bind the one you're performing the spell with."

"And binding him will stop him from what? Helping me destroy the snakewoman who's feasting on my friend?"

"No. He never intended on helping you do that."

"Bullshit. You're lying. Just like you lied about trying to kill Ric in the hotel room." Sophie stood and shoved Julius Caesar aside, heading for the door. Before she pulled it open, he caught her by the waist and hauled her backward until her back was pressed against all six-foot-something, 250 pounds of frustrated vampire. It was an intimidating place to be, especially with his seven-incher poking her in the backside. "Let me go."

"I'm not lying now and I wasn't lying then. I won't let you go until I have a chance to show you something."

"Buddy, I've seen everything you have, and although I'm impressed, I'm not that impressed. So if you don't mind, I'd like to leave, get these scratches and bites cleaned up before I get rabies."

His laughter made his belly bounce against her spine. "You can't catch rabies from those dogs."

"Who's to say?" She struggled to break free from his

hold, but like Ric, the man had the strength of a hundred men. She was growing to dislike the Immortals. The whole lot of them. Nothing but trouble. Bullies. Liars.

"Ric doesn't have to know who performed the binding spell," he whispered in her ear. "I would tell no one."

She shook her head, scrunched her shoulder up to block her ear. "No way. I hate secrets. I haven't lied to Ric and I don't want to start now. Especially about something so important."

"That's very honorable, considering how many lies he's told you, how many secrets he's kept," Julian challenged.

"There were reasons, I'm sure. He'll explain when the time's right."

"This way," he said, pulling on her arm. "I should've shown you this an hour ago." He opened the door, letting a second man inside, a very tall, very strong-looking man with deep auburn hair, then forced her to turn around.

The red-haired man walked by her like she wasn't even in the room and blew a stream of air at the wall. It went up instantly, consumed by a deep red flame. That was some trick, the most impressive illusion she'd ever seen in person.

Or so she thought.

When a transparent circle formed in the wall's center revealing a scene right out of her worst nightmare, her heart stopped. Again.

"Ric?" she whispered, alternately staring and blinking, trying to determine whether what she saw was real—God, she hoped not!—or some kind of illusion.

"He can't hear you," the red-haired man said.

She ran closer, flattened her palm on the wall. It felt cool to the touch, smooth, just like a regular, everyday, drywall type of wall. She couldn't tear her eyes away from the scene before her. Ric was lying on a concrete floor, nude. Margaret was next to him, running her hands up and down his torso, her head thrown back, her long hair brushing against her bare rear end. Ric had one hand on her hip. Small white marks surrounded his fingertips.

Sophie shook her head. "This is a trick. A mean one, too. He would never . . ." Her eyes burned. Her stomach rushed up into her throat. "He would never get naked with her. Not if he had a choice in the matter!"

"He's performing a spell," Julian explained, pointing at Margaret's face. "See? You can't hear her but you can see her mouth moving."

"No." This couldn't be real. "You're lying."

"I can't lie. She's performing an abolition spell, to destroy the shield and spear."

"Why? That makes no sense. He was looking for them too. He wouldn't want them destroyed." Or would he? Was that why he'd been searching for them in the first place?

"He's destroying them because he doesn't want you to kill the lamia."

"He can't do that. My friend will die and he knows how much that'll hurt me. He promised to help me. Why would he want to stop me now?"

"Are you so sure he ever wanted to help you?"

No. I'm not sure of anything anymore. "Yes. Maybe it's Margaret. Has she put him under some kind of spell? I've seen how powerful those lamia things are."

As Sophie watched, confused, angry, hurt, Ric pushed Margaret away from him, and looking mildly annoyed, Margaret walked out of the room.

"There. See?" she said with mild triumph. "He pushed her away." She held her breath as she watched to see what he'd do next.

Ric stood and turned to Barrett.

"Would you like to hear what they're saying?" the red-haired man asked.

She briefly considered saying no but put that option out of her mind immediately. She wasn't a coward. She'd already seen enough to shatter her heart into a million gazillion jagged, razor-sharp shards. Her insides were being ripped apart. What would eavesdropping on a conversation do to make things worse? She closed her eyes and nodded. "Yes." She would finally know what kinds of secrets he'd been keeping from her.

The red-haired man muttered some gobbledygook and the wall shimmered again. Then as if a switch had been flipped, the sounds of the room beyond the wall filtered into the room in which she stood.

"You haven't completed the spell." That was Barrett, Ric's brother. She knew she hadn't liked him! Jerk! "You must complete the spell."

"I . . . I will. I just need a minute."

"I don't understand why this is such a difficult decision," Barrett insisted. "It wasn't like you'd planned on actually helping her. You've always intended to follow your plan. You used her to help you find the spear. You knew a human would be more likely to find it than an Immortal."

No!

Ric turned and stared blindly at the wall between them and for an instant she wondered if he could see her.

"Yeah. I know." He dropped his head into his hands. "You're right."

"You lied to me?" she whispered. "You slept with me, and made promises and used me and lied to me and . . . and . . . I hate you," she said on a sob. "Lying, secret-keeping, bloodsucking double-crosser."

The transparent window closed in on itself, shutting out the sight of Ric's guilty face, the sound of his voice. That was a good thing. She knew she couldn't stomach another second looking at him.

"He lied to me," she repeated, over and over, still unable to fully accept what she'd seen and heard.

"He's going to complete the abolition spell to destroy the spear and shield unless you stop him first."

"And we have to . . . to . . . you know to do that?" Her lip curled up in mild disgust. She'd never had a one-night fling with a stranger. Never even considered it. "Are you absolutely positive there isn't another way? Could I give a drop of blood even?" she asked, recalling the time she'd donated some blood to Ric to save his life. "I mean, the sight of blood makes me all queasy, but if it meant we wouldn't have to . . . I can't say it! . . . I'm willing to poke myself again. I don't think I could . . . sex right now. Ugh. Nothing personal, of course."

"Of course," Julian looked genuinely solemn. "But I'm afraid there's no other way."

"Darn!"

"He's going to destroy the relics."

She wrapped her arms around herself, tried to stop the shaking that was rattling her teeth. "I know, I know."

He held her shoulders gently, but even the small bit of contact was painful. She didn't want him to touch her. Not anywhere. "Without the relics you have no chance of saving your friend."

Sophie shrugged away from Julian, hating the feel of his hands on her. "I know!" She paced across the room, her mind clogged, her insides twisted and torn. She couldn't think, couldn't feel, couldn't breathe. She needed room. Air.

Julian followed on her heels. "He has gotten worse, hasn't he?"

Angry, she whirled around and glared at him. "Yes. But I wonder why you're so willing to help me?"

"Because I had a friend once, many years ago. He was a human. Married Lisse, despite my pleas. She killed him, within months of their wedding. I was powerless to stop her then." He visibly swallowed. "But I'm not powerless now. Together we can stop her."

His confession cooled her storming emotions somewhat. "I'm sorry about your friend."

He reached for her again, and this time, she let him touch her. He held her hands in his so very gently. "My friend's been gone a long time and although a shadow of the pain remains at his loss, it's not as bad as it once was. But for you, how much worse will that pain be knowing you had the chance to save him? The guilt for having been afraid to do what you could. What will that do to you?"

She recalled the last time she'd been afraid to help someone she loved. Had let a few self-manufactured excuses stand in the way of saving a life. A dear life.

When she'd first found out about Dao, she'd made a promise not to let anything stand in the way of saving him, yet here she was, faltering, wasting time while Ric was doing God knew what with that lamia, performing the ritual that would stop her.

She swallowed a sigh of regret. This was the way of the Immortals. If sex was the only way to conjure the power needed to set the spell in motion, then sex would be what she'd do.

It was a matter of life or death. Dao's life was worth it.

Besides, it wasn't like she owed Ric anything. They hadn't completed the wedding steps; she was quite sure of that. So they weren't married. He was clearly not considering their arrangement an exclusive type of relationship. Hell, he was willing to let her friend die, despite the fact that she'd told him how important it was to her.

Who knew? Maybe this handsome Ancient One would do something for her that Ric would never have been able or willing to do—help her.

After all the risks she'd taken, what was one more?

"Okay." She swallowed the burning in her throat and prayed a little vomit wouldn't stop the spell from working. "I'll do it. For Dao."

Chapter 18

The gods help him, Ric couldn't go through with it. Despite the price he'd likely pay, he wouldn't complete the spell.

He had to help Sophie. He loved her. Whatever happened as a result of slaying the lamia he'd worry about later.

First, he had to find her before she bound him. That wouldn't be an easy task. Although he was still free from the metal cuffs that had secured him to the floor, there was a Guardian to get past, and his brother, before he'd make it out the door. And since he hadn't fed in a while and they'd begun the abolition spell, which drained his strength, he knew he couldn't just force his way past them.

He paced back and forth trying to think of some way to distract them, trick them. All he needed was a split second to slip through the door. What would distract them? He glanced around the room. There was a tall metal shelf standing against the wall. What if he knocked it over? If he did it just so, he'd make a pile of rubble that might slow Barrett and the Guardian down for a second or two.

Where was Margaret? In his state, if he bumped into her on the other side of that door, he'd be cooked. She was much older than he. And even though she would be drained from the partially completed spell too, she was stronger.

If only he knew where the spear and shield were!

Time was running out. He could sense it. Deep in his bones. He had to make his move right now.

Knowing this was probably his only chance, Ric lunged for the shelf, caught the vertical support in his fist, and pulled. The contents came crashing to the floor, and just as he hoped, they created a handy pile of rubble between Barrett and the Guardian and him. He dashed for the door, leaving them shouting and scrambling over the heap.

Once out into the main part of the basement, he shut the door behind him and shoved a heavy chest up against it to buy him a few extra seconds. Then he sprinted for the stairs. He took them two at a time.

From the vision, he knew Sophie had been in a bedroom. But which one? There were probably one or two on the main floor and another couple upstairs. And if he made the wrong choice, thanks to the layout of the house, he'd be blocked by his pursuers, would never make it to her. They were already working on getting through that blocked door downstairs.

As he ran, he reached for her with his mind, gently testing the delicate connection they'd formed between them by having taken that unwritten fourth step. It was as delicate as a single strand of spider's web. So fragile it wouldn't take any effort at all to snap it.

He found her mind at the other end. Rage and hurt buzzed along their connection and burned through his body. Her rage. Her hurt. Betrayal. Loss.

Fearing she'd break the connection at any moment, he tried to connect with her senses. He felt Julian's fingers on her skin. Felt the warmth of his breath on her neck. He struggled to see through her eyes, but they were closed tightly.

He stopped running and stomped his feet, hard. The sound reached him through her ears.

Above. She was upstairs.

He turned right, dashed through the doorway that closed the upstairs off from the ground floor, and locked the door from the inside. The little brass bolt wouldn't stop Barrett and the Guardian for long.

"Sophie! Stop!" he shouted as he ran up the stairs. "I love you. Please stop."

She was on the bed, still dressed. Julian was lying on top of her. She opened her eyes and glared at him when he ran into the room. "Get out," she said on a low growl.

"You don't have to do this," Ric said, taking a single step forward. "I'm here to help you. I know you don't believe me and I don't blame you. If you saw . . , if they showed you . . . But I'm telling the truth. I didn't complete the spell with Margaret, even though it could cost my brother his life."

Surprise swept over Sophie's face.

Julian sat back on his knees and looked at him. "I believe what he's saying."

Sophie scrambled to sit up. She handed Ric a sheet to cover with.

"I swear," Ric explained as he wrapped himself toga style, "I didn't want to do it at all. But I felt trapped."

"You lied to me." Her bottom lip quivered. Her eyes filled with tears. He felt his own eyes burning as he looked into hers, read the pain there, the anguish.

"I wasn't completely honest with you. You're right. At one point I wanted to use the spear and shield for my own purposes, to save my people. But I know that I can't help them, not just because it would cause untold destruction to who knows how many Immortals, but because I want to help you. I want to keep my word. We can still save your friend but time is running out." As if on cue, Barrett and the Guardian started working on the flimsy door down below. "They're coming to stop me. The relics must be here somewhere."

Sophie looked confused as she eyed Ric, then turned

her questioning gaze to Julian. She trusted the Ancient One more than him. That fact burned Ric's heart. But he could understand why.

Julian smiled. "Go with him."

She nodded, stood, and walked into Ric's arms.

It was the most wonderful feeling to have her in his arms again. The world was right.

The door below gave and he reluctantly released her, then pulled her toward the windows overlooking the front of the house. "This way."

"Do we have to jump out of another window?" Sophie said with a semismile.

"With Barrett and the Guardian hot on our heels? I don't think we have another choice."

"I'll hold them off as long as I can," Julian said, standing at the top of the stairs and shooing them toward the window. "Hurry. Go for the shed."

"Fine. But this is the last time. I swear." She looped her arm around his neck and wrapped her legs around his waist. "Have I told you I hate heights almost as much as I hate blood?"

"No." Ric pushed up the window and jumped. They landed with a tooth-jarring jolt on the front lawn and Ric started running toward the street with Sophie clinging to his front like a monkey.

She yanked on his hair. "Wait! Stop!"

"What? Barrett's faster than me. Always has been. I really don't want him catching me."

"Julian said to head for the shed. That's in the back of the house. I figure there must be a reason he told us to go there."

"I don't know."

Could he trust Julian? Julian had been trying to bind him. Julian had tried to kill him. Julian had tried to take Sophie from him. More than once.

"I trust him, Ric."

"I know you do. But I'm not sure I can."

Sophie unwrapped her legs from his waist. "He wouldn't send me there if it meant I'd be hurt. I know it."

Ric lowered her to the ground. "But he tried to kill me. He's tried to take you."

"He still says that wasn't him in the hotel room. I don't know how that could be, but I believe him. It's tough not knowing whom to trust, isn't it?"

"Yes."

"I gave you another chance."

Yes, she had.

Ric nodded, took Sophie's hand in his, and squeezed. "Okay." Side by side, they ran around the side of the house. Ric lifted Sophie over the fence, then jumped it and met her at the shed door.

They pulled it open just as Barrett and the Guardian rounded the corner, coming from the opposite side of the house.

"Quick!" Ric kicked the door open, then helped Sophie inside the cramped, dark interior. He glanced around the space, filled with gardening tools, a riding lawn mower, sacks of potting soil. There was no sign of a spear, a shield, or an exit. "Dead end. He lied. Dammit."

Sophie gasped. "No." She dropped to the floor on her knees and covered her face with her hands. "No more lies!" She vaguely heard Ric swear and scramble to brace the door, which was being battered from outside, but she was too lost in her thoughts to really pay attention. Julian couldn't have lied. He'd never lied to her. There had to be a way out of there, or there was a clue about the spear and shield hidden somewhere, something important. Unfortunately, the second Ric shut the door, the little bit of moonlight that had been coming inside was cut off, leaving her sitting on a dirty floor in the dark.

Working fast, she ran her hands over the gaping wood-plank floor searching for something, anything. A hiding place big enough for the relics to be slid between the planks. Toward the back, next to the lawn mower, her fingers closed around something that felt like a leather strap. She pulled and was caught by surprise as a heavy part of the floor lifted with it.

"Ric!" she yelled. "Here!"

"What? I'm kinda busy at the moment. Holding the door from being kicked in."

"There's stairs." She dropped her legs, found the first step, and half ran, half stumbled down several more. It was pitch-black. She had to feel with her fingers along the cold stone walls. They were lumpy and uneven, slick with slime like an old cave. "Ric!" she shouted as she kept going down, down, down. The air was heavy and thick, difficult to breathe, and smelly. Finally, she bumped smack-dab into a flat, hard surface, what she hoped was a door. "I'm at the bottom but I can't see." She frantically searched for a doorknob with her fingers, groping blindly, her heavy breathing echoing in the tight space.

And then she felt Ric's heat behind her and the worst of her fears eased.

"I can see it," said Ric.

There was a loud bang and then a creak and then a blade of light cut through the darkness as the door in front of them opened into a wide storeroom. Pushed gently from behind, Sophie stumbled into the room and grinned in triumph. "I knew Julian hadn't lied! This is it, isn't it? The dragon's lair."

"Sure looks like it is," Ric said behind her. After securing the door, which was slightly damaged by Ric's forceful entry, he stepped around her.

Rows and rows of glass-enclosed shelves filled the room, floor to ceiling. As Sophie ran to the first one, she saw that each relic was displayed and marked with a tag. "This shouldn't be too tough. They're all marked like a museum display."

"This seems too easy."

Sophie just shooed him toward another row of shelves. "You look over there, and I'll look here. It might take us a while to find them, but I just know they're here."

"They'd better be. Because otherwise we're in big trouble. That door isn't going to hold much longer."

Sophie cringed as the sound of heavy metal striking metal reverberated through the underground room, rattling the artifacts in the glass cases.

"It isn't here." Sophie stopped at the last case and spun around, dumbfounded. "How could it not be here?"

"It's here. Somewhere." Ric turned the corner around another row of shelves, disappearing from her view. "We're just looking in the wrong place."

Panic was making it impossible for Sophie to think. The big metal door at the front of the room was groaning against the battering the Guardian and Barrett were giving it. It wouldn't last much longer.

"We were performing an abolition spell," Ric said, coming into sight again at the end of a long row.

"Yes. I'm painfully aware of that fact. What does that have to do with anything?"

"Plenty. It means the artifacts would have to be positioned in a circle identical to the one I was in."

"Not in a case?"

"Maybe not."

"Okay." She started jogging up and down the rows again, this time looking for a circle of any kind. A circle painted on the ceiling, the floor, the walls, anywhere. Nothing. Just rows and rows of lighted glass-enclosed cases with gobs of crusty old bits and pieces of history. "Anything?"

"Not yet."

She ran to the end of one row and rounded the corner, then ran even faster up the second. At the very back, on the concrete wall, she found a large wooden-framed, circular shadow box hanging on the wall. It had some strange pictures or symbols etched into the wood frame. In the center, behind glass were a couple of strange-looking relics. What looked like a spearhead and a piece of rock with a scrap of wood with some metal protruding from it. Could it be? Oh, God, she hoped! "I think I found something!"

"Where?"

She tried to open the cover but it wouldn't budge. When the metal door at the entry groaned a warning that it was about to give, Sophie reached for the nearest hard thing she could find, wound up, and slammed it into the glass. It shattered, sending a spray of glass shards into the air, all over her face and arm, and onto the floor. Too scared to care whether she was bleeding to death or not, she dug at the ties holding the artifacts in place. Ric found her and hurried to help her remove the second one. And with each of them clutching an artifact to their chest, they ran the perimeter of the room looking for a way out.

Nothing.

And then the door gave and a very angry Guardian stormed into the room.

"Oh, God!" Sophie fought to stay conscious as all the blood remaining in her body drained to her toes.

Chapter 19

"Quick, behind me!" Ric stepped between Sophie and the obviously furious Guardian. Ric's body was stiff as steel, every muscle tight, ready. He held the chunk of rock in one hand and used his free hand to push Sophie behind him until his body completely shielded her.

The Guardian watched him with fierce eyes but didn't move.

Barrett rushed into the room behind the Guardian but quickly hurried around his side to give Ric a pleading look. "Ric, I can't believe you're going through with this. You know what it means."

"I'm not giving them to Ysgawyn. I'm helping Sophie. Even you don't know what'll happen. We have to take this risk. It's too important to Sophie not to."

"I'd hate to see you get hurt or killed."

"Me too. But I'm willing to take the chance. For Sophie. For her friend."

"You're such a martyr."

"No, I'm just in love." His gaze slid to the Guardian. Why hadn't he moved yet? That being had enough power in his pinky to send both him and Sophie into orbit. What was he waiting for?

Margaret dashed into the room hollering, "Stop him!"

The Guardian didn't remove his gaze from Ric's. "I can't," he hissed. "You know that."

"What do you mean you can't?" Margaret said, sounding bewildered. "You're the most powerful Immortal here. You could send those two to Hades with a sneeze."

"I can't destroy the relics."

"So, blast them in the knees."

"I can't use my powers against anyone who is in possession of those artifacts."

Margaret's face turned three shades of red and then one more.

"You get the spear and shield out of their hands, and then I can do something."

"And how am I supposed to do that?" she asked through gritted teeth. "Especially now that they may know you can't hurt them as long as they keep hugging them to their chests?"

The Guardian shrugged, glanced at Barrett in question, then stepped to the side, unblocking the door.

"What are you doing?!" Margaret shrieked.

"Letting them go," the Guardian responded. "You'll have to stop them some other way. It's out of my hands now."

Not sure if he believed the Guardian, Ric kept Sophie snug against his back as he shuffled his way between the Guardian and Margaret. Once Sophie was at the entry and heading up the stairs, he relaxed somewhat, turned his back on all three Immortals watching them, and followed her up the stairs.

When they emerged from the shed, he took her hand in his and they headed back to the car. He made sure they both held one of the weapons in their laps, in case the Guardian decided to follow them. Once they were back on the main road, he breathed a sigh of relief, the first breath he'd taken in a very long time.

"Where are we going?" Sophie asked.

"Back to the hotel for our stuff, I guess. But I don't think we should stay there. Barrett and Margaret'll be looking for us."

"I'm sorry about your brother."

"There's nothing to be sorry for. He's doing what he thinks is best. He wants to protect me, just like he did when we were kids. He's always wanted to protect me."

"I guess it's not such a bad thing when you put it that way."

"He's really a good guy. It probably doesn't look like it right now, but he is."

She leaned closer until the scent of her filled his nostrils and her head rested softly on his shoulder. Despite all the stress pulling at his insides, he smiled. Balancing the rock with the shield embedded in it on his lap, he lifted his arm, wrapped it around her bare shoulder, and pulled her snug against his side—or as snug as the bucket seats of his car allowed. "I haven't really absorbed everything that happened back there yet. It's all very confusing. Did you say that you love me?"

"Yes," he said, his heart thumping heavily in his chest. He'd forgotten how that felt, to have blood coursing through his system, his heart beating. What was she thinking? He mentally reached out for her mind, followed the thin thread between them but found her thoughts shut off from him.

"What does this mean for us?"

"What?"

"The fact that we love each other."

His heart soared. She was going to forgive him. She really, honestly loved him. She wasn't saying it during a moment of duress. "Anything you want it to. Anything, that is, but marriage. I won't make you take that final step. I know how hard it would be. How much you'd be giving up. I won't make you do that. We can be together anyway. Every day. Every night. If you want."

224 / *Tawny Taylor*

"Okay."

They drove a mile or two. Her head grew heavy on his shoulder and a soft buzzing snore sounded in his ear. He left her sleeping in the passenger seat, locked the car and made sure she had the spearhead securely clutched in her fist, went up to the room, gathered their belongings, and checked out.

She was still asleep when he returned.

Thoughts churned through Ric's mind as he drove them back east toward Detroit. He'd finally found the spear and shield and yet he was no closer to finding a cure for his people than when they'd started their search.

But so many more things had happened. Good things. Surprising things. Most notably, he'd fallen deeply in love with Sophie, who'd turned out to be a whole lot stronger, braver, and more capable than even she knew she was.

He was simply in awe of her.

Over the centuries there had been a number of women. Most hadn't lasted long. Many had fallen short of his expectations, not that that was their fault. It was always him. With an incomparable past woman having set the standard so high, most women would fall far short.

But not Sophie. She was everything he craved in a wife. His body, soul, and spirit clamored to be one with her, to find the completion he could only have through her.

Yet, he knew it couldn't be. He would have to resist, even if he suffered for the rest of her natural life for it. Even if he had to watch in agony as she drew her last breath. Even if he had to live with the heartache of having loved her and lost her to natural death for the rest of his unnatural life. Maybe it would take centuries, but he would wither and die too, fall to the Second Death, just as his clan members had before him. It was only a matter of time.

It wasn't fair to ask her for more, to make her suffer the same fate he was facing.

He had a feeling she was doubting her earlier decision regarding completing the marriage ritual. It was something he saw in her eyes. Heard in her voice. But he had to stay strong. Had to keep her safe. Had to refuse, no matter how much his whole being ached for it to happen.

Damn, he was in for a lot of pain. But it was still better than what he'd face if he turned her.

Sophie hadn't pretended to sleep in who knew how long, since she was a kid. Was it the mature thing to do? Maybe not. But it was necessary.

But she needed the break, a chance to gather the thoughts bouncing around in her head like Super Balls blasted from a cannon. She could hardly get a grasp on all the events of the past few days. She didn't even know how she felt at the moment. She was rather numb. But she knew herself well enough to know that she was on the edge and could easily overreact to some benign comment Ric was about to make at any moment. She had to spare both of them that agony.

And so, she spent the next several hours exploring her mind and heart trying to sort out her feelings. About Ric as a man. About Ric as a vampire. About Dao's cure and what it could cost Ric if what she gathered from the conversation with his brother was true.

Could she live with herself if something happened to Ric while they tried to save Dao? She doubted it.

It was at that moment, her head resting on Ric's firm shoulder, that she made her decision.

She would steal the relics and go to Dao's house without Ric.

She had no idea what she was supposed to do with them once she got there. Maybe a visit to her boss was in order when they got back in town. He'd know what she was supposed to do with them . . . she hoped.

Because one thing was absolutely clear: she could not

let Ric risk his life or his brother's life for Dao. As Dao's friend, that was her risk to take, not Ric's.

She knew he wouldn't understand. That he'd be furious. He'd probably yell and turn red and she hated it when he was hurt and angry at her. But that beat the hell out of watching him die. She'd been down that road once. She'd die herself before making a repeat trip.

Finally, the car stopped, from the look of it, several hours before sunrise. Now dressed in a pair of shorts and a T-shirt, Ric carried her into his house and laid her on the bed. She gently shifted her weight, preparing herself for a stealth maneuver to slip out. Unfortunately, Ric was still there, close enough to feel her movement and tighten his grip.

She'd have to wait a while.

"Where you going?" Ric said, sounding sleepy and sexy and tempting. "It may seem careless, but I want you to stay here, at least until I get the relics inside and we can figure out what exactly we're supposed to do with them. I figure dawn is best. The lamia is at her weakest at sunrise."

"Sounds like a plan. I just hope we're not too late. But rest assured, I'm not going anywhere. Just making an adjustment." She squirmed a bit when he settled beside her, and she flopped a leg over his. All kinds of parts warmed, thanks to the contact. Her body was in for some celebration.

Maybe that was what they both needed. Ric was dead to the world after lovemaking. She rubbed against him like a happy pussycat.

"Mmmm," he said. "You keep doing that and I'll have to make an adjustment too."

She slid her leg up until it met with the lump in his shorts. "Oops. What did I just bump?" she said with exaggerated innocence. A smile pulled at her mouth.

Ric growled, grabbed her hand, and pushed it into his pants. "This. That's what."

"Oh, dear. I certainly didn't mean to cause you any discomfort," she teased. Her fingers closed around his shaft. Her thumb stroked over the head. "Is there anything I can do to make it better?"

Ric grunted. "I could think of a thing or two." One of his hands fisted her hair at her nape. The other went to her throat. He drew a line with his fingertip from her ear to her collarbone, then traced the same line with his tongue. When he nipped on the hollow between her neck and shoulder, she shivered. Goose bumps coated her upper body. Liquid heat pulsed through her body in slow, pleasant waves, warming her from head to toe. She tightened her grip on his erection and stroked. Up and down. Up and down.

"You know just how to touch me, woman." Not waiting for her to respond, Ric unzipped his shorts and rolled Sophie onto her back. He wedged his hips between her thighs and kissed her. Like his touches, his kiss was slow and thorough, with a hint of the restraint he was clearly trying so hard to exercise. She could feel his muscles trembling. She could feel the stiff erection grinding against her belly. Could feel the temptation coursing through his body as his tongue slipped into her mouth to taste her.

It was as if their senses were tied together. She could taste herself as he tasted her, sweet and wet, like a ripe apple. She could hear her own soft moans as he heard them, sexy little hiccups and sighs. She could feel the need coiling inside his body, round and round, fed by the tastes and touches and sounds her body supplied him.

The end result of their blended senses was intoxicating. Overwhelming.

His kiss grew more urgent, more demanding. Slow, erotic strokes of his tongue gave way to quick, rhythmic thrusts. Instead of soft lips and gentle pressure, his mouth grew firm and demanding. The change stirred her desire. Sparks of heat shot through her body, igniting little blazes in her chest, stomach, sex.

Clothes. Too many clothes. She writhed underneath him, her mouth drinking in his flavor, her breath mixed with his. She pulled at his underwear, but thanks to the fact that his entire front was squashed against hers, she couldn't get them down. She groaned in frustration, the sound echoing in his mouth, and in her head.

He broke the kiss, doing more damage to her neck and ear with tongue and teeth. "What's wrong, sweetness?"

"Clothes."

"Oh. I agree. We have too many clothes on. Yes." He levered himself off her with two thick arms, then sat back on his knees. His eyelids were heavy as he looked down upon her, but they didn't hide the raw hunger in his eyes. Nothing could hide that.

He ran all ten fingertips down her body, starting at her shoulders. They skimmed over her breasts through her cotton shirt, teasing her nipples to aching hardness before stopping at the hem and curling.

The shirt came off with minimal effort. Pants too. Still, even though there wasn't a bit of skin that wasn't exposed to the air, she was burning up. It was his expression, the hunger she saw in his eyes. The way his lips curled at the corners. The way his tongue darted out occasionally to trace a damp line along his bottom lip. The tension she saw in his jawline.

"Your turn," she said on a sigh.

Ric crossed his arms over his chest and yanked his shirt up over his head.

Glory, the things his arms and shoulders did when he moved! A giant lump formed in Sophie's throat. A lump made out of something hard. It was no use trying to swallow it either. Her mouth was dry as dust. When he pulled his pants down, the lump slipped south, landing with a heavy thunk in her belly.

Ric's body was perfect, lean and hard and one hundred

percent male. A soft dusting of hair covered his legs, arms. She longed to trace the sexy line of hair arrowing down from his belly button to the nest at the base of his privates. She ached to taste his skin. She hungered to feel the weight of his testicles in her palm, to measure the girth of his erection with her sex.

She lifted her shoulders off the bed, her arms outstretched, her fingers just short of their target. But he gently pressed her back down. "No. Will you touch yourself for me? I want to watch."

"Oh. I . . . I've never . . . done that with someone watching."

"You trust me, don't you? After everything. And you know I think your body is the most beautiful, most exquisite thing on earth, right? Because I do. I love to look at you. To look at all of you."

His sweet words touched her heart and stoked her desire. He wanted to watch her masturbate. He wanted to see her do something so intimate she'd never even admitted to another human being she'd done it, at least no human being with a face. She'd purchased her one and only vibrator from a mail-order catalogue so she wouldn't be embarrassed.

"Please," he said, his eyes as pleading as his voice. "Take it one step at a time. Okay? Open your legs for me. Close your eyes if you need to."

Sophie wanted to please him so much! More than she'd ever wanted to please another person in her life. More than she wanted to protect her fragile ego. She let her eyelids shutter her eyes, closing herself in safe, reassuring blackness, then let her knees fall apart.

"Oh yes, that's it," he whispered. "We won't ever again hide from each other. No more secrets. I promise."

She was so thrilled to hear him make that promise, the guilt of what she was about to do ballooned. Here he was, asking her to open herself completely to him. Here he was, promising to share everything with her from now on. And here she was, plotting how to run away from him.

The heat in her body cooled to a mild simmer.

"Let me see your sex, sweetness. I know it's wet and ready for me." He gently eased her knees farther apart.

Even though her mind was still drifting in the wrong direction, down the highway of guilt to the land of What-the-heck-am-I-doing? her body was zooming down another road, a direct route to the city of Bliss. Nothing like being in two places at once.

She tried to knock her brain into submission, knowing a trip down Guilt Lane wasn't going to serve any purpose right now; reached between her legs; and parted her vulva.

She heard Ric's breath catch in his throat and realized the significance of such a simple reaction—since he didn't breathe too often. Her lips pulled back into a tense smile as she lightly teased herself with a forefinger.

"Oh yes. That's the way. I can see your juices. You're so wet. So ready." The mattress springs squeaked as he leaned closer to whisper, "Now tell me, what are you thinking about?"

She stopped stroking for one, two, three seconds, then resumed. What was she thinking about? Lying to him. Running away and taking on a creature she had no idea how to defeat. Saving him from untold danger. Sparing him from paying the consequences of using the spear and shield. The fact that the minutes were ticking by and she had no idea if Dao was still alive or not.

Ironic. She'd spent all this time angry and frustrated with him for keeping secrets, for not telling her everything, and now she was considering doing the same to him.

Thank goodness he couldn't read her mind at that moment!

"I'm thinking . . . about you. About your tongue swirling over my sex in soft, slow circles like this." She mimicked the circular motions with her fingertip. Blades of pleasure licked up her spine, despite her worries. "And this." She lifted her other hand to her breast and drew the same slow circles over her nipple. A sigh slipped through her lips. The thoughts swarming her mind fled.

"Oh, yeah," Ric said.

Oh, yeah.

She scissored her fingers apart, parting her labia wider, and left her breast for better territory, down below. Two hands to her privates, one stroking her nub, one teasing her tight canal. She slid a finger inside and gripped it with her inner muscles, groaning against the building tension working through her muscles. Face. Chest. Arms. Legs. Stomach. Her hand trembled. She bit her lip and increased the pressure on her clitoris, occasionally dragging wetness up from her vagina to keep it lubricated.

She ached for a touch from Ric, even an innocent one. She was so hot, so ready, yet unfulfilled. The vision of herself lying on the bed, legs parted, hands stroking played through her mind like a live-feed video. It made her hot. It made her desperate. "Please," she whimpered. "Please touch me."

"Thank you," he said, so close his breath warmed her face. "Thank you for opening to me." He pressed his palms against her knees, spreading them until her inner thigh muscles burned. Her hands were replaced with his. He knew exactly how to touch her, how much pressure, what speed. He played her body with the skill of a concert pianist. Lovemaking was a true art form when performed by Ric.

It wasn't long before she was sure she'd die if he didn't bury his thick rod inside her before the next beat of her heart. She was sure it would stop. And her lungs would quit. And her brain would die from lack of oxygen. And life would be over.

His fingers were stroking, thrusting, teasing, tormenting.

"Now," she commanded. "Now, before I die."

He hooked his arms under her knees and dragged her to the edge of the bed. And with a single thrust, he entered her.

She cried out, overwhelmed by the bliss of being filled. Thankful for an instant of relief before her body demanded more. She clenched her inner muscles around him and rode the waves of pleasure as they washed through her body. The waves quickened with each thrust, building in strength until they practically knocked the air from her lungs. She dragged in each breath, gulped it like it was her last.

Ric pulled out unexpectedly, and Sophie shouted, "No!" He gripped her hips with his hands and pulled, easing her over onto her stomach. Her legs slid down the side of the bed until her feet hit the floor. He gripped a fistful of her hair and pulled until she arched her back and thrust her rear end up in the air.

"Look at that bottom. Oh, yeah." He parted her cheeks and probed her bottom with the head of his cock. It found its way home with a single swift stroke, along the way dragging against sensitive parts of her anatomy that had been sorely lacking attention until then.

She fisted the covers twisted over the bed and rocked back and forth, meeting his thrusts to increase both their pleasure. Oh, the ecstasy! Her whole body, from toe to forehead and everywhere in between, was quaking. The first tingles of a building climax spread through her sex, then swept up into her belly.

Just before the last, fluttering spasm, Ric joined her in paradise, thrusting hard with each beat of his climax. He huffed with each inward thrust, repeating her name, over and over like it was the word that brought his pleasure, not the act of making love.

Finally, he slumped forward, feeling heavy and boneless on Sophie's back. "I love you, baby," he said to her shoulder. His erection softened and slipped from her body. She smiled into the mattress, then nudged him with her bottom.

"I love you too. But you're heavy, buster. Unlike you, I need to breathe. That's a bit of a challenge when I'm smooshed like this."

"Sorry." He lifted his heavy frame from her and then dropped it on the bed, spread-eagle, facedown. Oh, yeah. He was worn out, just the way she'd wanted him. "Just give me a minute to rest and . . . then I'll . . . we'll . . . leave . . . before . . ."

Silence. He was out.

Now, she could go to the bathroom, get herself cleaned up, and sneak out undetected. She'd be at Dao's long before he woke up. With her gone, and the relics, she figured Ric would be safe from his brother and the Guardian.

Her plan was flawless except for one small detail: being so sneaky and secretive was killing her. Here she'd just made love to the man, told him she loved him.

I hate secrets. Her words echoed through her head.

But what other choice did she have? Let him come with her, take a risk with his life, or with his people's lives, all to save one guy he'd never even met before?

Never in her life had she let another person take those kinds of risks for her. No. She had to do this alone, face the lamia that was sucking the life from her friend. It was the right thing to do, the right decision for everyone's sake.

She hoped Ric would find it in his heart to forgive her. If she survived.

She collected her clothes, purse and snatched the car keys from Ric's pants pocket. Then, before she chickened out, she pressed a kiss to his cheek and headed for the door, whispering, "This is my battle now. I hope you understand. I love you. I really, really love you."

Chapter 20

"I was beginning to think I'd never see you alive again." At dawn, Tim met Sophie at her desk, his gaze anxious as he met hers; then he dropped it to the dusty relics sitting on her desktop. "Are these the spear and shield? Did you find them?"

"Yes. I mean, I think they are. I guess I could be wrong."

"Oh, wow!" he said, sounding like a kid who'd just been shown the latest video game system. He picked up the spearhead and studied it. "I can't believe you found them."

"Neither can I. But now I have a question. What do I do with them? I have maybe fifteen minutes to figure it out. Julian said Dao would last no more than thirty-six hours from the time he first became confused. He's gotta be near death."

"I don't know," Tim answered, not taking his eyes off the little piece of carved rock or flint or whatever it was. "I don't know what you're supposed to do with them."

"But you told me I needed them. I figured you'd know what I'd need to do with them once I got them."

"Nope. I just read about it on the Web. Some guy said lamiae can be destroyed only with these two artifacts. How, he didn't say."

"Can you e-mail him?"

"No. He posted it on a bulletin board. I don't even know his e-mail address."

"Damn it," Sophie said, slumping into her chair. "I'm pretty sure Ric would know, but I don't want to ask him."

"Why not?"

"Long story."

"How about sharing the highlights, like who Ric is?" Tim rested his rear end on Sophie's desk and turned to inspect the shield.

"Ric is just a guy."

"Just?" Tim lifted his head for a moment to deliver a single raised-eyebrow, "yeah, right" expression.

"Yeah. Just a guy who was helping me find these."

"Sounds like a pretty good guy to me. Why wouldn't you want him to help you fight the lamia?"

"Because . . . because this is my battle, not his."

Tim set the shield back on her desk and drilled her with his paranormal ghost-hunter-on-the-hunt scrutinizing gaze. "You're in love with him."

"Yeah. So?"

"Does he love you?"

"It doesn't matter. I mean, it does, but not when it comes to Dao and Lisse. I need to take care of this on my own."

Tim stood and shook his head. "You've de-balled the poor guy."

"Have not!"

"You're not letting him be a man. Does he know you're doing this on your own?"

"Probably by now he does."

Tim shook his head even harder. "I'm guessing he's going to be pissed."

"Yeah. I know. But I couldn't let him do this. There was too much at stake, too many things that could've gone wrong."

"So you figured you'd protect him by doing it on your own."

"Yes. Exactly."

"What do you think he'll be feeling if something happens to you because you were too damn stubborn to accept his help?"

"Um . . ." She thought about that one for a few minutes, tried to put herself in his shoes. The resulting image wasn't a pleasant one. "Bad."

"Badder than bad. Call him."

"But I don't want anything to happen to him."

"Yeah, I know. But sometimes you have to risk losing everything to gain everything. If that makes sense."

"Yes. Yes it does." Her mind still not made up, Sophie took up the relics and headed out of the office. She needed to think, maybe do some reading.

The library was open.

She hid the relics carefully in Ric's car trunk, then drove to the library, not even bothering to go home yet. She half expected Ric to show up at her house any time now and she wasn't ready to deal with him yet. She wasn't sure if she was still going through with her plan to take on Lisse alone or wait for Ric.

The fear of losing him, of having something terrible happen, was definitely steering her toward the go-it-alone route.

She wandered the aisle where she'd first met him, her mind and body replaying the memory of how those first few moments had felt. Her body tingled all over as the memories played through her mind. Fragments of conversation. The quirk of his lips. The glitter in his eyes. The feel of his strong, hard body against hers.

She missed him. Something fierce. So bad, in fact, that she could swear she felt him near her right then, sensing him like when she entered a room and sensed someone staring at her. A buzzing, skittering, electric feeling that zipped up and down her spine.

"Sophie," she heard him say. She spun around. Her heart stopped.

"Ric." His eyes were filled with rage. His jaw clenched so tight a thin muscle there bulged. "I told myself I wouldn't look for you, but dammit, I couldn't help it. Why? Why'd you sneak out like that? After everything? After we made love and I promised not to keep any secrets?"

"I know, I know." She held her hands in front of her chest, fending him off, back stepping into a shelf full of books.

"What were you thinking? Can you tell me that?" he asked, closing the distance between them until she couldn't think, couldn't breathe, couldn't speak.

"Eep."

"Huh?"

Her mouth was dry again. He seemed to have that effect on her a lot. "I . . ." She sidled sideways, her spine dragging along the lumpy surface of book spines. "I was thinking about you."

"How could you say that?"

"Because it's the truth. I saw the hell you were going through when you'd thought about using the spear and shield to get your cure. I heard it all."

The anger in his eyes cooled a tiny bit.

She continued, "If you use those things, you'll die, or your brother'll die, or someone's going to die and I won't be responsible for that if I can help it. Dao's my friend. He needs my help, not yours. And if I can do this myself, I'm going to. Because I'm willing to lose my life for my friend. But I'm not willing to lose you for him." Her nose burned. Her eyes too. She sniffed and ran the back of her hand over her eyes. She wouldn't cry. Not now. Not here. "You were supposed to stay asleep for a while. Give me a head start."

"I was up before you left the hotel."

"Obviously."

He closed his hands around her upper arms. "I love you. Don't you understand that? I'd do anything for you. I'd die for you."

"But I don't want you to. I just want my friend to be okay. That's all. And I don't want anyone else to be hurt in the process."

"Sometimes you have to risk everything to get everything."

She froze. "You been talking to Tim?"

"Who's Tim?"

She shook her head to clear it. Her thoughts were not on the topic at hand. They were wandering. "No one. My boss. He said the same thing today when I went to talk to him."

"Smart guy." His thumbs rubbed her inner arms. Who knew inner arms could be so sensitive? She was about ready to melt.

"Yeah," she said on a sigh.

"Are we ready now?"

"Ready?"

"To go take care of that lamia. You aren't still insisting on doing it alone, are you?"

"Yes."

"Yes?" he repeated, looking confused.

"Yes, I'm ready. And no, I won't insist on facing her on my own. If you make me one promise."

"Tell me what you want and I'll see what I can do."

"Promise me nothing'll happen to you. That you won't break some law that'll land you in vampire prison or get yourself killed or hurt."

"Sweetheart, I can't make a promise like that."

Her heart sank.

"But I will promise you one thing."

Her heavy-as-lead heart lightened a smidge. "Oh?"

"I promise to do everything in my power to keep those things from happening. Okay?"

It wasn't good enough, but it was what it was. It was realistic. "Okay."

"Now, let's go get her before afternoon arrives. You don't want to take on a lamia after dark. Have you talked to your friend recently?"

"Yes. Yesterday."

"And?"

"He's still alive but he didn't remember me."

"Then we'd better hurry. Some of the damage may not be reversible."

"Okay." Sophie put her hand in Ric's and together they ran to the car. It felt so good to have him by her side again. She just hoped it wouldn't be the last time.

She directed him to Dao's house, too nervous to drive herself. When they parked outside of the house, she asked, "Do you know what we're supposed to do with those things in the back?"

"I'm a Wissenschaft. We believe in science. I have no idea."

"Great."

"We'll wing it. Between the two of us, we ought to be able to figure it out."

"I hope so. She's one scary snakewoman."

"I can tell you this—all vampires, muses included, are susceptible to death if their hearts are pierced. So I'm thinking we should go for the heart."

"With that little scrap of chiseled rock?" she asked, motioning to the spearhead. "Yikes. I was hoping we wouldn't have to get that close to her. What if she spits venom or something?"

"I'm assuming that's what the shield is for." He handed the hunk of rock with the wood embedded in it to her. "Here. I want you to hold on to this."

"What about you?"

"I'll take my chances."

"I hate this." Her hands shook. Her legs were rubbery. She felt like a giant block of cement had been dropped on her shoulders. Yes, she wanted to save Dao. She loved him. She had vowed to help him. But the thought of losing Ric was killing her. What would she do if he was truly hurt or worse?

"We'll be okay. Don't worry. Just concentrate. That's important right now."

Sophie nodded and tipped her chin to look up at him. "If something happens, I want you to know, I love you. I love you more than I've ever loved anyone. And this is killing me inside."

Ric pressed his palms to her cheeks and slanted his mouth over hers in a soft, sweet kiss. His lips worked gently over hers, first on one corner of her mouth and then the other. "I love you too. More than I've ever loved anyone. So much that when I found out you'd left me, I thought I'd die. So much that the thought of you taking this risk by yourself made me want to move the heavens and the earth to get here to stop you. We will never again face danger alone. I will always be here by your side. No matter what happens today."

She didn't quite understand what he meant by that but she nodded her understanding anyway. Then, the shield clutched to her chest, her heart in her throat, and her stomach dragging down around her toes, she followed Ric up the walk to Dao's front door.

This was it.

"What are you doing?!" Sophie yelled just before Ric hit the front door with his shoulder. Taken by surprise, he tried to stop, but the momentum pushed him forward into the door anyway. It didn't give.

He grimaced. Now the inhabitants of the house would know they were coming. So much for the element of surprise. "I was trying to bust in the door so we could take them by surprise."

"I have a key." She held a key in her fingers to illustrate, then gently shoved him aside to use it. Sheesh, make a guy feel like a brainless lug. She turned the lock softly, like she was trying to be quiet. He didn't bother telling her that it was too late, that her friend and his muse wife had to know they were on their way in by now.

The door swung silently open. Ric took the lead, stepping into the living room. He motioned for Sophie to leave the door open, in case a quick exit was necessary. His body was tense, ready for a battle with a pissed-off lamia. The spearhead was securely gripped in his fist. Sophie motioned toward the hallway at the end of the living room and he nodded and headed that way. The doors lining the corridor were all closed. She pointed at the first one and mouthed, "In here."

"Ready?"

She nodded.

He tightened his grip on the spearhead, turned the doorknob, and pushed the door open.

The room inside was very dark, but he could make out the shapes of two bodies in the bed.

"I can't see a thing," Sophie whispered next to him. "Should I flip on the light?"

"Yes."

The room was instantly awash in blinding white light. The two bodies in the bed shot to a sitting position like dummies fixed to springs in a haunted house. One lamia in her human form—which Ric had to admit was quite lovely—and a skinny, bedraggled-looking Asian man.

The lamia took one look at Ric and smiled. "We have company. How nice. Hello, Ric."

"Hello."

"Mmmm," the lamia said, assessing him with cold eyes. "My sister was right. You *are* something."

"I'd take that as a compliment if it wasn't for the fact that you're sitting next to your husband," he said, feeling like a hunk of beef in a butcher's window.

"What do you have there, lover?" the lamia cooed, pointing at his fist.

"Just a little something. I brought it just for you."

"How thoughtful." She stood. Nude. Lovely. Long legs, slim body with curves in all the right places. Full breasts. "Aren't you going to show it to me?" she asked in open invitation. She was making this too easy. She had to know something he didn't.

Ric tensed his shoulder and arm muscles and leapt forward, swinging with all his might, her left breast his target. The blade struck her skin, then bounced away, like it had hit hard rubber. His arm and shoulder muscles jerked painfully from the impact. The spearhead went flying through the air and Sophie screamed behind him.

He heard a thunk, scrambling. He spun on his heel, catching the two women wrestling for the dropped spearhead. The shield lay on the floor, forgotten. He grabbed the lamia by the shoulders and yanked, giving Sophie a chance to snatch the spear from the floor in the nick of time.

The lamia hissed and spit in his face. He reached for the shield to block the venom with one hand, but the lamia knocked it away. Instantly, his skin was on fire. He heard himself howling and released the lamia to frantically rub away the excruciating burn. "The shield!"

"Ric?" Sophie said beside him.

He couldn't see her. Couldn't see anything. The pain was almost unbearable. He staggered, his arms out in front of him, and walked back toward the exit. "Sophie! Run!"

"No."

"I can't see. I can't . . . help you." He tried to pry his eyes open but they wouldn't budge.

"This is my battle," Sophie said.

"What a brave, foolish girl," the lamia hissed. "It's a shame I'll have to kill her."

Ric howled in rage and threw himself in the direction of her voice.

Chapter 21

Ric was blind, swinging wildly at Lisse but doing absolutely no damage. In fact, he was doing nothing but wearing himself out. Dao staggered to his feet, gave Sophie a blank stare, and then lunged at Ric's back, clawing at him like a ticked-off bear.

Ric howled and turned, swinging blindly at Dao.

Sophie screamed.

Ric stopped.

Dao stopped.

Lisse stopped.

They all stood and looked at her—well, all but Ric, whose eyes were still clamped tightly closed—like she was going to tell them all what to do.

"You. Men. Get out," Sophie barked, hauling the shield to her chest.

"I won't leave my wife here defenseless," Dao said through gritted teeth. "A couple of crazed strangers come into my bedroom and I'm supposed to stand idly by and watch them attack my wife?"

"Yes." Sophie nodded. "Don't you remember me? I'm not a stranger. I'm Sophie. Your best friend."

"Don't listen to her, my love," Lisse said.

"I don't know you."

Ric swung, knocking Dao to the ground.

Lisse screeched and spit at Ric again.

Sophie saw red. No snakewoman spat venom at her man! She swung her arm in a wide arc aiming for the same area Ric had. But the stone blade didn't even cut the skin. It bounced like a stone off a tire. "What the fuck?"

"You can't kill me," Lisse scoffed. "You're a human."

Sophie didn't want to believe the lamia. She hadn't come all this way to fail. What did she mean she couldn't kill her? They had the magic spear. They had the magic shield. What more could they need?

"Liar." She jumped forward again, spear aimed right for the heartless snake's chest. Lisse didn't even try to block it. Again, the blade bounced off her chest, wrenching Sophie's shoulder. She huffed her frustration. Her fear, at the hunger she saw in the lamia's eyes as it looked at Ric.

"I think next I'll take that one. He's delightful."

"He's taken, bitch."

Lisse smiled, displaying two elongated canines. "Who's going to stop me? You?"

"Yes."

"I told you, you can't. Only a newly born Immortal has the strength to kill me, even with the Romakh. Our friend here is too old."

"Only a newly born . . ." Sophie repeated, turning to look at Ric.

He seemed to read her mind. He shook his head. "No. I won't let you. I love you."

"He's my friend. I can't save him if I don't."

"Isn't this sweet. The little lady thinks she can become an Immortal and kill me? All for her dear friend who couldn't give a shit whether she lives or dies."

"Shut up!" Sophie said in a low growl, her mind whirling round and round.

Lisse knelt beside Ric. "He's a Wissenschaft. My venom might kill him if I took a little taste." She dodged a blind swing from Ric and caught his wrist, then dragged her flickering tongue up his arm from palm to elbow. "Oh, he's sweet." Smiling, she dragged a fingernail over his skin. A crimson trail followed the line she'd drawn.

"No!"

Lisse licked the trail away. "Oh, yes. Delightful. You know, he was wrong to have once thought a lamia can't wed a Wissenschaft. He could make a nice husband." Lisse leaned forward and kissed his lips. He fought for a brief second, then sagged against the wall.

"No." Sophie stood frozen, scared, confused. If she completed the wedding ritual with Ric, she'd be an Immortal. He'd pretty much made that clear. But what was the final step? And did she want to take it? Could she take it? Did she have the strength? The courage? What would happen to her? What would happen to Ric? And Dao?

Ric moaned and slumped forward, lifeless.

"Ric!" She knew she couldn't take another moment to think, couldn't wait. Her choice had been made for her. Not only for Dao, who was starting to stir and was taking in the scene before him with rage-filled eyes, but also for Ric, who was falling under the lamia's spell. She caught his hand, closed her eyes, and sucked at the red blood dripping from his wrist.

To hell with life. To hell with fear.

When the salty blood hit the back of her throat, she gagged. But out of fear and rage, she forced it down. A flare of heat blasted through her belly, like she'd swallowed a lit firecracker. She forced another mouthful down her throat. God, it burned. Worse than shots of 200-proof liquor. Her insides were boiling. Her blood was like volcanic lava rushing through her body, sending the agony to every cell from the top of her head to her toenails.

She heard Ric yell below the loud thud of her slowing heart. The world grew hazy and dark. She staggered, dropping the shield. She fell to her knees.

The lamia stood over her, smiling. "Too late, baby doll. Your Wissenschaft's mine."

Sophie felt the strength draining from her. Felt her soul lifting out of her heavy body. It whirled around the room and then plunged inside Ric's body. But it was a shell— empty, lifeless, cold. Ric was gone. Where? Her spirit shot from him again, returned to her body. She tested her arms, legs. They were heavy, weak but could still move. "Ric?"

He was gone. She'd lost him. Lost Dao. Lost her own life. Lost everything. She dropped her head, letting her forehead rest against the shield's cool surface. "Oh, God, help me. I'm too late." The shield heated, as if a flame had ignited inside.

Then she felt Ric fill her, felt his strength surging through her veins. She felt strong. She felt powerful. She felt new. She pretended to stagger to her feet, the spear clutched in her fist, and tripped on her own foot, falling forward. Lisse lifted her hands to push her away, but she didn't block Sophie's strike to her chest.

It was a clean shot. This time the blade sank in. Frigid air blasted from the wound and Lisse's body crumpled to the ground like a deflated balloon.

Dao screamed behind Sophie, scrambled to his feet, then shook his head and stared at her, confusion pulling his face into a mask of tension. "Sophie? What happened? What's going on?"

Sophie hugged Dao. "I'll explain in a minute." She kneeled next to Ric's limp, cold body; palmed his cheeks; and kissed him. She felt his spirit rush through her mouth and out into his body. He stirred under her. Tears blurred her vision.

She'd done it; they'd done it. The lamia was gone. Dao was alive.

And she was now officially a vampire, or so she assumed.

"I guess there's no more Ben & Jerry's for me, unless they make a new flavor—AB positive."

Ric's chuckle was the sweetest sound on earth. "Not exactly. You see, you kind of skipped a part in that last step. Which means you're not a real, full-fledged vampire. You're a little bit human and a little bit vampire."

"Oh?"

"But we are Joined and you know what this means, don't you?"

Oh no! More secrets?

"Noooo."

"It means you're stuck with me for the next, oh, I'd say five hundred years or so. I hope you can deal with my snoring."

Sophie kissed the daylights out of him. "No problem. I'll wear earplugs. I'm just grateful for your being alive . . . or dead . . . or undead."

"Sophie, what the heck are you talking about?" Dao asked incredulously. "Since when did you start believing in vampires?"

"Oh . . . about four or five days ago, when I met this incredibly handsome guy in the library who just happens to be a real vampire." She then held her index finger to her lips and whispered, "It's a secret. My secret vampire."

"Sounds like a great story title." Dao said, heading toward the door. "Mind if I go do some writing? I've just been inspired."

"No way. I've just had a spark of inspiration myself," Sophie said, pulling Ric to his feet. "First stop is the bathroom to clear up those eyes. I want you to see me when we're making love. All of me," whispered Sophie.

"I'm all for that plan."

"I thought you would be. If there's anything I learned

the last couple of weeks, it's that real vampires never say no to a good thing. And speaking of good things, I'm starving. How about some Ben and Jerry's? I don't know what being a half human, half vampire means, but I've got a taste for some Chocolate Therapy."